Shortliste

"Friedman has a keen eye for the ridiculous [but] [illegible] here, too. [She] understands the temptations and the hazards of allowing yourself to get trapped in the past."

The Gazette (Montreal)

"Friedman acquits herself as a fluid, entertaining stylist with a gift for zippy but believable dialogue.... Friedman's writing here is fast and fun, but when she slows the wisecracking and delves into the sources of her characters' grief, she is capable of resonant writing."

Quill & Quire

"Breezy, sardonic and confident, *Then Again* brings to mind earlier examples of troubled adolescence — it's filled with jolts of recognition that the adult world is awry. There's more than a little Holden Caufield lurking in Michelle Schafer, with a touch of Sylvia Plath's Esther Greenwood thrown in."

The Ottawa Xpress

"Toronto debut novelist Elyse Friedman hooks the reader immediately and keeps the suspense high.... Friedman is a witty and edgy writer who has a knack for painting engaging character descriptions."

Times-Colonist (Victoria)

"Friedman has a wonderful ability for describing pleasure both small and vast. A sly humour that simply won't yield."

Ben Hamper, author of *The New York Times* bestseller *Rivethead*

"Newcomer Elyse Friedman scores with *Then Again*, the story of three siblings who revisit their dysfunctional childhood at a bizarre 'blast from the past' party. This is a darkly comic novel dripping with a delicious horror-movie sense of foreboding."

En Route

Then Again

Elyse Friedman

VINTAGE CANADA
A Division of Random House of Canada Limited

VINTAGE CANADA EDITION, 2000

Published in Canada by Vintage Canada, a division of Random House of Canada Limited, in 2000. First published in hardcover in Canada by Random House Canada, Toronto, in 1999. Distributed by Random House of Canada Limited, Toronto.

Canadian Cataloguing in Publication Data

Friedman, Elyse, 1963–
Then again

ISBN 0-679-31068-1

I. Title.

PS8561.R4924T43 2000 C813'.54 C00-931166-1
PR9199.3.F74T43 2000

Cover design: Scott Christie of Pylon Design Associates

Printed and bound in the United States of America

2 4 6 8 9 7 5 3 1

To Annette, Otto, Robyn & Danny,
with love.

—

I knew that my brother was peculiar — my entire family was peculiar — but when I received an invitation to a "Blast from the Past" party to be held at the suburban home in which we were raised, I couldn't help feeling that perhaps he had finally crossed the line from amusingly eccentric to disturbingly weird. It wasn't just the fact that the soiree was to be held in a house that had been sold after my parents' death close to twenty years ago, or even that the invitation had been hand-delivered by a girl who was obviously done up to look exactly like me at the age of sixteen — waist-length red hair parted in the middle, tube top, Levi's straight-legs, Roots inverted-heel suede shoes, Player's Extra Light dangling from the snarly, lip-glossed mouth; it was that the latest tabloid tale circulating about my brother suddenly seemed as if it might have some credence. I had dismissed it as bogus, and I could almost always tell which ones were true.

It's funny, when you're weird and poor, your strangeness options aren't that great. You can drool and touch yourself in public, bark at passing cars, collect string, giggle maniacally while microwaving your houseplants, disrobe in the frozen-food section of the local supermarket... But when you're weird and obscenely rich, well, then the world is truly your oyster. If you felt like it you could hire the Rockettes to kick the crap out of your neighbour's prize-winning roses. You could rent Disneyland for an evening and hand hundreds of your closest friends paint guns to fire at the hapless Mickeys and Goofys wandering about. You could throw a Japanese dinner party in which each place setting consists of an Asian virgin sitting cross-legged on the table with slices of sashimi glistening between her thighs. You could hire contractors to literally turn a friend's house inside out: William Morris and oil paintings on the exterior, brick and grass and patio stones where the living room used to be. All of these things my brother Joel has done. For laughs. For kicks. He has a well-developed imagination and way too much expendable cash.

—

I can hear the phone ringing in the bookstore. It's a long-distance ring, which means it's either my brother or my sister calling. I decide not to go down and get it. I'm not ready to hear from them yet. Besides, Martin will be here any minute. He's going to cook dinner for me. I will endure his vaguely nourishing vegetarian meal. I will endure his wistful reminiscences of backpacking through Thailand. I will even endure his ridiculous felt jester cap (the kind that all the nonconformists wear) and his handwoven Guatemalan sweater that smells like wet gerbils. All of this I will endure because when the rice and sprouts are adequately digested — about thirty seconds after consumption — and the dishes have been cleared away, twenty-six-year-old Martin will strip off his cap, his sweater and his 100-percent-hemp pants. Then twenty-six-year-old Martin will have sex with thirty-six-year-old me. He'll grab me hard by the hair and bend me forward over the wooden table. He'll hold my hands tight behind my back, reach under my skirt and yank the panties down around my ankles. He'll kick my legs apart, growl *sexy bitch slut* in my ear and fuck me like the rapist he is at heart.

Soon after, Martin will leave without having to be asked. He will hook up with his pierced-face girlfriend in some Osborne Village bar. They will drink microbrewery ale and talk about ozone layer and rain forest, about teaching English in Tokyo or Prague. I will sit in the dark smoking cigarettes, luxuriating in the return of gorgeous silence all around me. Maybe maybe I will pour some Bushmills and think about ugly Frank McCollum, the only one I love or even like.

—

The phone is ringing again. It's Marla. I can tell. There's a hysterical edge to it. High-pitched. Insistent. I throw on sweats and head downstairs. I pick it up before coffee. First mistake of the day.

"Hello?"

"Jesus Christ, Michelle, I've been trying to get you *forever*! Can you fuckin' believe this Joel business? I mean the Blast from the Past thing, not the Maple Leaf Gardens thing — although that's *another* story. You got an invitation, didn't you? 'Cause if you didn't get one on Friday you're definitely gonna get one today. Unless he's just trying to screw with *my* head, which is extremely possible, knowing Joel. Though I seriously hope not, 'cause I just can't fucking handle something like that right now. Not alone, anyway. I mean, Jesus, that's all I need."

My sister talks fast. She does a lot of things fast. She chews fast. She smokes fast. She walks fast. She reminds me of a squirrel. Furry. Nervous. Scurrying here and there. Rubbing her little hands together. Chattering.

"I got one on Friday," I say, studying the ceiling tiles. They look like flattened-out golf balls. Some are stained yellow around the edges.

"Oh, thank Christ! I'd hate to think he was cooking up something like this for just me. I mean, the more I hear about him in the news, the more paranoid I get. I mean, do you think that Maple Leaf Gardens thing is true or what? Oh! Hold on a sec, I've got a call. One sec!"

I put the receiver on the counter and start making coffee. It's almost noon; I usually open around eleven. Happily, my customers have given up any real hope of punctuality or consistency. In fact, I suspect that a lot of them think it's "quaint" or "cool" that I open or close whenever I feel like it. Fine by me. They can think whatever they want as long as I can bag ten hours of sleep every night and come and go as I please.

"Hello? Hello? Michelle! Helloooooo!!! Pick up!"

The blue receiver is shrieking at me from the counter. It's like a creature lying on its side with everything but the tongue paralyzed. I have the urge to submerge it in the sink full of soapy water, but instead I pick it up and place it next to my ear.

"Yeah."

"Sorry 'bout that! It was my friend Louise. You don't know her. She just had an ectopic pregnancy — this is all I need right now — but I told her I'd call her back. So, where were we?

"We—"

"Oh yeah! I was going to ask you how you got your invitation. Mine was delivered by a girl who looked *exactly* like me *circa* 1975, I swear to God! It was fucking eerie. She had everything from the bad perm to the white painter's pants *and* she reeked of Love's Fresh Lemon! Remember that stuff? I used to *love* that stuff. I mean, shit, I don't even think that stuff's on the market any more! They must have used Lemon Pledge or something. So did you get yours from a look-alike?"

"Yeah, sh—"

"Because I was wondering how detailed they got with yours. I mean, the long hair, they could use a wig, but what did they do about the arms? Did they have, like, fake cuts all up the arms or what? Probably not, right? I bet Joel doesn't even remember that. God, that was weird, Michelle. I mean, why did you do that, anyway?"

"Well..." I hear a manic clicking sound in the background.

"Fuck! These childproof lighters drive me insane! Are you still smoking?"

"Yeah." I try to focus on the sound of the coffee brewing. It's dark and throaty. A large purring cat. Black.

"Don't you *hate* these fucking childproof lighters? I say let the rug rats sizzle. Just kidding! I swear to God, though, I got dragged to a Rush anniversary concert the other night and at the end of the show all these people were trying to light their lighters and it was just, like, the entire auditorium filled with sparks. It was *hilarious*!"

"Listen, Mar, I gotta go. I've got a customer here."

"Right... You still have the bookstore, eh?"

"Yeah."

"You wouldn't believe what I've been up to! I took a real estate course. I'm a real estate agent. Can you believe that?"

"Yeah, I guess so."

"I can't. It's too weird! Guess whose house I just listed?"

"Actually, Mar, I really gotta go." I'm starting to feel bad. Edgy. Like a dog with the fur combed the wrong way and one ear bent back.

"Well, we'll have plenty of time to gab this weekend. You're going, right?"

"I don't know."

"Oh my God, you *have* to go! I cannot go alone! Besides, you don't want to piss off Joel, do you? I don't think that would be wise. Especially after the Jaguar thing. I mean, this is probably his way of showing that he forgives you for that. Besides, aren't you just *dying* to see what he's got planned? I mean, Joel throws some pretty wacky parties, and this is the first time we've been invited. Tell me you're not curious."

"Of course I'm curious."

"So, you'll come? C'mon, 'Chelle. Please, please, please..."

"I'll think about it, OK?" Second mistake of the day.

"Great! I'll call tomorrow and convince you! God, it was great talking with you again. It's been too long, Michelle. Why don't we talk more often? Oh yeah, before I forget, what do you think about this Maple Leaf Gardens business?"

"Well—"

"Ah Jeez! I don't fucking believe this, I've got another call coming in. Sorry! We'll talk later, OK? Bye."

Dial tone.

A young man tries the locked front door and peers at me through the glass. I wave him away. Too soon for more humans. I pour myself a coffee and go back to bed with the *Globe and Mail*.

—

I like to read the paper, though most of it bores me. It allows me, an agoraphobic, to go out into the world without having to leave my room. Sometimes, amidst the corrupt politicians, the endless inquiries, the deficit, the constitution and the rising tide of whatever whatever there'll be something really interesting, like the two girls who were killed in the canoe when the boy in the speedboat slammed into them. He survived. He was trying to splash them.

I can see the boy all sunburnt and shirtless in the powerboat. Motor revving. Loud. Fast. Skipping across the lake. Churning up the sparkling water. In the canoe, his cousin Amanda and her best friend Kate. Whispering secrets. Paddling softly.

Good cousin Amanda with the zinc oxide on her freckled nose, the droopy sun hat and those same canvas sneakers summer after summer. Good cousin Amanda with the startling new best friend Kate. Gorgeous Kate, who looks like a model. Perfect Kate, who needs to be splashed. Buttery blonde Kate, whose toenails are painted pink and whose baby blue two-piece has a tiny skirt that just barely covers her bum.

There he is, racing across the water towards them, his heart bursting with love and exhilaration, anticipating the glorious shrieks of fear and delight as he gets closer and louder and bigger and scarier, as he veers at the last possible second and sprays a magnificent white wave all over the girls. All over pretending-to-be-furious Amanda. All over beautiful straight-backed Kate. He's hooting already, just thinking about how he'll turn and wave goodbye — *adiós muchachas!* — smug and laughing as he speeds away. Leaving Amanda shouting and shaking her fist. Leaving Kate drenched and dripping in the honey sun.

Of course, he never does get the chance to wave goodbye.

I can see him at the funeral, sitting stiff in a scratchy suit. The head held up but the eyes downturned. The chest pressed in, hollowed out. The mother sitting close, clutching hard the limp hand that isn't in a cast.

That was a good one. I clipped it. I have a file of newspaper stories that I'm going to give to a good writer to write about if I can ever find one around here. I hold monthly open-mic readings to try and root one out, but so far it's just been a lot of "my grandmother was a saint" or "my McJob sucks" sort of thing. Too bad, because I clipped a really good one recently. The one about the man and woman in Quebec who hired thugs to break the legs of their teenage neighbour who would always always squeal the tires of his 1986 Pontiac Grand Le Mans. Every single time he left the house he would squeal those Grand Le Mans tires. No matter how much the man or the woman pleaded with the teenager or his guardian aunt, even after they told about the man going slowly bonkers and having to swallow nerve pills because of the stress of the noise, the kid would jump jaunty into that '86 Pontiac and squeal those souped-up Grand Le Mans tires.

I can picture the man sitting pale and jittery in his La-Z-Boy, lifting fork carefully to mouth. Now the hand jerks spasmodically and freezes in mid-air. Close-up on omelette morsel quivering as ears perk to the soft thud of car door followed by the roar of ignition. Cutlery goes crashing onto the TV tray as the man braces himself for the inevitable. Mouth clamps shut, throat closes, veins bulge in sweat-popping forehead, nails sink deep into burgundy vinyl La-Z-Boy arms... SCREEEEEEEEEEEEEEEECH! ***O you fucking cocksucking bastard***. Defeated again! And again and again and again. Tears of rage, frustration and screaming hate sting the eyes as he begins to sob and crumble and fumble for the nerve pills. Here comes the wife from the kitchen with a glass of cool water and a little pink dot in her upturned hand. She is murmuring soft, soothing words. She is wondering if she'll ever get her husband back. *Please, Marcel, let's just move. I mean, why don't we just sell the house and get the hell out of here?* ***Because then HE WINS! For Christ's sake, can't you see that?!***

I can see the wife and husband lying in bed at night fantasizing about all the things they could do to the Pontiac Grand Le Mans: *slash the tires, scratch the paint, snap off the side mirrors, Dippity-do in the gas tank, dead skunks in the glovebox, cow pies in the trunk, take a crowbar to the windshield, hire a crane to drop a safe on top, rent a flame-thrower and sizzle the fucker, better yet, tar and feather the bastard, blow it up, drive over it with a monster truck, tow it to the wrecking yard, photograph it getting munched then mail the eight-by-tens to that good-for-nothing snot-nosed son-of-a-bitch punk!*

I try to imagine how many squeals it took before the fantasies shifted from the car to the boy: *plant some drugs on him then call the cops, train a pit bull to attack him, mail him a box of steaming monkey turds, hire someone to beat the shit out of him, yeah, hire someone to punch his fucking face in, no, hire someone to break his goddamned legs! without legs, you can't squeal the tires of a Pontiac Grand Le Mans...* And how many more squeals before the wife was actually withdrawing the thousand dollars from the bank account and the husband was meeting the hooded man from the Mega Survival Paramilitary School in a remote wooded area of Île Perrot?

I think about that fateful day. About the repressed glee, the giggly satisfaction bubbling beneath the surface as the man and the woman hop happily about their daily tasks, watching and waiting for news of the legs. *look look: a police car next door! listen listen: the guardian aunt crying! quick quick: cop coming up walk, assume mask of bewildered concern!* I wonder how hard the pounding of the hearts and whether or not there was an urge to laugh. Mostly, though, I try to envision the dizzy wave of hot nausea passing through flesh as they take in the news: seventeen-year-old Daniel Légère — shot in the back, strangled with a wire garrotte, stabbed fourteen times, throat slit ear to ear.

It seems the director of the Mega Survival Paramilitary School got a little carried away.

I wonder, as he gulped his nerve pills and waited for the authorities to close in, if the man ever prayed to God to please please let him once again hear that terrible riff of rubber spinning hard against pavement. Or perhaps he just figured: *at least in prison it will be quiet.*

No such luck with today's papers. The only remotely interesting tidbit is a small item in the *Globe*'s Arts section about the event my brother held at Maple Leaf Gardens. It seems that Jason Beale, the guest who leaked the alleged goings-on in the first place, has unequivocally retracted his story.

—

This is what supposedly happened five weeks ago at Maple Leaf Gardens. My brother rented the arena for an evening and invited a dozen of his childhood peers to an event that was billed as "The Big Game Celebration." This much, at least, is true.

The guests were guys he hadn't seen or even talked to since he was thirteen years old, neighbourhood kids — road hockey, smokes in the ravine, hanging out at the plaza, that sort of thing. I was surprised he even remembered them, let alone tracked them down for a reunion. Apparently, he hired a private detective to locate them all. The ones who no longer lived in Toronto were provided with first-class airline tickets, rental cars and accommodation. Joel made sure everybody would show up.

Jason Beale showed up. Jason Beale was a catering manager at the Ramada Inn in North York. He must have viewed the reunion as a wonderful opportunity. Not only was it a chance for him to pal around with a bona fide celebrity (and the one guy from his past who had really, really made good), it was also the perfect opening to hit Joel up for some investment moolah. Jason Beale had invented a board game that was going to make him fabulously rich. I had seen him on CBC's *Venture* several months ago. He had gone so far as to have the prototype made, but he didn't have the cash to bring the game to the market. It had been collecting dust for almost two years. This was his big chance.

The first part of the evening sounded pretty straightforward. The boys drank beer and got all caught up. Then they laced on the skates and suited up for a game of hockey on that beautiful Zambonied-within-an-inch-of-its-life regulation ice. Everyone except Joel played. Apparently, he slipped away to watch the proceedings from the press box and never came back down.

After the game, the winners drank Dom Pérignon from a tinny replica of the Stanley Cup. Then everyone sipped cognac, puffed on Cohibas and waited impatiently for the "special show" to begin. And soon enough it did.

> *lights fade to black as softly whirring machines spill smoke onto the ice. now, music. tortured sax rips through the room. opening strains of tom waits's "temptation" resonates to the rafters. on first drumbeat red spotlight falls around peroxide blonde in skating garb. tight and purple. the men shout hurrah. blonde glides and slithers slowly across the ice. the music plays. now she's peeling off a long satin glove. now a quick twirl reveals naked ass and cunt. the men, hot and sweaty in the stands, cheer and chew on cigars. now the sparkly top pops open. implants bob as she weaves around the crease. men hoot and howl. now here comes a brunette in gold lamé. she's carrying a platter and a briefcase and a bag. she skates to centre ice and sets the platter down on the ground. then the briefcase. then the bag. peroxide glides to centre ice. she lifts her dainty purple skirt, squats over the platter and begins to grunt. the men stop cheering. some mutter, some giggle nervously, some are silent. the brunette opens the briefcase. it's full of cash. now a voice comes on over the music over the p.a.:"congratulations, friends," says the voice, "you have provided me with some happiness. in return, i'm going to give you a chance for happiness." the brunette removes a small stack of paper cups from the plastic bag and starts scooping. "can you guess," asks the voice, "what it is that i want you to do?" the brunette is nearly finished. she places twelve tiny spoons in the twelve tiny cups. "i want you each to leave here a little bit happier. but happiness, as we all know, has a price..."*

According to Jason Beale, every man except him went home with $250,000. But now Jason Beale has retracted his fantastic story. It'll be interesting to see if Jason Beale's board game soon goes to market.

—

Unlike everyone else in my family, my brother Joel always had a knack for making money. He started at the age of eight with packets of Kool-Aid stolen from the corner Safeway and sold in the schoolyard. He introduced the dip 'n' lick method of consumption, and soon half the kids in the neighbourhood were walking around with bright purple or orange or green index fingers and lips.

His next big venture was pimping. He started a peep show in our garage. For five cents you could flip through one of my father's *Playboys*. For twenty cents, Joel's girlfriend Becky would lift up her shirt. She'd show her underpants for a dime. Becky didn't get a piece of the take, but Joel would treat her to a Lola afterwards.

Joel always had at least one scheme on the go. At first he stashed his profits in a shoebox in his bedroom closet. He never kept track of the amount, and Marla and I used to raid it occasionally (some things never change) for cigarette money. One day he dug a hole in the drywall behind a framed picture of an Inuit boy that hung above his bed. This was his "wall-safe." I used to check in there regularly. Not for cash, for poetry. Joel used to write poems. They were terrible for a while. Then they got pretty good. And then they got terrible again.

Joel's most successful early enterprise was drug smuggling. He started when he was thirteen. It began when the older boys whom he bought his joints from offered to send him on an all-expenses-paid vacation to beautiful Negril, Jamaica, *and* pay him a thousand dollars in cash. All he had to do was swallow ten condoms full of hash-oil a couple of hours before boarding his flight home. When he got back to Toronto he would eat Ex-Lax and hand over the loot. Simple enough. Joel went three times. The first time he swallowed ten condoms and collected his thousand dollars. The second time he swallowed eleven condoms: ten for them, one for him. The third time he swallowed a dozen. This gave him enough cash to start his very own smuggling ring. Before long he had a fair bit of money stashed.

He took some of the profits and started a punk band called Hey,

Nice Slacks, a three-chord outfit that played a lot of pseudo-angry, tongue-in-cheek type of stuff. Loud. The group put out a couple of cassettes and even cut a 45. A-side was their most popular song, "He Couldn't Agree With Me More," a snappy little number about compliance and conformity. B-side was some kind of musical weirdness called "Tanked for the Memories." It was basically a wall of discordant noise that featured gut-wrenching shrieks, wailing guitar feedback and an unbearable solo in which Joel (a.k.a. Mister Swanky) trashed a Hammond organ. First he leaned all over the keyboard — "Lady of Spain" on a bad acid trip — then he pushed all the beat buttons simultaneously so the thing didn't know whether to mambo, rumba, cha-cha or samba. Then he took a sledgehammer to the beast until it was just sort of wheezing somewhere in the cacophonous background. Surprisingly, they sold quite a few copies and began to garner a loyal cult following. My guess is that Joel would have eventually ended up with some kind of record deal if he hadn't "retired" from the music biz.

Joel abandoned music in a bid to become a writer. A screenwriter. His first screenplay was about a nice Jewish boy from the suburbs who starts a drug-smuggling ring to finance his fledgling rock 'n' roll career. In the movie, the love interest/backup singer dies when one of the hash-oil-filled condoms she's transporting bursts in her belly, and the nice Jewish boy pays for his crimes with an extended jail term, a broken heart and eternal remorse. In real life Joel sold the option to a Hollywood studio and launched a successful screenwriting career that would lead to much fame and, thanks to some phenomenally savvy investing in newfangled companies like Apple, Corel and Microsoft, much fortune as well. As for the backup singer/love interest, the authorities simply didn't have enough evidence to prove that she wasn't acting on her own. Good thing Joel went in for homemade wall-safes instead of bank accounts.

—

It's peaceful here in the bookstore. Very peaceful. A boy is sipping mint tea and reading a magazine. A girl is eating a butter tart and looking out the window. Garrick Ohlsson is massaging the ivories. Gently.

I have a CD player that will spin up to ten discs. I have four speakers positioned strategically around the room. I have one CD. Chopin's nocturnes. It's the only music I can stand to listen to. Every other music hurts. The nocturnes don't. When I hear them I smell autumn leaves and woodsmoke and pumpkin flesh. Soothing.

Some of the regulars seem to be getting a little sick of it. Try Alanis, they say, or Beethoven. At the very least toss in a mazurka once in a while, or a lousy polonaise. No, I say. Can't do it. Some others don't mind. They like it. They understand that it's just part of the room. Like the fat burgundy sofa in the corner, like the air.

To me it's the same deal as the hours I keep — if the patrons don't like it, they're free to nibble their Nanaimo bars elsewhere. I'm not trying to get rich or win a customer service award. This isn't Wal-Mart. But most don't mind the music or even the irregular hours. It's the pricing that really seems to annoy them. They think it's completely arbitrary, but it isn't. It's actually quite methodical. Here's how I work it: Books that I've never read are sold at the regular price. Books that I like sell for 15 percent off the competitor's retail price. Books that I dislike have a 10-percent premium tacked on. And then there is a small handful of authors whose work I sell at cost. I keep those books together on a special shelf set apart from the rest. I like to glance over every once in a while just to see them standing there. Existing. They stand so beautifully and silently, warming up the room with a soft apricot light. It makes me feel OK and sometimes even happy.

My brother freaked out when I bought this place. Joel assumed that I wanted to leave Winnipeg, so he sent me a car. He sent me a dreamy, creamy Jaguar convertible with buttery nut brown seats and gleaming walnut dash and air conditioning and compact disc player and power everything and shiny chrome you-name-it. It was gorgeous and fabulous and smelled divine, like maple fudge and leather jacket, like pipe tobacco and new skipping rope. I sent him a thank-you card, then I sold the thing. A car — any car — is not exactly the first item on the agoraphobic's wish list. Besides, driving a spanking new Jaguar around the Peg is tantamount to wearing the crown jewels to McDonald's. If you need people to stop and gawk, OK, OK. But I didn't need that. What I needed was a place to reside and hide and tug out some semblance of a living. A bookstore. Yeah. A bookstore with an apartment above where I could stare out the window at minus forty or giant sky or lush green bower of towering elm.

So why would I fly away and leave, even for a weekend? To see my sister? To reconnect with my brother? There's really no point. To satisfy a needling curiosity? I'm bound to find out what goes on anyway, if not from Marla, from TV or tabloids. No, there is only one good reason why I would gobble Klonopin, crawl out of my cave and brave the flight home to Toronto. That reason is Frank McCollum.

There is, I can't help thinking, a small chance that my brother has somehow arranged for him to be present at this Blast from the Past thingy. A slim wispy slip of a chance.

That's good enough for me.

—

The first thing I noticed about Frank McCollum was his bare naked ass. He had wandered into the female ward by accident — typical McCollum, no sense of direction — and had failed to notice that his gown had come untied. So, there's this scrawny butt shuffling by, all pale and dotted with zits, and for the first time in about six months I laugh.

McCollum never backpacked through Asia.

McCollum never had an ear/scrotum/nipple pierced.

McCollum never made frequent unnecessary calls from a cell phone.

Of course, I can't say for certain that these things are so, and McCollum would think I was being a real hard-ass for pointing them out anyway. Unlike me, he doesn't harbour a lot of unkind thoughts about mankind. He's extremely forgiving of human frailty. To a point.

We met in the smoking lounge. Back then you could still smoke in hospitals. The good old days. McCollum was sitting there all bandaged up, reading a dilapidated copy of *Equinox*. I was sucking on cig after cig, picking foam bits out of the orange vinyl armchair and sneaking peeks at him. He was, without a doubt, one of the ugliest young men I had ever laid orbs on. Even hunched in his wheelchair he seemed alarmingly tall, at least six foot four and painfully gangly. His nose was huge and fleshy and crookedly hooked. It drooped down over a tiny mouth, far too small to contain the snaggly mess of tombstone teeth trying to get out. The chin was non-existent, the Adam's apple monstrous and pointy — a tomahawk lodged in his throat. The hair was particularly ludicrous — a brambly mass that couldn't make up its mind how to behave. Some of it stuck up and out in kinky sproings. Chunks of it lay flat and matted in little drifts. The hair couldn't even decide what colour to be. It wasn't red and it wasn't blond and it certainly wasn't brown. It was a combination of all of those, a kind of fake-looking doll's-hair shade of ginger. The skin — Jesus God! — was beyond bad, pale and pockmarked and covered in scabs and oozing boils of various sizes. I remember there was a particularly ripe one squatting plump over his left eyebrow. Every time he furrowed his brow (something in *Equinox* made him furrow every now and again) a column of pus would protrude a teensy bit, threatening to volcano into the tangled eyebrow hair. Then McCollum would unfurrow and the pus would recede back into the mound. It was maddening to watch, like a roll of bubble wrap just dangling there in front of you. I had the urge to vault over the teak table and commence a squeezing, popping frenzy.

I butted out my last smoke and stood up to leave. Then, for some reason, I sat back down. That's when McCollum looked at me and said: "This is the only quiet place."

The voice was warm and sweet. Oatmeal. Brown sugar.

I tried a smile, but it came out stiff and twisted. The one I got back was easier and genuine, and it made me finally notice the most remarkable feature: the eyes. Small and green, practically slits really, but shining with an extraordinary light. And different. Even with the smile, the left eye looked sad. When the smile disappeared the right eye went right on looking twinkly and mischievous. I liked the overall effect. For the first time in a long time I felt like talking.

We began.

—

I soon discovered that the boy I'd been meeting in the smoking lounge every day for a week was none other than Frank McCollum. *The* Frank McCollum, whose suicide attempt had become legendary on the ward. We'd had shooters and pill-poppers and jumpers, but no pill-popping jumping shooters. McCollum had swallowed a motherlode of Valium, stuck a pistol in his mouth and leaped off a fifth-storey balcony. Fortunately, his "foolproof" method didn't even come close to working. The jump jarred his hand, causing the bullet to go out through his cheek. The pills made the jump sloppy (he landed in a shrub two feet shy of the concrete) and loosened him up, resulting in less bone breakage. The gunshot, of course, alerted the neighbours. Everyone and their grandma called 911. An ambulance arrived in more than enough time to get his crazy stomach pumped out. McCollum broke a leg and his collarbone and cracked a few ribs. There's a tiny pucker mark on his left cheek where the bullet left his face, but you can hardly see it for the acne.

After we had left the hospital and moved in together, I asked McCollum why he did it. He wouldn't say, but he told me that on the morning of that sad stupid day he took a One-A-Day vitamin with his breakfast.

—

I have no luck. This is the first time I've enjoyed the privilege of flying anywhere first class. This has also got to be the first time the first-class section on a flight from Winnipeg to Toronto has been filled to capacity.

Filled to capacity with pet-food salesmen.

With every Scotch on the rocks they get a little bit louder, a little more boisterous. The flight attendant keeps smiling. She keeps smiling, but she looks as if she's about to lunge for a parachute and bail out the emergency door. If only the nerves could hold up as well as the hairspray.

I have the nocturnes on the Walkman and a tumbler of Bush. I chewed half a Klonny before boarding to take care of any inner turbulence. I would probably be just fine if it weren't for the three-hundred-pound pet-food salesman standing next to my seat, yucking it up with his buds across the aisle. He came from behind the navy curtain as soon as the seat-belt lights were switched off. He has been standing here drinking ever since. The three-hundred-pound pet-food salesman is like a beverage cart in slacks. There is literally a wall of gabardine-covered flesh sealing me into my seat. When the plane jostles, the wall bumps the side of my head or brushes my cheek. The plane jostles a lot. The gabardine is beginning to chafe a divot in my flesh. Chapped face. I suck on Nicorettes and fantasize about plunging the tiny plastic sword from my cocktail into the pet-food salesman's massive thigh. The capper is, I can't even turn away because the world's oldest human is passed out in the window seat beside me. Her mouth is hanging down and open, a terrible sulphur stench coming up from the lungs and mingling with her lilac talcum. Thick and sick.

I am trapped.

Of course, anyone else would say something. Joel would. Marla definitely would. I consider saying something to the stewardess. I know that a few whispered words would be enough to have the three-hundred-pound pet-food salesman trotted back to his seat in economy. It's true what they say, the squeaky wheel gets the grease. Unfortunately, I've never been the squeaky type.

I close my eyes and press my wrists to my nose, inhaling the clean soap smell. I try to think about something else. I try to go somewhere good in my mind.

—

Sunday afternoon. July.

Blue sky. Poofy clouds.

Frank McCollum is coming up Pinecrest Avenue, pushing a wire shopping cart that says FOOD CITY on the side. He's half-whistling, half-singing something. What is it? "Love Land" by Charles Wright. His white T-shirt is flapping like a sail in the breeze. His hair is buzzing electric in the sunlight.

The neighbours are out in full force today. They are ferreting the yellow dots out of their square green lawns. They are levelling off the hedges. They are polishing up the hubcaps. They pretend not to stare at McCollum as he lopes long-legged towards number 5, as he navigates his shopping-cart vessel up the Schafers' cracked driveway. I'm on the porch hiding behind the clematis, but McCollum sees me right away. He waves to me through the foliage. *Ready?* he says. *Aye aye, Captain!*

We go up to my room. McCollum takes the Lloyds plastic stereophonic and two speakers. I take the garbage bag full of clothes and paperbacks and my pillow. I think about saying something to my mother, but she's in the bedroom with the door closed. That means migraine. Do Not Enter.

The rest of them are in the family room doing what they do. Full volume. McCollum pretends not to notice, but I can tell he's thinking, *Is it always like this?*

I say goodbye to the dog, then we ship out. We decide to take Canada's longest street. Yonge Street. We start at Steeles and move south. McCollum sings "Love Land" until Sheppard. Then we get Popsicles. Orange and yellow. As we walk along, not talking, I find myself smiling. I find that I cannot stop smiling. Even at Lawrence, even at Eglinton, I'm still beaming like a bedlamite.

We pass Davisville. On one side, the Mount Pleasant Cemetery. On the other, a cluster of apartment buildings. Vertical. Horizontal. It's only a matter of time, really. I imagine the buildings tipping forward, the inhabitants tumbling out and rolling across Yonge Street into their graves. McCollum directs my attention to some of the names carved on the stone tablets — DICK, PRONG, BOYLE — and I'm smiling again. At Summerhill we find a lamp on the curb. The shade is gone. The base is a lime green plaster poodle with a chipped bouffant and an astonished expression on its loopy face. Someone has painted the nose with red nail polish.

"Every home needs a dog," says McCollum. "C'mon, boy." He puts "Fang" in the shopping cart and we carry on.

Three and a half hours after setting sail, we have arrived at Bloor Street. Downtown. The New World. A man in a shiny leopard-spot jumpsuit minces by on high heels. A woman with a bleach-blonde Afro stands on the corner torturing the bagpipes. Nobody looks twice.

"We're almost home," says McCollum.

"Yes," I say. And we head west.

Sooner than I think, we have arrived at our street. Grace Street. Sloping, curved and sun-dappled. Tangled vines and fat red rose bushes; narrow brick Victorians wedged tall and tight together; teeny lawns decorated with candy-coloured shrines to the Virgin Mary (sparrow drinks water collected in smooth plaster palm); yellow cat snoozes on wooden railing; black cat blinks and looks the other way; stocky men in porkpie hats huddle together and smoke tough cigars;

widows whisper on porches, their hands working crochet needles, lacy white circles spreading slowly across the thick black laps.

We stop in front of number 27. Painted red brick with pea green eaves and creamy vanilla trim. Nice.

McCollum leads me down a narrow path to the back. I'm surprised to find that there is no grass in the yard at all. The entire thing has been turned into a garden. A garden garden, not a flower garden. I suddenly realize that, other than corn, I have never seen food growing in real life. I look at the different rows of squat leafy tufts, slender feathery plumes, pale coiling tendrils, and have no idea what any of them will turn out to be.

We go down a small flight of concrete stairs to the basement door. McCollum fumbles for his key ring, then drops it on the ground by a rusty metal drain. He scoops it up and fishes forever for the right key.

"It's a little tricky," he says, and clears his throat. I watch him fiddle endlessly with the lock. He turns the key left and then right and then left and then right again. "OK," he says, "before we go in I want to warn you again, this ain't the Taj Mahal..." Something finally clicks.

"Well, I ain't Mumtaz Mahal, so don't worry about it."

McCollum swings the door open and we step inside. He pulls a tiny chain on a bare light bulb and I see that we are standing in a small, dank storage cellar. Well, I'm standing. McCollum is more than a little hunched over, the ceiling being about six feet two inches high. We are surrounded by shelves upon shelves of pickled and preserved everything in every conceivable shape and size of jar. There are artichoke hearts in Kraft peanut-butter jars, banana peppers in industrial-sized mayonnaise jars, cucumbers, peaches, yellow beans, green tomatoes, beets, plums, cauliflower, red peppers, broccoli bits, something I can't identify that looks suspiciously like human parts, and gallons upon gallons of tomato sauce and homemade red wine. It smells good. Wet cement.

"Right through here," says McCollum.

I follow him into the main room where, I'm relieved to discover, he can stand fully upright with at least two inches to spare (including hair loft).

"Well... What do you think?"

My initial impression is that whoever put the place together was inordinately — no, obsessively — no, *criminally* fond of brown. Everything in the tiny, windowless room is chocolate brown. From the fake-wood-panelled walls to the dirty velour sofa, to the flat, rough carpeting, to the crocheted Phentex bedspread, to the hoop-skirt wannabe lampshade... brown, brown, brown. In the middle of the room — a giant brown fridge is humming a distinctly brown tune.

I open the bathroom door. It's not the bathroom, it's a cupboard. The shelves are covered in peeling checkered MACtac (brown) and mouse excreta (also brown). I open another door. The bathroom. The floor, miraculously, is pink. And the tub is white! But the toilet and the sink and the roaches scurrying to their dark hiding places... all brown.

I feel tears coming up in my eyes.

"Well...?" says McCollum. He's chewing hard on a hangnail that has begun to bleed.

"It's perfect," I say. "It's the most perfect place in the world." I wipe away the tears of relief and happiness and fill my arms with McCollum's bony torso. I'm about to push him gently onto the brown Phentex bedspread and kiss his ridiculous lips for the very first time when a honey-voice breaks through and tells me to please put my seat into the upright position and fasten my seat belt in preparation for the final descent.

—

Just as I expected, Joel has arranged for someone to meet me at the airport. A rumpled limo-driver with a greasy comb-over is waiting by the baggage carousel with a sign. MICHELLE SCHAFER. He scoops my blue suitcase and we head to the car.

As I step out of the climate-controlled airport, a gust of hot August wind slaps me in the face. The foul-smelling Toronto air is a shock after the cool sweetness of Winnipeg. Now another blast and I notice that the limo-driver's comb-over has been lifted like a farmhouse roof in a tornado. The Brylcreemed flap teeters precariously in an almost vertical position, threatening to flop completely over to the wrong side. Just in time, the driver claps the thing back onto his scalp and holds it in place, using his free hand to toss my suitcase in the trunk and open the door for me.

"I'll have the air on in a second, Miss."

"That'd be great. Thanks." I try to find the smile that acknowledges his courtesy and not his hair predicament. For both our sakes I put up the little black window that separates passenger from chauffeur; I've had more than enough human contact for one day. I close my eyes, sink into the soft velour seats and fantasize about holing up in my hotel room with TV and terry cloth robe and room service and mini-bar. First, a shower — definitely — then a nice cold beer or two. Chase that with a Toblerone bar and an entire jar of those cashews or, if they have them, macadamia nuts. Yum. Or maybe I'll order a toasted clubhouse sandwich with french fries and a dill pickle, and maybe there'll be something great on the tube, something in Technicolor, like an old Doris Day comedy. I'll kick the phone off the hook and lie in bed eating french fries and smoking cigarettes and watching Doris Day get hustled into the sack by Rock Hudson or Cary Grant. Yeah.

I pick up the plastic phone that connects me to the driver. "Hello... Excuse me."

"Yes, Miss?"

"Could you please tell me which hotel we're going to?" I'm sure Joel has selected a nice one, but I'm curious now.

"We aren't going to a hotel, Miss."

"We aren't?"

"No, Miss. I am to take you to 5 Pinecrest Avenue."

"*What?* Tonight? I believe that's not until tomorrow night. Are you sure?"

"Yes, Miss. I am to pick you up at the airport and take you directly to 5 Pinecrest Avenue."

"Oh... OK. Um — do you happen to know if anyone else will be there?"

"I'm afraid I don't know, Miss."

"Well, have you taken anyone else there today?"

"I'm afraid I'm not at liberty to say, Miss."

"So you *have* taken someone else there today? Could you please just tell me if it was a man or a woman?"

"I'm very sorry, but I'm not at liberty to say anything about it, Miss." Joel's orders, obviously.

"All right... Thanks anyway."

I hang up the phone and reach for the cut glass decanter. I'm not ready for this yet. I pour myself a deep glass of cheap Scotch and stare out the window at the grim and increasingly familiar scenery.

—

The front lawn is mud. Just mud. Cracked and hard like a mini badlands.

"Don't worry," says my father. "By the time we move in, this will be a beautiful lawn just like that one." He points to the house next door, on the corner.

I look up at my mom. She is leaning against the baby blue Oldsmobile, rocking Joel in her arms. She is gazing at the model home on the corner and she is smiling.

It turns out he's wrong, though. When we move in, the lawn is still mud. It's mud all the way until the following spring, when the developer finally lays down sod. But the sod doesn't take. It turns brown and they have to roll it up and carry it away on their shoulders. Eventually they replace it and the second batch finally works, but even ten years later, after ten seasons of my father's rigorous attention — pesticides, herbicides, mowing and weeding within an inch of its life — it still doesn't look anything like that baby on the corner.

—

"Here we are, Miss." The driver hands me the keys to the house, then carries my suitcase to the front door and sets it down. I try to pay him, but he insists that it's all been taken care of. Off he goes. I light a smoke and stroll to the curb.

Pinecrest Avenue looks a lot shorter than it used to. There are only about seven houses on our side of the street and about nine on the other side. On one end of Pinecrest is the park and Briarway Elementary School (both looking much smaller than I recall). On the other end is the Texaco station and the plaza (I'll have to wander down later and see if anything's still there). I can't quite put my finger on it, but there's something distinctly unsettling about the way the old place looks. The other homes on the street are slightly different than I remember them. The colours of paint have changed, there are different blinds and drapes in the windows, different landscaping on the lawns. Our house looks *exactly* as it was. Brick two-storey detached, avocado green garage door, trim and shingles, cement porch with wrought iron railing, small garden just in front of that with evergreen shrubs and marigolds and clematis and alyssum, young weeping willow smack dab in the centre of the lawn. Suddenly I feel a cold chill in the forearms and back of the neck as I realize what is disturbing about our house. It's the willow tree and the shrubs in the garden. They haven't changed at all in two decades. They haven't grown any bigger.

Impossible.

I look and look, but it doesn't make any sense. I can only conclude that, for some reason, Joel has arranged for whatever was there a couple of weeks ago to be ripped out and replaced with whatever was there twenty years ago. I try to examine the soil, but I can't really tell in this light. It's already started to get dark. I bury my cig into the warm earth and head inside.

There are no lights on in the house. I palm the wall in the void of the vestibule trying to remember where the switch is. I feel scared and nervous, as if something is lurking inside, waiting. As my fingers find the switch and flick it up, I half-expect my family to leap out in front of me and scream *Surprise!* They don't, but what I see before me is surprising enough. Like the garden, the house has been rigged up to look exactly as it did twenty years ago. The pale green linoleum floor, the avocado green carpeting on the stairs, the immaculate off-white hallway walls have all been freshly done — I can tell by the smell and the pristine condition. Over by the plant stand where we put the mail, those giant black-and-white Simpsons baby portraits of Marla and me and Joel are back, hanging one, two, three, exactly where they should be.

"Hello?" My voice resonates through the house. No answer. I guess I'm the first to arrive. The first to tour this strange museum. Off I go.

Turn to the right into the large open-concept living room/dining room. True to form, it has been stripped bare — nothing on the hardwood floors, nothing on the white walls. The only object in the hollow room is a dinky upright piano painted hospital green and pressed against the wall by the bay window where the baby grand was going to stand. Yeah right. I can't believe after all these years I'm still seeing my mother's phantom *House & Garden* visions — the soft Oriental carpets, the fat silk sofas, the gleaming mahogany dining-room set... My parents plunged themselves into severe debt when they bought this house and couldn't afford to furnish the thing. They did it slowly over the years, room by room, but they never made it this far. Marla and Joel and I used to play Nerf soccer or fetch with the dog, or running and sliding across the floor in our socks. We liked it the way it was, but our mother hated it. The one thing she did manage to purchase for the room was a pair of expensive champagne-coloured drapes, heavy and thick, so the neighbours couldn't look in and see the emptiness. I try the middle C on the piano. It's muted. Dead. Joel, obviously, has thought of every detail.

I move through the dining room into the kitchen. It looks familiar and strange. Dark oak cupboards. Avocado green stove. Avocado green fridge. There is a jar of Taster's Choice on the counter beside the kettle. There is a box of Honeycombs on the windowsill. I open the fridge and stare at the contents. Baloney, baby dills, mustard, ketchup, whole wheat bread, apple juice, margarine, Cool Whip. In the freezer, a stack of Swanson TV dinners: Salisbury Steak, Southern Fried Chicken. I roll a pickle into a slice of baloney, like I used to, and stand there in the fridge light, eating it.

Suddenly I get the feeling that I'm not alone. Like I'm being watched. A wave of heat passes over my body.

"Hello?" No answer. I look into the family room. Nobody.

I turn on the TV to drown out the sound of my heart. It's an old black-and-white, barely working. The screen comes alive with the broken image of Jimmy Stewart with his leg in a cast. *Rear Window*. Jesus! I switch it off and fumble for my smokes. I don't like this. I don't like this at all. There is no way in hell that I'm going to be able to go up those stairs. Not tonight. Not alone. I mean, God only knows what kind of death scene Joel has re-created in my parents' bathroom. Maybe the whole point of this elaborate exercise is so that I'll be the one to find my father this time. Maybe all of this is some kind of cruel payback for not being around when the real shit hit the fan. Oh well. If the house is really the way it used to be, then the world's largest bottle of Johnnie Walker is still squatting in its fat wooden cradle on the rec-room bar. Time to crack that pig.

I try the basement door, but for some reason it's locked from the inside. Bolted shut. What the hell? Maybe the furniture and belongings of the current owner are being stashed down there.

Maybe not.

I leave the lights on in the family room and stretch out on the sofa. As I lie there staring at the stucco ceiling, I realize that the most peculiar thing about the house is not what is the same but what is different.

For the first time ever, it is quiet.

—

I am running across the street towards the school. My hair, still damp, smells like Herbal Essences. My arms are white with baby powder and my mouth is smeared thick with wild cherry Lip Smackers. Andrea is waiting for me on the sidewalk. She's wearing the baby blue angora sweater and matching blue eyeshadow. Beautiful. She smells like jasmine with a faint topnote of Kitty Litter. Always that hint of cat box about her. She lights a Salem Menthol and grins.

Tonight I will advance to the next level. Tonight is B.J. night. I've done hand jobs, been felt up, Richard Bederman fingered me in his parents' walk-in closet, but I've yet to try a blow job. Andrea has done it all. All. She had sex when she was twelve years old. In Thornhill with a pizza delivery man. At almost fourteen I am the world's oldest virgin.

We stroll casually to the school, where the boys hang out. Terry Rosenberg, David Snider, Steven Jacobs, Sid Cooperman. They know why we're there and before long the standard exchange crops up:

"Ah, suck my dick."

"Whip it out."

"Self serve."

This is where it begins or ends. Tonight it begins with me leading Terry Rosenberg into the field behind the school. I don't particularly like Terry Rosenberg and he doesn't particularly like me, but he needs to rack up a blow job and so do I. Fair enough.

We move into the fields and lie down on the cold grass. It smells good. Sweet and fresh. Terry grabs at my flesh and kisses me. Kissing is not what I'm here for. I unzip his pants and take it out. His cock feels warm in my hand. I bend down and slip the head into my mouth. It tastes all right. Salty and clean. I move down the shaft as far as I can go. As I slide back up, he comes. This is too easy, I think, swallowing a little and letting a little dribble out onto my sleeve. I make a mental note to show the spot to Andrea. Proof.

Afterwards, Terry doesn't want to kiss me any more. But he does give me his jean jacket to wear while we share a cig before heading back. He tries to make conversation, but I just smoke and smoke. There's no point. Rosenberg's an idiot. A follower. A blur in a crowd scene in a watercolour. And I am a SLUT. All conversation must soon cease anyway. I smile politely and go to collect Andrea. I feel pretty good. Only one more step to go before I'll be up to speed and ready. Ready for the one I love. The one I haven't yet met.

On the way to the plaza Andrea asks if I like Terry. I lie and tell her that I do. I've noticed that Andrea eventually sleeps with anyone I "like." So, what the fuck. Let Terry get screwed this time.

—

"Hell isn't other people. It's other people in laundromats!" Once again, an old Italian woman has scooped the Dry-o-Mat Triple Loader a nanosecond before I could get to it. McCollum stands there grinning, with his arms full of wet sweaters. He actually looks pleased.

"That's not hell, that's poetry," he says.

"Poetry? Please! How is that poetry?"

"Think about it. No matter when we come here, no matter what we do, whether we try to time it or just wing it, we are consistently outmanoeuvred for prime laundry space, be it the Wascomat Senior or a corner of the good folding table." McCollum waits for me to get it. I don't. "Look around," he says. "These women are the queens of clean. They've been coming here so long they are actually in sync with the cycles of the washers and dryers. It's like being in sync with the moon's cycles; it's unconscious and magical. The gears are in motion. The laundry gods are smiling. All is as it should be at the Tumblers Super Coin Cleaners." McCollum's shirt is soaked through from the soggy armload of clothing, but he doesn't seem to notice. He can see that I'm not entirely convinced. "We are but pups," he says, "rocking outside the rhythm of the thing. There's no use in getting frustrated. That only makes it worse. The machines are like horses, they can sense a prickly vibe, they know who's in control. The best course of action is just to sit back and admire this tiny miracle, this lepton of order in a universe of chaos, this living, breathing poetry in motion."

I search McCollum's eyes to see if he's kidding. Then I stop and look around. I watch the black-clad bodies shift from place to place; the swirling of the suds; the spinning colours; the doors opening in and out, up and down; the rolling of the carts; the wide expanse of cotton held in four hands, now two as it folded over and over into a crisp white square. All around is warmth and the whir of machine, and soon I see that he's right, and I'm no longer at the laundromat doing a dreary chore. I am at a strange and intricate ballet. It's a private performance and McCollum has kindly invited me to attend.

—

Something is entering my dream. Entering and tugging me out of sleep. Music. Chopin. It pads in softly like the ghost of a cat and melts into the ambience. Now it's filling the room. Creeping across the rug, like a stain, turning everything blue. Altering the images. I see hospital corridor. I see door opening to the left. Something is wrong. I want to continue dreaming, but the notes are pulling me out. They don't trickle the way they're supposed to. The vibrations whisper that these are not Garrick Ohlsson's steady hands. The notes falter and limp forward. Soft and sad. A tiny muffled thump for the middle C... I lurch into consciousness, bolt upright, heart hammering. *Where am I?* Stare wide-eyed into the darkness, straining to distinguish if the echo of music is real. It's gone. The house is settling. The room takes a shape I remember. Stumble down the hallway towards the source. My mother is not at the piano. *Of course she isn't, you fool!* The room is empty. Ringing with moonlight. The piano glows pale and green in the corner. Walk across the creaky hardwood and touch the bench, testing for warmth. *I must be crazy... or half asleep*. But it seemed to originate outside the dream. I'm almost sure of it. I think? Sit down at the small piano, close eyes and press hot forehead against the still, white keys.

—

In the morning light everything looks innocuous. The fifteen stairs leading to the second floor don't seem nearly as foreboding. Particularly since I've slept in my clothes, smell like airplane and desperately require a shower. I gulp Taster's Choice and head on up.

My bedroom is the same old shrine to bad '70s design. Gold shag carpeting, orange walls, white chipboard dresser and night table, white vinyl pull-down blind with little nylon tassels, lava lamp full of fat red globs, and the pièce de résistance, a photo wallpaper mural depicting a deserted beach with gently rolling waves. Top marks to Joel for locating one of these babies. It is identical to the one that was there, except this one has been applied properly and the palm trees aren't all wrinkled up and gluey around the edges, marring my view of paradise.

The only object out of place in the small room is the wardrobe. It is not a copy of the original but the very same one that stood there twenty years ago. The faces in the wood grain immediately suggest themselves to me the way they always did — the moose, the monkey, the old lady peeking over the flower. I'm not surprised that Joel kept this. It is antique and lovely. Much smaller than I remember. It is as high as my shoulder and stands on a five-inch pedestal, but I used to stand inside it with headroom to spare. Countless times I stood there in the dark among the hangers and the blouses, holding my breath and trying to think fuzzy blank thoughts so my brainwaves wouldn't act as a beacon and give me away. It wasn't the hitting I feared. A few whacks of the strap could easily be endured. But the noise... the shouting was unbearable. Oddly enough, it never occurred to him to look in there. He would tornado in, screaming, check under the bed, rifle through the closet and then storm off to do the same in Marla's and Joel's rooms. My father never found me in there. No one ever knew about this place. I press my lips against the wardrobe and inhale its good wood smell. I think I'll ask Joel if I can have it. Ship it home to Winnipeg if he doesn't mind parting with it. He probably won't.

In the shower I am reminded of other things. Embarrassing things. It was in this pale pink American Standard that I technically lost my virginity. Lost it in the bath to an economy-sized bottle of Tame. Well, not the whole bottle. Just the lid. I thought it would be a marvellous idea — in preparation for impending sexual intercourse — to try and loosen myself up a bit. I figured a penis was at least as big as the lid of a conditioner bottle. It took a few nights of concerted effort to work the thing in, but I finally made it. It didn't feel particularly good, though. I remember wondering what D.H. Lawrence and Erica Jong were going on about anyway.

As I'm towelling off I hear something in the house. Marla. As usual she announces her presence with a cross between a salutation and a sonorous bray. "Helloooo? Anybody home? Hello, hello, hello!"

I don't answer. I've never been capable of bellowing. I slip back to my room and dress quickly. A few moments later I hear Marla bounding up the stairs.

"Hello? Anybody here?"

I poke my head out the door. "Hi."

"Heeey!" Marla rushes down the hall and grabs me hard around the shoulders. "God, it's great to see you! It's been so long! Years! Can you believe this place? I mean, is this too weird or what?!"

"I know. It's bizarre."

"God, you look great, Michelle. I look so old. Do I look old or what?"

"No, you look good."

"Fat, right? And old!"

"*Fat?* Jesus, Marla, you're not starting that again, are you?" My sister is all of ninety pounds. Borderline anorexic.

"Just look at my stomach, OK? Look!" Marla lifts up her shirt and grab-grabs at the imaginary fat.

"You're not fat and you look good. I like your hair."

"Really? I hate it. I think it makes me look old. I'm gonna grow it out."

"I like it."

"Oh my God, this is too strange. I mean, *what the fuck?* Where's Joel? When did you get in? Look at you, you're so skinny!"

"Last night. I don't know where he is."

"Oh my God, c'mere! Look at this. Look at my room. I can't believe it. I loooved this room!" Marla launches herself onto the pink canopy bed and cuddles a white stuffed animal in her arms. "Remember this? I had a bunny just like this. Wow, check it out, all my Doodle Art!" All over the walls, framed Doodle Art posters. Joel has paid someone to doodle.

"He's certainly gone to a hell of a lot of trouble," I say, falling into the fat white beanbag chair in the corner. "I can't really figure out why."

"I don't know. But it's pretty cool, don't you think? I mean, it's nice to be able to come home. I miss that. You know, most people still have homes they can go to. Their parents still live in the same house they grew up in or, at the very least, still have a basement full of Kerplunk games and sleeping bags, you know what I mean?"

"I guess."

"I mean, we haven't had that for a long time. Everything's gone. It's kind of nice to see all this stuff again."

"It's not real, though."

"I refute you thus." Marla tosses the stuffed rabbit at me. It bounces off my head and lands on the pink shag, staring up at the ceiling with a demented, bucktoothed smile. Marla snatches it up and places it back on the bed. "God, I hope Joel shows up. I wish Mom and Dad could be here."

"Do you?"

"Don't you?"

"I haven't been in their room yet."

"And Freddy!" squeals Marla, ignoring my comment. "I wish Freddy was here!" Freddy was our dog. A dachshund. "Remember how he used to shock himself on the TV?"

"How could I forget?" Freddy used to walk around on the carpet in front of the television until he had built up a charge. Then he would touch his nose to the metal volume control, shock himself, sneeze indignantly and then do it all over again. Even the dog was fucked.

"Let's check out Joel's room." Marla leaps up from the bed.

"OK," I say. Joel's room is not my parents' room. Joel's room sounds like a good idea.

"Maybe there'll be a garbage bag full of Halloween candy in the closet. Remember that? Joel would horde it all year. Or the shoebox with the cash? Oh look. It looks so tiny!"

It is tiny. Tiny and blue. Above the narrow bed with its antique-car bedspread is a framed print of an Inuit boy. I lift it off its hook. Sure enough, a small rectangular hole has been dug out of the plaster behind it. Inside Joel's wall-safe is a piece of paper.

"Hey, what's that?" squeals Marla from inside Joel's closet.

"It's a note," I say, recognizing my brother's childish handwriting.

"What does it say?"

"It's a limerick. A weird limerick."

"Let's see." Marla plucks the page from my hand and begins to read. "There once was a man from LA, With money to burn, so they say. He bought an old place and filled up the space. Will he blow all his dough in one day?" She hands me back the note. "What the fuck does that mean?"

"I don't know."

Marla gets a cockeyed look on her face, goes back to the cupboard and resumes rooting around. Skates, hockey equipment and a Meccano set come flying out.

"Hey, look what I found." She holds up an old shoebox sealed shut with gaffer tape and covered in old decals: *Don't Eat Yellow Snow, Fly United, Keep On Truckin'*. "I wonder what's in here," she says, shaking the box. She sits down on the bed and starts working away at the tape.

I feel vaguely uneasy. I feel a sudden urge to gather my stuff and leave this house forever, but I can't take my eyes off my sister and the shoebox. Those long red nails digging away at the tape.

—

McCollum has more music than anyone I've ever met. Soul, bubble gum, rock 'n' roll, jazz, folk, country, opera, blues — over thirty milk-crates-full stacked up to the ceiling of our apartment. None of it is alphabetized or in any categorical order, but he always knows where everything is. At night we drink Bushmills and listen and listen. The Mothers of Invention, Marv Johnson, The Delfonics, Al Green, Chet Baker, Steve Goodman, Nina Simone, Lou Christie, the Strawberry Alarm Clock, Mario Lanza, Louis Armstrong, Howlin' Wolf, Leo Kottke, Joni Mitchell, Freddie and the Dreamers. McCollum says he didn't believe in any kind of a God until he heard Mel Carter sing "Hold Me, Thrill Me, Kiss Me."

Sometimes we take the portable tape recorder out to the front porch and listen to McCollum's homemade cassettes and watch the other people on their front porches, cooling off, playing cards, eating gelati, reading the paper. I like the way the little kids' pyjamas glow white and clean in the dusk as the sun slips away and the evening turns blue. I try not to watch the guy across the street working on his car. The black Camaro. Up on blocks since we moved here. All summer long he tinkers with that thing. Always without his shirt on. A coiled red bandana around his thick neck, his jeans all ripped and slung low. Sometimes he smiles at me and winks. Both McCollum and I pretend not to notice.

In the morning McCollum walks to the university, where he's studying to be an entomologist. He tells me how it is that spiders don't get caught in their own webs. He tells me how much weight an ant can carry on its back. He tells me that there are over 350,000 kinds of beetles in the world. His face glows with pride and happiness.

McCollum walks to the university and I walk to the donut shop. Olde Country Donuts. Yeah right. Lime green sprinkles in the Olde Country? Industrial-sized vats of synthetic strawberry goo? I wear an orange polyester smock and a hairnet. I serve the same greasy donuts to the same greasy customers day in and day out. I get free day-olds, half-priced coffee and the occasional ten-cent tip if I'm lucky.

I'm slightly embarrassed by the whole thing, but I see no alternative. Unlike McCollum, I have no idea what to do with my life. I think about all the things there are to be and I don't want to be any of them. Lawyer, secretary, window washer, botanist, chambermaid, engineer, zookeeper, chef. It all seems equally unfitting. School is definitely out of the question. I will never go back. Just the thought of it is enough to bring on a cyclone of anxiety. All those defeated, vaguely sadistic teachers camouflaged in their down-to-earth corduroy slacks and jackets, the throngs of robotic students dividing off like cancer cells into little vibrating clusters — jocks, hippies, stoners, nerds, rich kids, punks, geeks, freaks. Hell, I'd rather serve crullers, dodge Kelly and Tina, and watch the big dead clock do its slow-motion dance.

Kelly and Tina. The other counter girls at Olde Country Donuts. They have banded together against me in a completely natural and appropriate way. It has little to do with anything I've said or done (though I raised a couple of ultratweezed eyebrows when I announced on my first shift — in my best Patsy Cline drawl — that I was there to "put the cunt back in Olde Country"). It is more elemental than that.

They have sniffed me out, sensed something burnt and festering beneath the happy-chat surface. Something unseemly. It all makes for a rather dismal eight hours, full of Vise-Grip smile and sugar-coated stench.

It never ceases to surprise me when McCollum strides in after school with his arms full of bug books. He comes in every day, but it's always a shock. Like spotting a lemon tree in a coal mine. Like Fred Astaire stepping dapper into the monkey house.

—

My father ended his life in the same manner in which he did most everything. Loud. Forty-four Magnum in the mouth. Blew his brains out all over the bathroom. All over the pale lavender tiles. All over the blue metallic wallpaper with its patterned reproductions of nineteenth-century ads for hair-growth tonics, laudanum restoratives and licorice pastilles.

He had a fearsome weapon collection: sawed-off shotguns, semi-automatic rifles, hand grenades, crossbows. He slept with a foot-long steel rod under his pillow. "This time we'll be ready," he'd say to my mother as he oiled up one death gizmo or another. "This time I'll be waiting."

Preparation was very important to my father. The sooner he could prepare us children for the inevitable, the better. I was six years old when the bedtime stories began. Father sitting at the end of the bed in profile. Drink in hand, draining fast. Here we go, off to Hungary. Nineteen forty-something. The one about the dad being taken away. The one about eating the family pet. The one about being sent to the orphanage. The one about being taken from the orphanage. The one about the barefoot march through the snow to the ghetto. The one about the bodies stacked along the road like cordwood. The one about the baby swung by leg into wall. The one about the mother on the train to the camp. The one about Uncle Irvin. The one about the showers that weren't really showers. The one about Uncle George. The one about soap and hair and lampshades. The one about Auntie Eva. The one about twins and experiments. The one about cousin Joseph and cousin Alex. The one about cousin Joanna. Cousin Liosh. Uncle Ziggy. Auntie Rae.

Cousin Andrew. Cousin Ruth. All gone but not forgotten. Not for a moment. Not ever. Then it was lights out and *sweet dreams*. Sweet dreams. Lights out.

Nazis were everywhere in our house. On the bookshelves, in the piano, in the fireplace, the record player, the shower, the liquor cabinet, in my father's sewing machine in the basement where he stitched fur garments with hands that were meant for greater things. At the kitchen table at every meal. In every bite of food that wasn't there yesterday and probably wouldn't be there tomorrow. It was a big house but crowded.

Nights were the worst. Bad dreams or insomnia. I doubt if there was one night when all five slept peacefully. I remember reading for hours under the covers with a penlight. Anne Shirley and Anne Frank. Green Gables and Bergen-Belsen. Me, under the blankets somewhere in between in North York.

—

Marla peels back the tape and pops the lid off the shoebox. I see cash and paper.

"It's a shopping list," she says, "and one, two, three, four, five hundred dollars."

"Let's see." She hands me the list but hangs on to the cash. I read it aloud: "'Five T-bone steaks; five baking potatoes; ten corn on the cob; lettuce; tomatoes; cucumbers; salad dressing; sour cream; ice cream (butterscotch, Neapolitan); watermelon; diet Coke; whatever else you guys want. See you soon... Joel.'"

"You see, Michelle! This is what drives me nuts about Joel."

"What?"

"He is so fucking smug! I mean, how does he know we're going to find his little list hidden in the back of the cupboard?"

"Well, we did, didn't we?"

"Yeah, but what makes him so sure?" hisses Marla, pocketing the five hundred. "I'm tempted to seal it back in there and let his majesty order a fucking pizza when he arrives!"

"What difference does it make? At least we know he's showing up for dinner...and it'll be good to get out of here for a while."

"It just bugs me, that's all. He thinks he's so powerful just 'cause he's got dough. I mean, who died and left him lord of the fucking manor?!"

My brother hasn't even arrived and the bickering has begun.

"I feel like a walk anyway," I say. "I'll go, you wait here."

"No, I wanna come with. I just need to take a quick shower, OK? I'll be, like, twenty minutes, max."

"I'll wait on the porch."

Marla huffs off to the bathroom. I head outside for some air.

The neighbourhood has changed. The Jews and Italians have moved on, replaced by Chinese and East Indians. I watch the kids tricycling up and down the sidewalks, the parents washing cars, mowing lawns, sneaking surreptitious peeks at the redhead chain-smoking on the porch at number 5. The neighbourhood hasn't changed that much.

Across the street, a pregnant Asian woman is festooning a wrought iron entrance gate with paper streamers and balloons. Birthday party. This used to be the Marcheses' place, the biggest, most impressive house on Pinecrest, and the only one in which I was forbidden to babysit. It was hotly rumoured that Mr. Marchese was tangled up big-time with the Mob. Everyone believed. The fact that he started his car by remote control from inside his house and was frequently spotted making after-dark telephone calls at the pay phone outside Becker's did little to dispel the gossip.

Once, in the wee hours of a ludicrously hot summer night, Joel and I snuck out of the house, crept barefoot across the street and pasted a bumper sticker onto Mr. Marchese's navy blue Lincoln. *Mafia Staff Car. Keepa You Hands Off!* Joel had found it in a novelty shop at the Towne & Countrye mall and had let me in on it because he was too nervous to go it alone. We practically peed our polo pyjamas, trying to stifle our laughter at such a marvellously clever joke. In the morning we got up early and went outside to survey our handiwork. It was a Saturday, no later than 8 a.m. The car was in its same place in the driveway, but the sticker had vanished. Not even the slightest trace of gluey residue remained on the shiny chrome bumper. Mystery. *how did he know?* Danger. *did he know it was us?* Fear. *what would he do?* Intrigue. *when would he do it?* We waited and waited for the inevitable retribution. Joel thought kneecapping. I figured one bullet in the back of the head, KGB-style. For at least six months Marchese's Revenge fuelled our imaginations and paranoia, but nothing ever happened. Apparently, Mr. Marchese had more important matters to attend to — important matters that would eventually garner him a twelve-year jail term after being caught on tape in an undercover sting operation organized by the OPP and broadcast across Canada on *the fifth estate*. The rest of the Marcheses packed it up and moved away soon after, unable to handle the nudge-nudge, wink-wink of the Pinecrest residents.

The residents of Pinecrest. Most of the families appeared quite normal on the surface — 2.8 children, Pontiac, barbecue — but there was some serious strangeness going on behind all those double-paned windows and avocado green front doors. My short-lived career as babysitter afforded me an inside peek. A case in point, the Mandlebaums — grifters, essentially, who appeared to make their way by scalping tickets, going to the track and encouraging their three children to swindle as much as possible, whether that meant shoplifting from the mall or sneaking into movies via the fire exits. I accompanied them once to Ontario Place and was forced to enter like a Marine on a reconnaissance mission, crawling on my belly across the grass and squeezing under the fence. They seldom paid me on time and they never paid cash. It was Eaton's gift certificates or a ticket to a concert or a Leafs game. Once, they settled up with a carton of Pepperidge Farm frozen cakes that Mr. Mandlebaum had "found."

Next door to the Mandlebaums were the Bregmans — Amway salespeople and closet inventors. Their house was littered with elaborate pencil sketches for innovations such as "The Headache Helmet" (a rubberized contraption that resembled a bathing cap hooked up to two bicycle pumps) and "The Fry-Boy" (a vending machine that dispensed freshly cooked fries, with or without gravy). For a while the Bregmans got into this bizarre routine of feeding their border collie, Squeaky, various bits of indigestible matter: the top hat from the Monopoly game, a pencil eraser, a crocheted baby-booty. They would cunningly conceal these objects in a mound of dog food. Later, they would don Playtex rubber gloves and pick through the hapless hound's feces, examining the items and making notations on a chart titled "Degrees of Degradation." Why they did this, I'll never know. I only know that I wasn't allowed to let the dog out while I was there, and that the first thing the Bregmans would inquire about upon returning home was whether or not Squeaky had taken a dump (they called it a "goonk") and where they could find it. Another weird thing about them was that they called their daughter Peanut. Not just on occasion, but all the time. It was more than just a pet name or term of endearment. Everyone called her that. Even in school. Peanut Bregman. Nobody seemed to know what her real name was. When I asked her directly she would giggle and assure me that it was Cashew.

Next to the Bregmans were the Millers. Mr. Miller owned a small jewellery store. Mrs. Miller was a housewife. They had three young children and a cocker spaniel named Honey. The exterior of their home was a model of suburban integrity — perfectly groomed lawn, well-maintained facade, freshly paved driveway with shiny station wagon — a meticulously manicured mask for the malodorous interior of the house, which looked as if a dozen male college students had taken up residence after World War III. It was beyond squalid. It was an Augean stable strewn with overturned furniture, putrefying food, discarded toys, reeking diapers, piles of yellowing newspaper and mounds of fetid clothing. It shocked the hell out of me the first time I ventured inside. The vestibule — a harbinger of what lay ahead — was littered with broken crayons, snotty Kleenexes and decapitated action figures. The walls were covered in jammy hand smudges, and in the corner on the slate floor there was a big blob of lime Jell-O with a boot print in it. I waded through the muck into the kitchen, where I was instructed to wait for Mr. and Mrs. Miller, who were upstairs putting the finishing touches on their coiffure. I gawked, vaguely amused but mostly astonished, at the filth all around me. Every available surface, including the floor, was covered in stacks of dirty dishes and rotting food. There were two particularly memorable accent pieces (that in a gallery setting could have passed for avant-garde sculpture). One was a frying pan full of old cooking oil with a matted hairbrush submerged amongst the burnt food bits. The other was a cereal bowl half filled with a substance that at one time was probably porridge but had morphed into something blue and furry. It was garnished with a naked Barbie doll — her head and upper body immersed in the goo, her shapely, oatmeal-crowned legs sticking straight up to the ceiling.

"Help yourself to anything you want to eat," Mrs. Miller would chirp on her way out the door. *Yeah right*, I'd think to myself, *I'll be lucky if I can ever eat again*. I once discovered an old pizza box teeming with maggots underneath the living-room sofa. You had to be careful where you sat down in that place. The only good thing about babysitting for the Millers was that I could invite Andrea over for late-night food fights. We'd run around the main floor, laughing our asses off as we frisbeed Wagon Wheels at each other's heads or pelted one another with Fruity Pebbles. It was fun, and clean-up was a snap. We simply didn't bother. Oddly enough, the Millers never noticed.

One of the least offensive of the Pinecrest bunch were the Geffens, a family so incessantly plagued by accident and misfortune that it grew to be almost comical. The Geffens were continually breaking limbs, tumbling out of windows, overdosing on drugs or developing peculiar afflictions like Ménière's disease, edema and gout. I remember being summoned by Mrs. Geffen one evening to look after Jeffrey (recovering from German measles) and the twins, Rachel and Risa (immobilized after a school-bus crash left one with a broken arm and the other with a broken leg — extremely handy for distinguishing who was who). I was told that Mr. Geffen would be at home but unable to attend to his children since he had recently had three-quarters of his stomach surgically removed (cancer). Though suffering with a painful bout of arteriosclerosis obliterans, Mrs. Geffen rushed off to see about daughter Allison (who had been attacked by a young man with a blowtorch at a youth centre dance), but on her way careened into the back of a Mr. Poultree delivery van and was hospitalized with a concussion (and later sued by Mr. Poultree). Just another day in the life of the Geffens.

There was Mr. Jafine, who used to beat his wife and children with a tennis racket reserved solely for that purpose; crazy Mrs. Blatt, who felt it her duty to regularly inform me that my father was a "greeny" and my mother was a "hoo-er"; and old Mrs. Scinocca, who once did away with a litter of kittens by stuffing them into the leg of an old pair of pantyhose and holding them underwater (with the aid of a bathroom plunger) in the neighbour's built-in swimming pool.

When I think back on it, it was quite an achievement for us Schafers to be regarded as the freaks of Pinecrest Avenue.

"OK, let's boogie." Marla steps onto the porch and pulls the front door shut behind her. I butt out my smoke and scan the row of homogeneous houses, marvelling at their blank, unrevealing faces. Beige paper wrapping on a lurid novel.

—

McCollum doesn't want to go to the freak show. He's standing in the middle of the midway, frowning absently at the Tilt-A-Whirl.

"They've got a genuine sword swallower," I say, trying to tempt him towards the brightly coloured tent. He has other ideas.

"Let's go see the motorcycle daredevils again."

"I dunno..."

"Or the gorilla girl! Have you ever seen that?"

"Uh-uh." This is my first time at the Canadian National Exhibition. I haven't seen anything.

"Oh, the gorilla girl is the best!" He grabs my hand and pulls me along behind him. "You haven't lived until you've experienced the gorilla girl. She's like the Bugatti Royale of midway attractions."

I follow McCollum through the meandering maze of humans — weary couples eating snow cones and pushing strollers, sunburnt kids clutching balloons and candy-floss torches, young men with gigantic stuffed dogs and buffaloes balanced on their sinewy shoulders, clusters of teenage girls wearing CHUM Radio T-shirts and black felt top hats with their boyfriends' names written on them in silver sparkles. We make our way to the gorilla girl tent, where a grizzled barker takes our tickets and tells us to wait inside.

The tent is stiflingly hot and airless. We stand sweating and giggling in the dark until an ample crowd has trickled in through the khaki flap, then a scratchy tape recording of jungle drums and tropical bird shrieks fills the air, and a man's voice comes on...

Long ago, in the deepest, darkest jungles of Borneo, a she-creature — neither human nor ape — was born...

A light fades up on a cage that stands between two black velvet curtains. In the back of the cage, standing perfectly still, the gorilla girl — around twenty years old, blonde perm, chipped nail polish, Kmart bikini and white high-heeled pumps.

A creature with a strange and terrifying ability...

"And a strange and terrifying hairdo," whispers McCollum.

The ability to transform from human to beast using her extraordinary powers of concentration! Think gorilla, Sheena. Think gorilla! Think gorillaaaa...

Sheena stands there looking bored, vaguely malnourished and in need of judicious airbrushing.

Think gorillaaaa...

The transformation begins. Sheena's image starts to fade away, replaced slowly by the image of someone in a ratty gorilla suit.

"The Blue Jays' mascot would look more at home in the wild," sneers a woman in the crowd.

Within seconds, Sheena is gone (out back, having a smoke, no doubt) and the gorilla guy is hopping around and rattling the bars of the cage with as much vigour as someone earning five bucks an hour can muster.

Oh my God! She's going crazy. She's busting out! Run for your liiives!!!

The gorilla flings open the cage door, leaps down into the crowd and chases us out of the tent, back into the blinding white sun on the midway.

McCollum laughs and catches his breath. "Now that's entertainment!"

"Oh, we gotta see the freak show now," I say. "It's the perfect follow-up!"

"No, let's get something to eat," says McCollum. "I've got something special planned for dinner."

I wait outside the Food building on a singed patch of grass while McCollum braves the crowds crushing in and lining up for ten-cent spaghetti and five-cent Cokes and free samples of Billy Bee honey. Before too long McCollum emerges with his arms full of Tiny Tom donuts and Maple Leaf fudge and Switzer's beef knishes and Mennonite sausage.

"Where do you want to eat?" I ask him. All around us people blanket the lawn, stuffing their faces.

"Follow me," he says, with a mysterious smile.

We snake through the Foods of the World kiosks, stopping to pick up a Belgian waffle as we make our way over to the Alpine Way cable-car ride. I follow McCollum up the long ramp to the boarding area.

"But it only lasts about seven minutes," I say, hesitating at the entrance.

"O ye of little faith," snorts McCollum. He hands me the food, fishes a book of tickets and five bucks out of his pocket and approaches the tattooed carny operating the ride.

"We'd like to go back and forth a few times," says McCollum.

"Cool," says the carny, pocketing the fin. He swings a yellow car around the bend and holds it steady as we climb in. He slams the door shut and clamps the safety latch. The car lurches forward then settles into a steady skim high above the length of the fair.

"That was so very suave, McCollum!"

"I'm a classy guy, Schafer." McCollum spreads the food out on the seat opposite, reaches into his knapsack and pulls out a bottle of Chianti, a corkscrew and two wineglasses wrapped in a terry cloth dishtowel.

"Would mademoiselle care for some wine?"

"But of course, my good man!"

"I understand that this vintage goes exceedingly well with a fine maple fudge, but I'll leave it up to the lady's discerning palate." McCollum pours a splash of red into my glass.

I sip, suck, swirl, then pause before making my pronouncement: "Mmm, definitely better than a poke in the eye with a burnt stick. In other words, fill me up!"

McCollum pours. We raise our glasses in a toast to the gorilla girl as the occupants of the blue car passing in the opposite direction point and stare.

When we finally stumble off the ride, we are stuffed and pickled. We go to the Better Living Centre, where McCollum antagonizes the sales reps by folding himself up in Craftmatic adjustable beds, sitting on massage pillows and smashing unbreakable dishes. It's time to go home.

On our way to the Princes Gate we pass the freak show once more. A crowd has gathered around the Human Blockhead — a scrawny old man with a nicotine-stained bouffant who is trying to entice them inside. The Human Blockhead inserts a screwdriver into his nose, then hammers on the yellow plastic handle until he hits bone. The crowd groans, repulsed and delighted. The Human Blockhead removes the screwdriver, wipes the shaft with a crusty J Cloth and starts collecting tickets.

"How many tickets do we have left?"

"Four."

"Perfect! Let's check it out."

"Oh, I don't know..." McCollum is wavering.

"Come on... the Human Blockhead! That rivals the Gorilla Girl for utter silliness, don't you think?" The last few people are filing into the tent. I grab the tickets, tear off two and hand the others back to McCollum. "I gotta see this. I'll be right back."

I move through the multitude, manoeuvring my way up to the front of the stage. The Human Blockhead welcomes the crowd and warns us that what we are about to see is not for the squeamish. He advises those who are prone to fainting spells or anyone with a heart condition to leave now while they still can. The crowd titters. Nobody moves. The Human Blockhead introduces the first attraction: "Ladies and gentlemen, please welcome Pisces, the Amazing Fish Man!"

The Amazing Fish Man emerges from behind a curtain at the back of the tent and takes his place centre stage. He is a middle-aged man with a bad case of ichthyosis (though nothing that a case of Keri lotion wouldn't remedy). He is wearing a tiny turquoise Speedo. A set of green plastic gills has been clumsily glued to his neck. The crowd gawks at the Fish Man's dry, scaly skin as he turns this way and that, as the Human Blockhead goes through his spiel about the Fish Man's idyllic early years on the lost island of Atlantis. I search the Fish Man's eyes to see what he thinks about the whole deal, but he's got it down. In true fishy form, the eyes aren't giving anything away. When the people have had enough, the Fish Man goes back through the curtain behind the stage. From my vantage point I catch a glimpse of a black-and-white portable television with a half-eaten hot dog on top.

Now it's time for the Human Pin Cushion. He carries out a long strip of plywood perforated with thousands of nails. He strips off a dirty white tunic and lies down on the spiny bed. The people applaud. Now the Human Blockhead gets into the act. He places a plain sheet of plywood on top of the Human Pin Cushion and steps gingerly onto the surface. He begins to sing, laying on a bad Cockney accent: "I've Got a Lovely Bunch of Coconuts..." He begins to tap dance. The people applaud even louder. Blockhead hops off and removes the plywood. Pin Cushion leaps up, makes the victory sign with both hands and turns to display his muscular back, which is now covered with thousands of tiny pink indentations.

Next up is a woman billed as Ellie, The Ghoul Next Door. Curtains part and Ellie appears in a wheelchair. A murmur of shock and revulsion ripples through the audience as the twisted figure rolls slowly to centre stage. She speaks.

"Hi, my name is Eleanor Montgomery, but my friends call me Ellie. You've probably never seen anyone quite like me before."

She speaks the truth. Ellie is outrageously deformed. Her head is enormous — something like three feet in diameter — and grossly misshapen. The forehead bones bulge like sick cantaloupes. There is easily enough room above the eyebrows for another entire face. The head tilts down and rests on the left side of the body, which has somehow managed to grow at least three times as big as the right side. The hands and feet are monstrously large and, like the head, are blanketed in pale brown splotches of varying sizes. Hideous.

I feel bad. I suddenly wish I hadn't pushed my way to the front of the stage. I suddenly find myself thinking about McCollum. Ellie stares down the audience.

"I have what's known as hemihypertrophy and macrocephaly, with some lipolymphohemangiomas tossed in for good measure. That's quite a mouthful, isn't it? Heh, heh, heh. Yup, the doctors got so tongue-tied that they had to come up with another name: Proteus Syndrome. Does anyone here know who Proteus was?"

The crowd shuffles its feet.

"A Greek sea god," I say. "A shape-shifter."

"Now there's a young lady who knows her mythology! Right. But unlike Proteus, I pretty much stay the same shape these days. In fact, I pretty much lead a normal life..."

I think about McCollum. I think about six weeks sleeping together and no sex beyond kissing. I think about the grey sweatpants that he wears to bed every night and the locked bathroom door when he showers and dresses. I think about the naked body I've never seen.

"...married for eighteen years. My husband, God rest his soul, passed away in 1971. But I'm not alone. I have a beautiful and talented daughter, whom you are about to meet. Her name is Helen, and she is one of the few genuine sword swallowers in the world. After the show we'll be selling autographed postcards for fifty cents each. But right now please put your hands together for my beautiful daughter Helen!"

Much tense applause. The curtain parts and a young woman in a gauzy blue gown slips through. She is tall and slim and evenly featured. She has long red hair and clear green eyes. She is beautiful. The crowd breathes an inaudible sigh of relief.

Helen holds up a long silver sword for the audience to see. "How many people out there believe that I am a real sword swallower?"

No response from the crowd. Helen turns to Ellie. "Well, it looks like we have a lot of sceptics with us today." Ellie doesn't say anything. She is beaming at her daughter, practically shivering with pride. She looks like the cat that swallowed the caviar-stuffed canary.

"Well, perhaps this will convince them. Here..." Helen hands the sword to a man in the audience. "I think if you'll examine that carefully you'll find that it is one solid piece of tempered steel. Twenty-five inches long. No springs or gizmos or tricky bits whatsoever."

The man turns the sword over and over in his hands. He nods his head to signify approval.

"Please, pass it around."

The sword is circulated through the audience. More nods of approval. Eventually it is handed to me. I explore every inch with my fingertips. It is heavy and hard. One piece. Real.

Helen reaches out for the blade. She wipes it down with rubbing alcohol and tilts back her head. "Don't worry, it only hurts when I laugh."

She opens her mouth wide, and slowly, slowly lowers the sword into her throat... then down, down through the throat into the belly. When the blade can go no further, she raises her hands in the air.

Wild applause. Ellie rolls to the front of the stage. "Now, just in case there's any doubting Thomases left out there, I'm going to ask a volunteer to come forward to pull out the sword."

Hands shoot up all around me.

"But you have to do it very slowly and you have to be very *very* careful!"

Ellie scans the audience, searching for the most trustworthy candidate, scrutinizing the faces for kindness, for compassion. Her eyes hold on me for more than a moment, then continue roving. She fixes her gaze at the back of the room.

"You, sir!" she says, pointing a gargantuan finger.

The people, with their hands still in the air, turn and look to the entrance of the tent, where McCollum stands slouched with his arms folded across his chest. The crowd parts as he moves towards the stage. Helen bends slowly forward at the hips, rigid with her offering. A brief look into each other's eyes, then, with impossibly gentle hands, McCollum deftly pulls the blade from the young woman's body.

—

Five steaks. I'm picking out five T-bone steaks from the meat counter at the corner Safeway. "Five steaks for three people... it seems a bit excessive, don't you think?" I try to sound offhand about my observation. I try to keep the tiny quaver of hope and excitement out of my voice.

"Are you kidding? Joel is the king of excess. I'm surprised he hasn't installed a gold-plated veal-hut in the backyard. Or one of those guys from Japan to massage and slaughter a Kobe cow just in time for dinner." Marla tosses one of the steaks back into the display case. "Actually, I don't even want one. I'm on a low-fat diet. Fat is the culprit, you know." She waits for me to take the bait and launch into the anorexia lecture, but something inside of me hardens and rebels.

"It just occurs to me that maybe there'll be other people showing up. Maybe Joel has arranged for a couple other people to come." I steer the cart towards dairy. A Muzak version of "Daniel" is being piped out of the ceiling.

"Yeah! Maybe he's bringing home two eligible Hollywood bachelors for his spinster sisters! You're not seeing anyone, are you?"

"No."

"Me either. Surprise, surprise. OK, I'll take Matt Dillon and you can have... let's see, who would be good for you...?"

I don't answer. I'm rolling fast past the sour cream. Marla grabs my arm and looks hard into my flushed face. "Oh my God, Michelle, you can't be serious!"

"What?"

"You're not *still* thinking about what's his name, are you?"

"No. Not really..."

"Oh my God, you're obsessed! I thought that was finally resolved."

"It is."

"I mean, when's the last time you saw the guy?"

"Six years ago. In Winnipeg. You know the story."

"Right. So you haven't had a real conversation with the jerk for, like, twenty years or something. I'd say it's time to let it go."

"He's not a jerk." The words pop automatic from my mouth even though I know there's no point.

"Oy vey! *I* would never let myself get that obsessed with a man. I mean, I was in love with Brian, *deeply* in love, but when we split, we split. That was it. I moved on. I'm just not the obsessive type." Marla drops a container of low-fat yogourt into the cart. "You know he's totally religious now. He has, like, seven kids or something. Did you know that?"

"No."

"Yeah. He moved to Israel. Lives in the West Bank. Weird, eh? I mean, imagine if I'd stayed with him. I'd be wandering around the desert with a shmatte on my head."

"Hmm."

"Listen, you'd better just forget about it. There's no way Joel would be shipping your long-lost boyfriend home. He's too selfish to even think of that. If anything, he's bringing a couple of personal assistants along to impress us."

"Well, what about the Maple Leaf Gardens thing? He already shipped home everyone he wanted to see from the past. It's not beyond the realm of possibility."

"You know, I've been thinking about that, and as much as I've always hated that Jason Beale, I don't think he'd make up a story like that. I believe him."

"I don't know."

"Joel is into power. That night wasn't about seeing old friends; that was about seeing old friends squirm."

"I disagree. I think he really wanted to see them. And even if the other part is true, it's not like he held a gun to their heads. They could have walked out."

"You think so?"

"Of course. Wouldn't you?"

"I'm not so sure. I've eaten a lot of shit in my life and, believe me, it was for a lot less than a quarter of a million bucks. I mean, that's pretty much financial security, right?" Marla drops two cartons of ice cream into the cart. "Uch, I can't believe he eats this junk! To tell you the truth, I think that's what this whole weekend is about. I think he's gonna pull something similar with us. You know, offer us bags of cash and make us go through some humiliating ritual to get it."

"If that's the case, I'm out of here."

"Yeah, we'll see about that. Everyone has their price, Michelle. I mean, think about what he said in the limerick: 'There once was a man from LA, blah blah blah... Then he blew all his dough in one day.' Maybe Joel is planning to pull a Cat Stevens or something. Pack it all in and go join a monastery. But first he's gonna dole out the dough and have some twisted fun doing it."

"Well—"

"Which, in all honesty, is fine by me. Whatever it is, I am up for it, baby."

"Oh, really?"

"Yes, really. I am sick to death of working crappy jobs. I've been working crappy jobs since I was eighteen years old. I'm tired, Michelle. Very tired..." Marla adopts a far-off, droopy-eyed gaze and sighs wearily.

"But Joel has helped you out over the years. What about the catering business? And the PR company and the photography studio?"

My sister whirls around, her face mangled with rage, all teeth and vein and bulging eyes. "Oh fine! Just throw that in my face, OK?! Fine! I'm a fucking failure, all right?!"

I shrink away from the pierce of her voice. A high sick sound that shakes the aisle and hardens every cell in my body.

"Marla the fucking loser, OK! Here..." Marla tears the five hundred dollars out of her pocket and flings it at my head. "You happy now? Sadistic bitch!" Marla spins around and storms away on little legs, the butt cheeks popping fast and furious, the sandals click-clicking on the hard linoleum gleam.

I stand for a moment unable to move, trying to swallow. I listen to the Muzak. I listen to her absence. Then I pick up the money with cement fingers, double-check the shopping list and proceed evenly towards the checkout counter. I know that when I get outside, Marla will be waiting. She'll flick her cigarette, smile and offer to help me with the bags. She'll chatter aimlessly about one thing or another. Maybe crack a few jokes or see if I want to grab an egg roll at the old Chinese restaurant. In her mind it is over and done with. She has forgiven me. She feels much better now.

—

Barbie Benstein doesn't tap me any longer. All through grade seven, all through grade eight, she'd sit behind me in every class, tapping on my shoulder with a pointy-nailed index finger. Tapping for answers with a fat stupid finger. Tap tap tap...*who is Arch Duke Ferdinand?* Tap tap tap...*where is the Beaufort Sea?* Tap tap tap...*the square root of 441?* Tap tap tap...*the difference between frog and toad?* I would half-turn my head and hiss-whisper the answers, anything to kill the vibe of fat bewilderment buzzing at the back of my neck like a warm cloud of flies. But now she no longer taps. She sits far away and avoids my eye. Just like Melissa Fisher and Stacey Greenbaum and all the rest of them. I have freed myself. Freed myself with ripped jeans and lumber jacket and airplane bottles of vodka in the bathroom at recess and skipped-period spliffs with Paul and John and Ryder and hanging at the OH complex after school. Ontario Housing. Poor and white. Black Sabbath, Led Zeppelin, Molson Ex, Export "A". Rain-soaked empties on tiny cement porches. Mothers smoking cigarettes at dirty kitchen tables, the fathers long gone long gone. Through the ravine and over the bridge, I have crossed to the other side. I am no longer someone to be tapped. I am someone to be feared.

I hang with the toughs in the park at the complex. All winter long we stand for hours in the cold. We smoke and smoke. Pot, cigs, whatever. Sometimes there is acid, peyote, mushrooms. Sometimes there is beer. Always there is Ryder with his torn and skinny jeans, with his rough arms circling warm around my waist and his stale tobacco lips brushing coarse against mine. Sweet and stupid and borderline dangerous, Ryder stands shivering with his threadbare jacket draped over my shoulders, looking for the next person with drugs, looking for someone to beat up, looking like a Kmart version of Christ with his flowing blond locks and his blank blue eyes.

Tonight there is someplace warm to go. A basement party. We make out on a pile of coats in a dark corner, then slip into the furnace room when it becomes available. Ryder strips off his clothes and spreads them out on the cement floor. I marvel at the taut body graffitied with navy blue homemade tattoos, the tangle of golden pubic hairs, the hard uncircumcised penis. I undress and lie down. We fuck. I have learned how to buck up against him, how to make myself come. He likes when I do it. He says some girls just lie there like corpses. Afterwards I feel warm and remarkably calm. Not much to say. Back to the party. We sip Southern Comfort and smoke another joint, then I let him walk me halfway home. Just as far as the bridge. A quick kiss goodnight and I lumber drunk into the ravine, slouching back through the woods to my secret Jewish existence.

When I get home the house is still shaking. Something about *pigsties* and *lice*. Blaring accusations. Bat-screech denials. I don't want to know. I slip off my sneakers and make for the stairs. Halfway up on stockinged feet I am caught.

Is that you? Where the hell have you been?! Father hurricanes into the hallway, clutching a dirty dinner plate. Marla and Joel in his wake, wild-eyed and frantic.

Andrea's, I murmur.

That's not true! Andrea called here! shrieks Marla.

Father roars forward, coming at me with the plate. *Did you do this?!* he thunders, waving it in my face. I stare at the thing, bewildered and stoned. Then, suddenly, the tiny dried mustard smear registers. I remember what I forgot. A couple of days ago, lying on the couch watching *The Flintstones*. I eat a baloney sandwich before dinner. I hear him coming up from the basement. I slide the plate under the couch.

...*no*, I whisper.

A wail of overlapping outrage explodes in the hall. Joel, Marla. Marla, Joel. *She's lying, I swear to...! I didn't fuckin' do it...! She just proved she's a liar...! Look at her, she's a slob...!* And the father right in my face, purple with rage, a sick beer stench leaking hot from the terrible mouth.

You want maggots and lice? Is that what you want? A shaking hand clenched in a pluck dabs at my hair and my neck. *You want cockroaches and maggots and lice?* Dab dab dab. *Have you ever seen a louse? I have. I have!*

Look what she's wearing!

She's lying, she did it!

Shut up, you... Your mother is trying to sleep!

Attention momentarily diverted, I back away slowly. One stair, two stair...

What the hell have you got on?! What are you, a derelict, some kind of a pig? Father grabs hold of the rips in my jeans and yanks. Tearing denim, piercing scream from Marla and I'm standing there, shredded, white legs exposed.

A moment of enormous silence. Then... Joel begins to laugh. Now they're all laughing. I watch the faces twist from one extreme to the other as the house peals with a manic three-toned howling. Marla and Joel clutch each other for support. Tears squirt down my father's red face. I turn and walk thickly up the stairs, trailing a train of denim like some kind of zombie bride. Now they're at it again. Already. Another short-lived truce.

Zombie past my mother, who is trying to sleep, past the closed door, down the hall to my room. The brain is squirming hot and crazy. I require relief. First the window, push it open, let the burning snow blow in blow in. Now the headphones and the stereo as loud as it can go. *Break On Through.* Now the razor on flesh. Roll the sleeves and sink it in. Not too deep. Just enough. A glorious release. A wonderful gush. All along the top of the forearms, a fabulous easing. The lines, like tiny valves, releasing steam, pressure and blood.

Downstairs in the hall they whirl and claw, shriek and shred.

Me in dark bedroom, emptying onto the rug.

Mom in dark bedroom, growing the tumour.

—

One of my favourite things. Going alone somewhere with my mother. Today we are going to Daiter's and Health Bread and maybe maybe to the library. I have stayed home from school with another headache. My mother knows that I don't have a headache and I know she knows, but we don't say anything. It's no big deal. Brenlee Megler and I are the browners in the class. The teachers say I can skip from grade four to grade six if my parents agree.

In the car we listen to the radio. My mother sings along. "There's a Kind of Hush." I close my eyes and watch the sun patterns dance glad across my eyelids. Or I stick my head just a little out the window and tilt it back to watch the sky rolling by. Branches, wires, street lights, birds. I like to see things from unusual angles. Sometimes I'll make the sky be the foreground and the branches be the background. Sometimes I'll look down at the moving pavement and pretend that I am so tall and gigantic that even walking at a normal gait the ground is racing that fast beneath me. Sometimes I'll stare at the crinkly blue dashboard and imagine what I would see if I was the tiniest speck of a bug trying to traverse the mountainous plastic terrain. And sometimes I just watch my mother sing, her shoulders hunched and moving with the music, her head tilted dreamy to one side. When we get to where we're going it is almost always too soon.

First, Daiter's. My job is to pick the cottage cheese, an old ritual that I am almost too old for. For a while I truly believed that I had some magical power to divine the freshest, most delicious piece of cottage cheese. Now I do it for tradition's sake. We proceed directly to the back of the store, to the white counter lined with giant yellow cheese wheels, slabs of marble halvah and bags of wrinkly green pistachios. It smells good in here, like sour cream and smoked fish and worn hardwood and clean linoleum. We exchange greetings with the man in the white cotton apron. He says my mom and I look like sisters. He says he likes me in green. He tells my mother that I have "intelligent eyes." A little slice of halvah for me to nibble, then he shuffles to the fridge and fishes out three heavy cheesecloth sacks. He unties and untwirls the first one, holding it open for me to evaluate. I sniff and consider. No, not quite right. My mother watches me, quietly amused. I move on to the second piece. Sniff, squeeze, oh yes, this is definitely the one. The man pops the white slab out of the cheesecloth onto a large rectangle of clean waxed paper, folds it shut and seals it with a sticky price label. We buy chive cream cheese, dill pickles and a tiny piece of smoked sable, then it's off to Health Bread for sweet yellow challah, poppy-seed bagels and a cinnamon buffalo bun to share in the car.

Today we will go to the library. Five books for me. I can't get enough. *A Wrinkle in Time*, *Rina Goes Riding*, *Emily of New Moon*, *Papa Says* and *Little Men*. I love the smell of the yellowing pages, the dull KA-CHUNK of the machine at the checkout desk. Now we sneak into the basement. Quiet quiet. Sneak into the auditorium with its rows of metal bridge chairs and its baby grand piano. I lie across three chairs pushed close together and select my first escape. Mom adjusts the creaky piano bench, test tests the middle C and gently fills the room with music. Blissfully quiet music.

As the nocturne plays, Rina feeds apples to her golden palomino. Tiny, tart apples on a flattened palm. She is dreaming about victory in the upcoming race. She is velvety stroking the beast's soft muzzle.

—

My marks have plummeted faster than Nancy Greene on Whistler. I no longer see the point in school or anything. I would quit if I could, but I'm too young. Under sixteen you need parental consent, and my parents still cling to the belief that I'm going to be a doctor or a lawyer or a doctor. Just a phase, they think, just a phase. So I go to school, but I don't stay there. I usually make it to English; the rest depend on how I'm feeling. Science is a total joke, taught by Mr. Szostak the phys. ed. teacher. He wears a lab coat over his navy Adidas sweatsuit and doesn't even pretend to comprehend the mimeographed module from which he recites. When the frog tongues and hamster hearts go flying across the lab, he retreats to his glassed-in mini-office, chews on his whistle and tries not to notice. Math has ceased to make sense since I dropped my first microdot. Patterns have disappeared. Logic has flown. History is all what and never why, and so a bore. Geography is colouring, decorating maps with pencil crayons. Marks for neatness. Shameful for grade eight. The teacher is a zero with a wonky glass eye. When she says "Yes?" to someone with their hand raised, six people blurt out the answer. Typing is less than useless. I ignore the assignments and amuse myself by tapping out whatever the hell I please on the hideous piss-yellow paper.

To Whom It May Concern,

I saw the best minds of my generation destroyed by
    mildness, well-fed serene swaddled,
conducting themselves through the Holt Renfrew streets at dawn
    looking for a sugar-free Fresca.

Yours Truly,

Michelle Schafer

Art was all right until the class destroyed my term project, a mosaic of the Last Supper rendered entirely in fruit-flavoured Chiclets. It took me months to glue the bastards in place. I spent every last cent I had on gum from Shoppers Drug Mart. Even resorted to shoplifting to finish the damn background. Stealing Chiclets — it's like trying to steal rattles. The thing survived one day in the classroom before it was picked clean. The teacher got a good laugh out of that one. I haven't been back since. Home Ec. is ridiculous. Cooking and sewing. I was put on notice for squirting dishwashing liquid into Marnie Bloom's pancake batter, and finally suspended after my A-line denim skirt assignment mysteriously mutated into a fetching denim straitjacket.

Phys. Ed. is out of the question. Do the Hustle. Leap over a bar. Trot around the track. Yeah right. French — *mon Dieu* — is more than I can bear. The teacher is a sadistic little troll, four foot nine and pushing half a century old. She wears adorable little girly frocks, usually pink, always frothy, and does her greasy grey-streaked hair in two long braids. The aging offspring of Heidi and Grandpa Munster, she delights in mocking the awkward accents of the recently immigrated.

So I go to school, but I don't stay there. I head to the pool hall or the OH complex in search of Ryder. Or John or Paul or Hinkley for that matter. Sex is my refuge. A wonderful distraction. A temporary clouding of the thoughts that are consuming me. I am dying. The world is a dismal place. I feel abnormal. Removed. Like a spectator at an ugly and absurd play. A black comedy with an incomprehensible plot and a cast of weak, stupid and evil characters. Ordinary men are executioners lying in wait. Everything is behaviour except, perhaps, brutality. The way people dress, talk, act and live strikes me as elaborate collusion, a collective agreement based on nothing. Rigid and unreal. I don't understand why they continue to play along. I cannot play along.

The more detached I become from humans and their modes of behaviour, the more magical and powerful I become. Strange things begin to happen. Birds come to me when I call them. Nighthawks and sparrows. A robin takes up residence in our backyard. It stands atop the wooden fence, waiting for me to show up. I walk to the middle of the lawn and wait for the signal. When the bird chirps, I whistle, raise my right arm to the side and then let it drop. After two or three times, the robin flies over and perches on my head. A few seconds later it darts to the fence on the opposite side of the yard and we do it all again. My mother watches concerned from the kitchen window up above. She sends Joel down to try it, but the bird takes off.

I am walking to the library when I have a sudden urge to fall down in the snow and taste it in my mouth. When the white melts away, there is a band of gold on my tongue. The inscription in the ring says *Sylvia*. When I get to the library I find a book discarded on my favourite chair in the corner. *The Bell Jar* by a writer named Sylvia Plath.

I am alone in my room, praying to God or Whatever to put me in touch with one person, just one real person — not a character in a book — whom I can stomach or love, when my father barges in on my latest arm-carving session. *What in the hell are you doing? What, you think you have troubles? You don't know what trouble is!* Three days later I am being admitted to the Toronto General Hospital psychiatric ward for a six-week assessment. Two weeks after that, McCollum takes a wrong turn and shuffles bare-assed down the hallway in front of me.

Magic.

—

When I get outside, Marla is waiting. She flicks her cigarette and offers to help me with the bags. I'm no martyr. I hand half of them over.

"Hey, you wanna grab an egg roll at the old Chinese place?"

"Nah, let's head back." My plan is to drop off the groceries then cab it over to the liquor store at the Towne & Countrye mall.

"See that girl's hair over there?" Marla gestures to a teenager sporting the latest TV do, a bad shag that bears the markings of a weed-whacker attack.

"Yeah."

"You think I should grow my hair out and get something like that?"

"I don't know."

"You think it would suit me?"

"Yeah, I guess."

"Or do you think I'm too old?"

"No."

"What's the matter with you?"

"Nothing."

"You want me to take another bag?"

"No, I'm fine."

"Fine!"

When we get halfway up Pinecrest I notice the car, a vintage baby blue Oldsmobile parked in the driveway of number 5.

"It looks like Joel has arrived."

"Oh my God, that's *exactly* like our old car!" Marla quickens her pace. "Remember our drives in the country?!"

"Yeah." Drive an hour north of Steeles. Listen to Marla/Joel/Father scream incessantly at each other, be forced to exclaim with childish delight every time we pass a cow or a cob of corn, grab a lousy hamburger at some divey roadside grease pit and then hightail it back to the burbs, staring hard out the window, imagining what it would be like to fling open the door and roll headfirst into the ditch.

Marla drops her bags and hops up onto the trunk of the car. She leans back on the rear windshield and closes her eyes. "Mmm,'member how we used to suntan on here. With baby oil!"

Before we killed the sun.

"Yeah, and remember how we used to go outside without protective suits and oxygen tanks!"

Marla opens one eye. "What?"

"Nothing," I say. "Just kidding." The adaptability of humans has always puzzled me. We'll accept anything, provided it comes on gradually.

"Just use sunscreen if you're so paranoid." Marla hops off the car, collects the bags and follows me to the door.

Key in the lock and then... barking. I swing the thing open and a dog sprints past me out the door onto the porch. A dachshund. Yapping and nipping at our heels.

"Freddy!!! Oooh, c'mere boy! Yes, attsa good boy, yes! Oh yes. Yukka tukka tukka. You're a good boy, aren't you? Little Freddy..." Marla scoops up the wriggling creature and smothers it with kisses. "Look, 'Chelle, it's Freddy!"

Marla releases the dog and it bolts back into the house. Now a voice calling out from deep inside: "Welcome home, girls, you're just in time!" Not Joel's voice. A woman's voice. Marla and I exchange a glance and proceed to the kitchen.

"Well, hello there, you two!"

I drop the bags on the kitchen floor. A woman who is the spitting image of my mother, a woman who is wearing my mother's clothing and beaming like a bedlamite stops stirring a pitcher of frozen orange juice and advances towards us with her arms outstretched.

"Oh my fucking God," mumbles Marla.

I take a step backwards and thrust out my hand for a formal shake. "I'm Michelle Schafer," I say, tersely, my body stiffening.

"I know who you are, silly. Always the joker, my Michelle!" The fake mom grabs my hand and yanks me into a rigid one-sided embrace. Then she moves on Marla. "Welcome home, bubelah."

To my astonishment Marla crumples into her arms and starts bawling. Wailing. Mouth wide open like a little baby. Tears and snot pouring down her twisted red face.

"Shhhhh," says the fake mom, stroking my sister's hair. "Shhhh..."

"This is ridiculous," I say, wrestling my sister from the stranger's grip. She feels tiny in my arms. A tiny toothpick bird. "Where the hell is Joel?"

"Joel will be home for dinner. Your father is outside fertilizing the lawn."

"My father is in the Dawes Road cemetery, fertilizing the lawn."

"What a way to talk! Here..." The fake mom goes for a box of Kleenex.

Marla pushes me away. I look out the window and, sure enough, a father replicant, alarmingly accurate at this distance, is futzing with a bag of fertilizer in the backyard.

"Look," I say, fumbling for a smoke and a match, "I realize you've probably been paid a lot of money and you're just doing your job, but it's enough already, OK? Joke's over. Time to go home."

"How many times do I have to tell you you shouldn't smoke, honey. It's bad for your health."

"Yeah, so is liver cancer, right Ma?"

"Shut up, Michelle!" Marla blows her nose into a peach-coloured tissue held by the fake mom.

"Now, now, no fighting. Let's just relax and have a nice lunch. Look, I got Daiter's cottage cheese. And Health Bread bagels! You can't get that in Winnipeg."

"It looks good," says Marla. "Let's just eat, Michelle."

"I'm not hungry," I lie. My heart is thumping like a bastard. I go for the White Pages and start looking up Air Canada. Five steaks. Five people. The writing is on the wall.

"What are you doing, honey?" asks the fake mom, slightly strained.

"I'm going home, sweetheart," I say, sucking hard on my cig.

"Don't you leave me here alone!" shouts Marla.

"I suggest you do the same," I say, dialling the number.

"Here, Joel wanted me to give you this." The fake mom fishes a note out of my dead mother's pants pocket and hands it to me.

I get a recording. "Thank you for calling Air Canada. For service in English press 1 . . ." No buttons on the old black dial. I wait and read the note: *Michelle, Please don't leave before I get there. There's something very important I need to discuss with you. Please! Love, Joel.*

I crumple the note and toss it on the counter. Put the receiver back in its cradle. The fake mom breathes a sigh of relief. She's too tall, I think to myself, the cheekbones are too high and the teeth are all wrong.

"You better stay," says Marla, smoothing out the note. "It's just a few hours."

I go for the basement door. It's still locked. "Why is the basement door locked?"

"I'm not sure," says the fake mom. "I think it's a surprise."

Great. More surprises.

"I'm going to the liquor store," I say. "Any requests?"

"Don't you want to have a little something to eat first?"

"I don't think so."

"Do you want to take the car?"

"Yes."

"Do you want to say hello to your father before you head off?"

"No."

—

Life in the basement with McCollum is strangely peaceful. I miss my mother, but that's nothing new. She calls once a week to see if I'm safe. That's all she can do. That's all she can do. Not once does she suggest that I move back home. She seems to understand that it's better where I am.

Women's lib is coming on strong. One day I say: Why don't you leave? Pack it in. Find a basement somewhere. Find some peace. No, she says, I am too old. The kids. Your father. Your father had a hard life. A victim of circumstance. You must understand.

My arms are slowly beginning to heal. Only the occasional new slash. McCollum is disturbed but not horrified by the gore. He seems to get it. Better than I.

One night, lights out, we take turns writing "inherently funny" words in the air with the glow of our cigarettes...*Minsk, Squat, Flab, Doodle*. McCollum whispers soft into my ear. "You know what I see when I look at your arms?"

"Pus?"

"No."

"A scabby image of the Virgin Mary?"

"Nope."

"What?"

"I see a painting or a story or a song."

"What do you mean?"

"I mean the message is OK, but the medium is all wrong."

"There is no message. It's sheer relief."

Twaddle, writes McCollum with his cigarette.

The next day he wrestles home a used IBM Selectric, two new ribbons and a package of white paper. When I plug the thing in, it purrs.

First I try the diary thing. That lasts a total of three days. When I look over my words I find them phony and clumsy and awful. I burn them in the sink. Wash the delicate black remnants down the drain. I try a few poems, but they also come off clunky. Florid. Hungarian. I stop trying. I begin firing off little notes to McCollum. Anything I can think of that he might find amusing. I slip them into his pockets and his bug books so that he'll find them during the day at school.

My Dearest Denise,

By the time you receive this, I will be long gone. Please don't try to find me, I won't be hiding in the linen closet with a month's supply of canned goods like the last time. I want to thank you for all you've done for me, darling. For opening my eyes to the beauty of life, for filling my days with love, for giving me the confidence to carry on with my work even after I was fired from the Orange Julius for gross incompetence.

I will always cherish the moments we shared: strolling hand in hand down the beach, rolling up little pieces of toilet paper and putting them in our eyes, doing the bird dance on your husband's grave...precious times that I will treasure forever. Enclosed you will find a little something for you to remember me by...my nose. You always said how you loved my nose. Well, I want you to have it, darling. Please don't cry, Denise. In time you will forget about me and go on with your life. This is as it should be. You are young, vivacious and built like a brick shithouse. Go out and love some more!

The light grows dim, dearest. I must now end this sad correspondence. Your obedient servant and truest of loves,

Rolph.

The Poodle

The poodle – nature's most perfect food – was invented by Otto Van Plotsberg in 1872. According to Van Plotsberg he had only just begun experimenting with kinky hair and extra toes when he happened upon the formula for poodles. Van Plotsberg's first poodles sported only one leg – a stumpy appendage protruding from the centre of the body. These crude early versions (commonly inverted and used as hat stands) were soon abandoned in favour of the superior French model, which featured a winning smile and four limbs positioned strategically around the torso. Thus began the dizzying proliferation of the modern-day poodle – hampered temporarily by a 1909 decree which stated that "Henceforth all poodles shall bear the name Svee," marking a slight decline in the population until the edict was overturned. Today, poodles inhabit every corner of the earth. Witness the African Killer Poodle, The Wild Poodles of Borneo, and the elusive Giant Swamp Poodle of Denchai.

Mickey Shane and The Case of the Missing Husband
Chapter 1

It was a night like any other in the big city – kind of dark, the letters "p.m." lit up on the clock radio. I was alone in my office catching up on some paperwork when I heard footsteps in the hall, footsteps that stopped outside my door. Through the fogged glass I could make out the silhouette of a dame. Either that or a man with no Adam's apple and unusually large breasts. She didn't bother to knock. She just walked right into my life.

"Mickey Shane, Private Dick?"

"Who wants to know?"

"I do."

"Er, OK...I'm Mickey Shane. What can I do for you, dollface?"

"First of all, you can call me by my name. It ain't dollface. It's Poopsie. Ms. Poopsie LaRue, Mr. Shane."

"All right, Ms. Poopsie LaRue Mister Shane, what can I do for you?"

"Look, maybe you'd just better call me Poopsie, OK?"

"Fine, Poopsie OK, spill it! As you can see I've got a lot of paperwork to do."

"You call origami paperwork?"

"What would you call it?" This Ms. Poopsie OK LaRue Mister Shane was no rocket scientist, but what a looker! Legs that went on for kilometres, curves in all the right places. Too bad about the pointy head and the herpe on her lip.

"I know what you're thinking, Mr. Shane. That's no herpe. I got my lip caught in a zipper."

"That's your business, sweetheart."

"And this is yours." She tossed an envelope on the desk. "Five hundred smackers and a coupon for a free creamy coleslaw from Kentucky Fried Chicken. I want you to find my husband," she said, reaching into her handbag. "Here's a recent photograph."

Just my luck. Of all the cases in all the world, I had to get stuck with the oldest one in the book: some slob goes out for a pound of mortadella and a roll of bubble wrap and never comes back. Still, you don't say no to five hundred samoleons when you're out of Nutella and the squirrels are pounding on your door.

"How long did you say your hubby has been missing?"

"Twenty three and a half hours. But I just know something's wrong. It's not like him to miss a tanning appointment. And he didn't show up at work today."

"Where's work?"

"The Wide Open Beaver."

"The strip joint over on Queen?"

"No, the daycare centre on Rose Briarway!"

Sarcastic cow. I was strapping on my piece and heading for the door when the wiseacre leaped up and grabbed me by the arm.

"You ain't goin' out like that, Shane."

"Relax, sweetheart, I always carry a piece."

"I ain't talkin' about the gun. It's your pants. You shouldn't wear white after Labour Day."

One thing's for sure, the broad had class. I wrestled

`her to the ground and kissed her full on the lips. Then I headed to the Wide Open Beaver to see what I could find out. (TO BE CONTINUED)`

McCollum keeps these missives in a pile in his underwear drawer. He says they make his day and to keep doing them. So I do. I enjoy it. I think them up during the day at the donut shop. Scrawl ideas on napkins whenever I can. It helps kill the clock. In some ways I feel as if I am edging towards a period of relative contentment. Hiding out in the basement with McCollum and his music. Me and the Selectric humming at the kitchen table, McCollum stretched out on the bed with his beetles and his trilobites. There is a definite calm. But there is also a definite tension. Something hanging heavy in the air between us. Looming large when the lights go out. Getting bigger and cloudier with every passing day. Sex. No sex.

Five months in the basement and still no sex.

At night we lie in bed in the dark, kissing. Sometimes I try to coax McCollum's hands to my breasts, my crotch. He lingers for a moment and then moves away as if by resolve. He pulls my hand aside when I try to touch his cock, though I've felt it stiff and hard against my wrist through the sweatpants. He pulls the searching hand aside and brings it quickly to his lips. He kisses the fingers passionately and presses the palm to his hot forehead, his eyes closed tight, his body tensed. I know I'm not supposed to say anything. So I don't. I lie awake or I go to sleep. I try not to think about it, but I think about it a lot.

One Bushmills-soaked night I break the unspoken pact with three terrible words: "What's the matter?"

McCollum flips over, his back to my face. "Nothing," he hisses. He lights a cigarette and lies there hunched in the dark. I watch the smoke curl up around his head.

"It's me, isn't it?" Lopsided tits. Fat ass.

McCollum laughs bitterly. "You?" he says, getting up and pulling on a sweater. "Hardly!" Socks, running shoes, ski jacket, toque and McCollum is out the door without another word.

I lie in the dark, trying not to panic. *I shouldn't have said anything. Shit! Why did I have to say something?*

I lie in the dark, drinking and thinking. *Maybe McCollum is gay.*

Maybe he loves me like a friend but not in that way. If McCollum was gay, would he get an erection? Would he kiss me the way he kisses me? Probably not. He knows I'm on the pill, so it isn't about that. Maybe it's a skin thing. Maybe he has acne on his penis. Is that possible? I don't think so. Maybe he's just afraid. I'm pretty sure he's a virgin. He told me that I'm his first real girlfriend. He knows I've had sex before. Maybe he's just afraid. Or maybe he had sex once and something bad happened... Jesus, maybe he was molested! He never talks about his family. Maybe he was sexually abused... O fuck, that must be it!

I get dressed and slip into the cold backyard. The garden is dead and black. McCollum is lying on his back in what used to be the tomato patch, staring at the sky. His giant feet, encased in enormous white tennis shoes, glow like Mr. and Mrs. Moby Dick at the end of the yard. I lie down beside him on the hard, bumpy soil and watch the first fat flakes of winter settle like drunken bumblebees in the streetlamp light. I take McCollum's hands and blow hot breath over the frozen fingers. I press a firm kiss on the hard-boned forehead and lay a softy on each eyelid.

"It's not what you're thinking," says McCollum, staring sharp into my eyes.

I don't say anything. I just keep looking.

"I know what you're thinking and it's not that. It's not any of that, I swear."

"OK," I say. I sink back onto the soil and wait for him to tell me something. I watch the snowflakes land and disappear. I think about how in the morning there will be no trace of their existence. Just like our words. After ten minutes of snow I'm shivering like crazy. I sit up and take McCollum's hand.

"Do you want to come inside?"

"Yes," he says. "Just give me a minute."

I go in and run a bath. Soak long in the hot water, chain-smoking soggy cigarettes and mulling things over. *I know what you're thinking and it's not that. It's not any of that, I swear.* OK, OK. I don't care what it is. Just come inside come inside come inside come inside.

When I get out, McCollum is in bed, pretending to be asleep. Relieved, I slip in quietly beside him, curl my hot body around his iciness and slowly slowly we drift off together.

In the morning McCollum is gone. Unusual. We like to walk together. I scan the surfaces for a note. Nothing. Off to the donut shop to sling crullers and wait for him to show up. The clock is a bastard. It says noon when it should say two. It says two-fifteen when I know it's at least three. *Who pissed in your Wheaties?* sneers Tina. *Here comes the employee of the month*, snarls Kelly. Finally finally four o'clock, but no sign of McCollum. Fear gives me the power to run all the way home. When I get there I don't remember how I got there. I cough and wheeze and fumble with the damn key, which doesn't want to go in the fucking lock. *Stop shaking for Christ's sake! Calm down, try again...*

B. Dylan on the stereo. McCollum alive and drunk. A new, half-drained bottle of Bushmills in his lap. I take a hit, wipe the sweat off my face and pass the bottle back.

"Hey," I say.

"Hey," says McCollum.

Take off my coat and lie down on the floor, a sweet relief flooding my veins. I'VE HEARD THE NEWBORN BABIES WAILING LIKE A MORNING DOVE, AND OLD MEN WITH BROKEN TEETH STRANDED WITHOUT LOVE, DO I UNDERSTAND YOUR QUESTION THEN IS IT HOPELESS AND FORLORN... Dylan. A bad sign. Of all the music this music is reserved for the blackest of blues. That's OK. I'm here now.

We pass the bottle back and forth and soon there is no light in the apartment save the stereo glow. Bob goes on about his visions of Johanna, the chimes of freedom flash and we end up on desolation row. The tape ends. I listen to the hum of the system. A good empty sound.

"There's something you don't know about me," says a voice in the dark after a while.

"OK," I say, waiting for the horrible and terrible.

McCollum stumbles to his feet and begins to undress. He takes off his shoes and his shirt and his sweatpants. He sits down on the edge of the bed in his underwear, lights a cigarette and then takes off the underwear too. I look over expecting to see I don't know what, something hideous and diseased, gaping wounds, teeth, wires, fur... but all I see are dimly lit white legs, a limp penis and two largeish testicles.

"Well..." says McCollum, "aren't you going to say anything?"

"I don't understand."

McCollum sighs, stamps out the cig and flicks on the lamp. "Look again," he says.

I squint in the harsh light, searching for what...what...? And then I notice something: the head of the cock is totally smooth, no opening, no aperture. McCollum lifts up the penis. There on the underside, halfway down the shrivelled shaft, a tiny little hole.

My brain says *wow*, and then my mouth says, "So?"

"So I'm a goddamned freak!" cries McCollum. "I can't even stand up to take a piss!" Strangled animal sobs surge from deep in the belly. A body shaking out of control. I turn off the light and push McCollum onto the bed.

"You fool," I whisper hot in his ear. "I can't believe this. It's nothing. Less than nothing, I swear!" A gasp for air. More shaking. I push the full weight of my body on top of his to quell the quakes. "Jesus Christ, McCollum, I couldn't care less if you pissed out of your forehead. I love your fucking guts, you idiot!"

The tortured sobbing goes on and on and on. I think I've never heard such a terrible true sound. Finally finally, one immense sigh and it stops cold.

"Oh God, I'm sorry...I need a Kleenex."

Run to the bathroom, madly unspool six feet of toilet paper, run back.

"Here..."

McCollum blows his nose and dries his face. "Could I have a cigarette?"

I light two, *Now Voyager* style, and pass one over. We lie in the dark, smoking. And then not smoking.

"So, do you hate me now?"

"Shut up!"

"You're disgusted, aren't you?"

"Yeah, this is how disgusted I am." I move in on McCollum, kiss the belly, the balls, the cock. He takes my head in his hands. *You don't have to do this*, he whispers. *I want to*, I say, grabbing his wrists, pulling them away from my head. Hold the tensed wrists in the air, lean in and take the scared cock soft into my mouth. Suck slowly and evenly. Slowly. Evenly. A minute, maybe less and the wrists slip naturally from my grasp and settle gently down on the bed. The body begins to ease and McCollum starts to grow.

—

If there's one thing I can't handle it's a shopping mall. My first and worst panic attack occurred in a mall. The Eaton Centre. I was seventeen years old at the time. Sweat-soaked pits, heart doing the Flintstone Flop, head all fuzzy and swimmy and light. I blacked out and went face down by the poster shop by the fountain. An ambulance ride to the emergency ward. A slew of tests. Blood, urine, electrocardiogram. "Nothing the matter with you," they said. "Healthy as a horse." Then they sent me home.

I circle the mall, in the yacht of an Oldsmobile, trying to remember where the damned liquor store is, trying to find the entrance that will afford me the quickest escape. I had forgotten that I was such a lousy driver. Nervous and distracted. I've narrowly avoided three accidents and one maiming of a pedestrian by the time I manage to inch the fat blue beast into a too-tight spot outside the Wal-Mart that used to be the Woolco.

The Towne & Countrye mall has changed. A massive and appalling turquoise entranceway thingy, reeking of the 1980s, has been slapped onto the main doors. The gates of po-mo hell. The name has changed too. It's now called the Four Corners Mall. I suppose north of Steeles at Yonge no longer qualifies as "country." The Towne and Endless Expanse of Hideous Subdivision Mall would have been apt. Probably have to go north of Major Mackenzie to find a decent patch of country these days.

I flick my cig, take a deep deep breath and walk into Wal-Mart. Air-conditioned discomfort. A blue-haired lady with a dazzling smile and a dizzyingly striped uniform jumps out in front of me and screams:

"Hi, welcome to Wal-Mart!"

"Hello," I say uncertainly, swivelling on my heel and hightailing it out the way I came. Walk half a block down to another entrance and try again. I'm still not good at malls. The crowds, the Muzak, the dead air, the sick lighting, the overabundance of gleaming products — a million shiny shoes, a trillion multicoloured sweaters, it's all too much for me.

I weave fast and dizzy down the aisle, ducking the Saturday people, searching frantically for the liquor store. Finally, a directory. The words shimmy in front of my eyes as I rapidly and randomly scan the list. Suzy Creamcheese, Pots 'n Stuff, Muffin Oven... Liquor Control Board of Ontario! OK, where the hell am I? *You Are Here*. OK, left, left, across from the pharmacy. Go!

Heart-racing, stroller-dodging dash to my destination. *Gin... Vodka... Whisky*! Right. Bushmills... Bushmills? No Bushmills. Jesus! Grab two Jameson, a Dalwhinnie and a Glenmorangie. Pick a line, pick a line, pick a line, pick a line. Which cashier looks the least witless? Which fucker is about to whip out a credit card or rummage endlessly for exact change? I have the world's worst line karma. Always always pick the wrong line. Always a price check or change the ribbon or doddering change-purse octogenarian or direct deposit malfunction or exchange or return or Air Miles card or personal cheque or shift change or "I'd like to speak to the manager" or lottery tickets — *scratch scratch scratch* while I'm back here sweating like a demon, blood pressure plummeting, on the verge of passing out. Come on buddy, move it!

Christ, I did it again! Watch the other line flow through, flow through... Contemplate the switch. Decide against it. Woman behind me keeps brushing me with her basket, nudging me with the basket. I could cheerfully wheel around and club her senseless with the Jameson. Come on, bonehead, move your ass! Damned cashier's missing a piece of his brain. Blink the sweat out of my eyes. Breathe... breathe... All right, all right, all right. $141.65. Here's $150.00. Keep the change. Jam the bottles into a bag. Skip the paper, just give me the plastic. Scan the mall for the nearest exit. Jog to the nearest exit, bottles clutched against my chest, bottles clanking against each other. Kick the door open and I'm out! Out.

I watch myself dissolve an Ativan under my tongue in the giant rear-view mirror of the Oldsmobile. My face is covered with big red splotches. They'll be gone in about twenty minutes. That wasn't so bad. Not too bad at all. The thing about panic attacks is once you know that you're having panic attacks you panic a lot less. If you don't know you're having a panic attack then you think you're going into cardiac arrest or you suspect that you've contracted some hideous

Ebola-like virus and you're certain that you are about to die so you panic a lot more.

It took me a preposterously long time to be properly diagnosed. I kept taking myself to the emergency ward and they kept sending me home, telling me I was fine. Perfectly fine. Had to switch hospitals after a while. Then again and again.

First I was convinced I had a weak heart. Five trips to Mount Sinai, two electrocardiograms and one echocardiogram later I realized that the doctors were probably right, there was nothing wrong with my ticker; in actual fact I was in the final stages of incurable brain cancer. But somehow, even with repeated electroencephalograms, the incompetent boobs at Toronto General couldn't locate the grapefruit-sized tumour that was obviously festering in my cranium. Ditto for the Wellesley and Doctors hospitals. Obviously I couldn't be suffering from brain cancer. What then? I bought myself a medical reference book and went to work. Barium enema and small bowel enema at North York General. Intravenous pyelogram at Branson Hospital. Upper GI series at Etobicoke General. Angiogram and bronchoscopy compliments of Sunnybrook. Eventually I end up in the emergency ward at Women's College Hospital, emaciated, blood-drained, irradiated and sleep-deprived, pleading with an intern for a full-body CAT scan.

"OK, I'll be back in a minute," he says.

Forty-five minutes later a weary-looking woman enters my cubicle and pulls the green curtain shut behind her.

"Hello, I'm Dr. Shore," says the woman, with an Australian accent.

"Are you from Australia?"

"Johannesburg," she says, with a South African accent. "So, what seems to be the trouble?"

"I don't know. That's the problem. There's something very wrong, but I have no idea what."

Dr. Shore scans her clipboard. "You've been experiencing palpitations and severe headaches for what... six months?"

"Yeah. About six or seven months."

"Headaches every day?"

"Yeah, and dizziness. A lot of dizziness."

"Well, that could be from all the painkillers you're taking."

"I'm not taking any painkillers."

"Why not?"

"I don't know... um, I don't know."

"You have stomach aches as well?"

"Yeah, and nausea and uh... pins and needles in my legs and sometimes my arms. But usually my legs."

"And chest pains?"

"Yeah. In the right side only, for some reason. And insomnia. I can't get to sleep, but that could be my heart. I keep focusing on my heartbeat and I can't get to sleep. Thank God for the *All-Night Show* on Channel 79."

"And diarrhea?"

"Yeah, I've had diarrhea for about four months now. I've lost about fifteen pounds."

"And burning urine?"

"Sometimes. It comes and goes."

Dr. Shore takes a deep breath and looks hard into my eyes. "Have you been under a lot of stress lately?"

For some reason her words are like a punch. A "wow" of electricity rings through my head. I suddenly feel as if I'm on the verge of tears. And I don't even cry.

"Well... not particularly. Not really."

"You're in school?"

"No. I work."

"What do you do?"

"I'm a slide rat," I say, stifling a small laugh.

"What does a slide rat do?"

"I mount slides. I put little pieces of film into little plastic and glass mounts. For multi-image slide shows, for a communications company."

Dr. Shore keeps staring into my eyes.

"It pays the bills," I say, to crack the silence.

"What about your family?"

"What about them?"

"What do they do?"

"Well, my sister was working at the company I'm at now. But she quit. She's down in Vancouver for a while. My brother is a musician. He's in the States for a while. Los Angeles." Lengthy pause.

"And your parents?"

"They passed away."

"When?"

"Um . . . let me think. Oh God, I can't think . . . Um, my father committed suicide about a year or so ago. My mom passed away about six months before that."

Something flickers across Dr. Shore's eyes. "What happened to your mother?" she asks.

"Cancer of the liver." I try to smile, but all I can do is lock my lips tight and nod my head. Nod nod my head.

"Well, it sounds to me like you've actually been under a great deal of stress." Again with the deep, dark stare.

"I guess so . . . But mostly from feeling sick. I mean, I'm really tired of feeling sick all the time. I'd just like to find out what's wrong with me so I could do something about it."

"Well, you've had a great number of tests and all of them have shown that you are physically healthy."

"Right. Which is why I think I should have a CAT scan. Obviously the tests have missed something, and I'd really just like to find out what's wrong already. I mean, I can barely get myself to work, let alone do anything else."

"Are you aware of the fact that mental stress can manifest itself in all kinds of physical ways?"

". . . I guess so. Not as bad as this, though."

"As bad, and much worse in some cases. You know, all of your symptoms strongly suggest that you are suffering from severe anxiety and panic attacks. Anxiety can cause headaches and palpitations, nausea, sleeplessness."

"Hmmm. But wouldn't it make sense to do a CAT scan just to rule out anything physical? I mean, wouldn't that make sense?"

"Not really. You're only eighteen years old. It's highly unlikely that there's anything seriously wrong with you, physically."

Heavy sigh. Exasperation.

"However, to put your mind at ease I will order the CAT scan, under one condition."

"What?"

"That you make an appointment to see Dr. Eric Ramu. He works at the Clarke Institute. They have a clinic designed specifically for panic attacks and anxiety. He's a very good doctor. I'll write you a referral before you leave, OK? Are you on a drug plan?"

"No."

"I'll have the nurse bring you some samples of diazepam. You can take one every four hours. Take two before you go to bed. It will help with palpitations and the headaches and you'll finally get some sleep. OK?"

"OK," I say. I figure the CAT scan will turn up the cancer or the answer and I won't have to bother with this Ramu business.

"OK," says Dr. Shore. She pauses, squeezes my arm reassuringly and gives me another big long look. Then the good doctor turns and disappears through the pale green curtains.

I slide the sleeve of my gown aside and look at the spot on my arm. No sign of the squeeze, no trace of redness or impression, just a slight tingling sensation. Just the slightest sensation of warmth.

—

It's Monday afternoon, four months to the day after my mother's funeral. I am lying in the brown basement, staring at nothing and everything, when I hear a knock at the door. The last time there was a knock at the door two movers came and carried away McCollum's music. Over thirty milk-crates full.

I jump up and hit the lights. Run into the bathroom and adjust my hair. Spritz a little perfume, slip quickly through the cold room and open up. It takes a nanosecond for my brain to register the real image as opposed to the hoped-for one. It is not McCollum. It is my father. Bizarre. He is standing in the doorway, holding a large cake box. He is wearing a summer suit.

"Hi, sweetie," he says, somewhat sheepishly.

"Hi," I say, confused by his presence and his manner. "Come on in."

"Oh boy," says my father, surveying the contents of the cold room, "would you look at all this food. This looks absolutely super. Do you ever sample this stuff?"

"We had some artichoke hearts once. Come on in."

"This is where you live?"

"Yup."

"It's dark. Why don't you turn on a light?"

"It's on."

"It's dark in here. You should get some lamps."

"Hmm."

"A few lamps or something. It's very dark."

"Fine, I'll get lamps. What's going on?"

"Can you open up a window in here? It's stuffy, Michelle. You want me to open up a window?"

"There are no windows," I say. "It's a basement."

"Well, you should leave the door open a bit. It's very smoky in here. Are you smoking now?"

"I've been smoking for four years."

"I don't like that, Michelle. That's no bloody good. You're going to stop that, aren't you?"

"Yeah."

"You don't have a washing machine?"

I glance at the piles of fetid clothing strewn around the apartment. "There's a laundromat on the corner. So, what's going on?"

My father gets this bittersweet smile on his face, a sloppy, sad-clown marzipan smile as he moves towards me with the cake box.

"Here," he says, "I brought you something."

I take the box and place it on the table next to the typewriter. Flip open the lid and stare at what's remaining of a large rectangular cake — a carved-up chunk from the left-hand side. The piece of cake says

Con

Pet

in pink icing.

"I don't get it," I say. "What is this?"

"Congratulations, Peter and Suzy. I got married yesterday."

"What?"

"I got married yesterday. I didn't think you kids would want to come."

"What are you talking about?"

"I know it's a shock. I didn't think you kids would want to know."

"You got married yesterday."

"Yes."

"Yesterday, you got married."

"That's correct."

"Who did you get married to?"

"Suzy Fish."

A moment to penetrate, and then laughter. I can't help myself.

"Suzy Fish?" I repeat, breaking out into a serious case of the yucks. It sounds like some kind of animated character. I picture my father strolling hand in fin down an underwater aisle with some red-lipped, long-lashed Disney creation.

"Yes, Suzy Fish. What's so funny?"

"Suzy Fish," I say, convulsing with laughter. "You married Suzy Fish."

"What the fuck is so funny?" says my father, folding his arms across his chest.

"Nothing," I say. And all of a sudden it's true. "How long have you known this woman?"

"Two months."

"Two months?"

"About two months."

"More than two months?!"

"No, two months. She's from Arizona. I'll have someplace warm to go now."

"Hmm." I look at my father. He looks at the floor. "You want something to drink?"

"What have you got?"

"Soda water, coffee... Irish whiskey."

"OK."

I pour a couple of shots. We drink them down.

"It has nothing to do with love, Michelle."

Another shot. We drink.

"What has it got to do with?"

"Companionship. I don't want to be alone. Nobody wants to be alone, Michelle."

"Well," I say, getting up, "thanks for the cake."

"That's it?"

"Yup."

"You're not going to wish me *mazel tov*?"

"What?"

"*Mazel tov*. You're not going to wish me *mazel tov*?"

"... *mazel tov*," I say.

"I'm still your father, you know."

"I know."

"Just a drop." My father pours himself another shot. "You want me to drive you over to the laundromat?"

"No, thank you."

"Bundle up this stuff, I'll take you over."

"I'll do it later."

"Why would you do it later when I can give you a lift now?"

"I'd prefer to do it later."

"This place is a mess, Michelle."

"I like it this way."

"You like living in a mess?"

"Yes."

"You enjoy wallowing in filth? You're gonna get bugs, cockroaches."

"Fine."

"Fine? Why don't you make the bed at least?"

"Why should I?"

"You'll feel better if you make the bed."

"You'll feel better if I make the bed. I'll feel about the same."

"Is there something the matter with you?"

"No."

"You should get some lamps in here."

"I will."

"Do you want some money?"

"No."

"A few bucks. Can I give you a few bucks?"

"I'm fine."

"How's fifty? Is fifty OK?"

"I don't want it. Please."

My father drops the money on the table. "You want me to take you to the laundromat?"

"No, thanks." I move towards the cold room.

"Quit smoking!"

"Yup."

"You can't mess around with that. That's dangerous business."

"Right."

"Boy, look at all this food. What are these, green tomatoes?"

"Yeah."

"That's just super. It's super, isn't it?"

"Yeah." I go for the door and swing it open.

"Have you spoken to your sister and brother?"

"I'm going to call them."

"You should call them."

"I'm going to."

"Can I use your bathroom?"

"It's broken."

"Your bathroom is broken?"

"Yeah. The landlord is coming in twenty minutes to fix it."

"All right. Never mind."

"Bye."

"Bye." My father leans in for a kiss. Old Spice. Too much. Now again with the sad gypsy smile.

"No one wants to be alone, Michelle."

"I'm going to get some lamps," I say, and then I shut the door, go wash my hands and take a piss.

The recently divorced and remarried Suzy Fish arrives at 5 Pinecrest with a tractor-trailer crammed full of shit. Overstuffed couches, velvet pillows, gilt-framed oil paintings, Persian rugs, lacquered china cabinets, twisted candelabras, decorative platters, oversized vases, jugs, sconces, cherubs, plate racks, loveseats, wing-backs, plant stands, ottomans, tiny embroidered footstools, giant brass coat racks, faux Louis XIV end tables, coffee tables, dining tables, occasional tables, curio cabinets, stereo cabinets, dressers, head-boards, marble mantel clock, mahogany grandfather clock, fake antique fireplace equipment, silk wall hangings, silk drapes, silk flowers, tasselled blinds, plaster pillars, velveteen lamps, china fig-urines, iron beer steins, Fabergé eggs, Lalique crystals, ceramic ash-trays, ornately framed mirrors, track lighting, exercise equipment, colour TVs, copper pots, Cuisinart, Hammond organ, vibrating recliner, lace tablecloths, lace bedspreads, lace-skirted toilet-paper dolls, monogrammed hand towels, half-shell soap dishes, candy dishes, gold leaf dishes, silver cutlery sets in wooden boxes, tea sets, tea trays, tea caddy, ceramic Kleenex-box covers and several Princess phones. No bookshelves though.

Joel hears them fucking at night. Suzy Fish through the wall. He goes down to the basement and cranks up the amp. Marshall amp. Five feet tall.

Suzy Fish moves it all in and nine weeks later she cleans it all out. Takes my mother's piano and the Passover dishes, the one good rug and the contents of the bank account.

My father hangs on to his weapon collection. This time he'll be ready.

—

I don't feel like going back. I don't want to go back yet. The Oldsmobile proceeds past Pinecrest Avenue, seemingly of its own volition. It continues along Steeles Avenue East, hangs a right on Leslie and pulls into the parking lot of the strip mall across the street from Zion Heights Junior High School.

The familiar stench of McDonald's draws me in. I order a Filet-O-Fish sandwich, scrape off what is commonly assumed to be sauce, and eat the thing in four bites. The last time I was here I was fifteen years old. Used to come in all the time with Andrea and cause shit. Used to stick our pickles on the wall. Stick them over the eyes of the Hamburglar, stick them on the tits of Mayor McCheese. Used to fill our plastic spoons with soft ice cream and catapult it at each other. We didn't care. The manager was around twenty years old. Overgrown. In a paper hat. We called him Lurch and ignored his pathetic demands or desperate pleas for us to vacate the premises. "We're still eating," we'd say, blowing smoke in his red face and pointing to half a fry sitting limp in the middle of the table. "Stop harassing the paying customers."

One day, as we sat pounding ketchup packets with our fists, he strode over and announced in a shaky, breaking voice: "I had a brain tumour removed last year. I'm a little slow. I can't help it." Then he rubbed the tears from his eyes with two enormous fists — just like in a cartoon — and walked quickly away. The last time I was here.

I drive the Oldsmobile across the street to the school parking lot, crack the Jameson and take a good hit. Just to kill whatever bacteria may have been lurking in the Filet-O-Fish. Strictly medicinal. Light a smoke, get out and wander over to the spot where I almost got beat up. Before I got tough.

I was a target. Part of the new crop of grade sevens. A bookworm. A redhead. And, according to some reports, a "little slut who sucks dick." It started with the twins, Chrissy and Kim, leaders of a small and select group of grade nine girls. Girls with good bone structure and Pearl Drops smiles. Girls with carefully tousled Farrah Fawcett hair. Girls with wide-set eyes under mint green eyeshadow. Girls who wore halter tops and chokers and platform shoes with wooden heels and blue jeans so tight it would require the jaws of life, or perhaps heat gun and scraper, to decamp from the denim grip.

Lunchtime. I'm at my locker, dropping off books, when I hear: "Hey, slut!" I look up.

"Hey, she looked! She is a fuckin' slut!"

Chrissy and Kim and Sharon Spence and some other Golden Girl are focused on me and laughing. I feel my face grow hot as I close the locker, click the lock and walk away. I don't walk fast and I don't walk slowly. A tense even pace and a warm tingle along my spine as I feel them following along behind me.

"Where you going, slut?"

"She's going to find some cock to suck."

More laughter. I don't say anything. Move towards the cafeteria, not daring to look back. Halfway through the caf I'm pelted with a shower of something small and hard. Coins. Pennies. They're throwing pennies at me.

"Hey, aren't you gonna pick them up? We thought you were a Jew!"

jew

This tiny and titanic word knocks the breath right out of my body. My heart goes staccato. I'm adrenalin and fire. I wheel around to shout something, but nothing will come out. I cannot say a word. What I can do is pluck a tray full of Este Minuskin's lunch from the end of a long cafeteria table and hurl it with all my might at the eight-legged blonde beast. It lands with a splendid crash just short of my target, spraying gravy and french fries and egg salad and Coca-Cola across the shoes and shins of my tormentors. A spontaneous cheer erupts in the caf. Even Este Minuskin joins in.

"You're dead!" shriek Chrissy and Kim in perfect hysterical unison.

Time to go, I think, making a dash for the exit, sprinting through the hall and hightailing it into the principal's office. Through the wire-reinforced window I see Chrissy and Kim and Sharon Spence and the other girl come to a breathless halt just outside the door.

"You're dead," mouths Chrissy with glistening pink lips. "You're fuckin' dead."

I discreetly give them the finger, and smile.

"Can I help you?" twangs the principal's secretary, hawk-eyeing me over cat's-eye glasses that hover between a poof of blue hair and a tightly pinched mouth.

"I don't think so," I say, after a millisecond of consideration.

At 3:35 I join the flow of bodies exiting the school. I try to make myself invisible, but I'm vibrating with a strange light that everyone can see. Outside in the parking lot an impressive crowd has already assembled.

"There she is!" yells someone in an after-school-special kind of way, and a hundred hungry eyes fix themselves upon me. I move with the jerky walk of the observed towards the approaching assembly. In a heartbeat I am engulfed and surrounded, ringed by four angry amazons and a bevy of blood-hungry onlookers.

Chrissy acts first. Knocks the book out of my arms. *Pride and Prejudice* goes down for the count. As I bend to pick up Jane, I get a hard kick in the tailbone, compliments of Sharon Spence. I feel no pain.

"Are you prepared to die?" asks Kim, warming up with a solid push against my shoulders. I fly backwards into The Other Girl, who pushes me back. As I catapult forward I catch a glimpse of Andrea's white visage through the sea of flapjack faces. Her eyebrows instantly furrow with sympathy, the tiny smile vanishes from her lips.

"You're gonna pay, you fuckin' slut bitch," snarls Chrissy, pushing me over towards Sharon Spence's waiting arms. As I pitch back and forth in the ever tightening circle, I find myself thinking abstract thoughts about the nature of friendship. Then, strangely, I find myself thinking about Prince Edward Island.

"Wake up, douche-bag," screams Kim, and I'm struck across the cheek with an open hand. Much laughter ensues. Now a body pushes through the crowd and breaks into the centre. Marla. My sister.

"What in the fuck is going on here?!" she demands, flicking her smoke with a short sharp move.

Chrissy steps up: "Mind your own business, asshole!"

"It is my business, *asshole*!" Marla, all tiny and compact, stares her down. The crowd makes a slight, instinctive adjustment.

"Why don't you let her fight her own fucking battles?!" snaps Sharon Spence.

"I intend to," says Marla. "I'm gonna stand back and watch her beat your fucking brains in." A laugh ripples through the crowd.

"Oh yeah?" says Chrissy. "We'd like to see that."

"The little chickenshit won't even fight back," squeals The Other Girl, crackling with giddiness.

"She's not fuckin' stupid," says Marla. "She's not gonna go four on one. She'll take on whoever wants to fight, but *one at a time*." Marla fires me a piercing look. "Right, Michelle?"

"Right."

"OK. One on one. Who wants to die first?"

The amazons scoff and laugh with disdain and bravado, but nobody volunteers.

"What, are you guys too chickenshit to fight a little grade seven on your own?"

"Go ahead," says Kim to The Other Girl. "We'll let you go first."

"Go ahead, Gillian," says Chrissy. "But save some for us."

"Yeah, save some for us," echoes Sharon Spence, looking noticeably relieved.

"I'll hold your book," says Marla, taking Jane from my hands and giving my shoulder a squeeze.

The crowd shuffles back half a step as Gillian and I assume the stance. She's the tallest amazon but, thankfully, also the skinniest.

"Kill her!" screams Sharon Spence with sudden unnerving fervour.

Gillian glances here and there around the circle, sucking up support, a half-smile spreading smug across her face. That's when I wind up and pop her full-fisted in the nose. A terrible crunchy cartilage sound and we're standing there, equally astonished, as blood squirts into the gaping O of her mouth.

"One more time!" squeals Marla above the crowd clamour, and I follow with a spastic jab to the stomach area.

Gillian crumples forward in slow motion, sags slackly to her knees and topples invertebrate onto her side. Her fluffy yellow hair looks wrong against the pavement. An uncomfortable contrast.

"All right, who's next?! Who's next? Come on, let's go!" Marla is all wide-eyed and hyper, clapping her hands and pat-patting me on the back.

Chrissy and Kim and Sharon Spence descend to the pavement and encircle their fallen comrade. Like pearls in a ring.

"Are you OK" murmurs Chrissy, soothingly.

"Are you all right?" whispers Kim, softly.

"She's fine," sneers Marla. "Nothing a little rhinoplasty won't fix. All right, who's up? Who's next in line?"

"Oh, just shut your face!" cries Sharon Spence, as the girls rise up slowly as one and shuffle off towards the school in a tender little huddle.

Now, Andrea pops 3-D out of the throng. She grabs my hand and pumps it up and down. "Way to go, Michelle." Up and down, up and down. "That was totally cool!"

"Got a smoke?" I say, staring her cold in the eye.

"Uh, no. I'm out." She pats her jean jacket pockets and looks down at the ground.

"Here," says Marla, handing me a cigarette and lighting it for me with her white lighter. She takes one herself and then puts the pack away, smiling all the while at Andrea. "Well," says Marla, jawing out two perfect smoke rings followed by a long steady column of grey, "see ya later."

"Oh. Yeah. See you guys later," says Andrea, blankly, walking away in no particular direction, melting back into the dispersing crowd.

Marla hands me my book and we head off across the schoolyard towards the bridge. The first time we've walked home together.

"God, Michelle, that was great! You fuckin' showed those bitches, man!"

"Thanks to you!"

"I can't believe you punched her right in the face. Oh man! That was too much. I mean, I knew you'd come out alive, but I didn't think you'd totally kick ass. I mean, holy shit!"

"I know. I don't even remember doing it!"

"I can't wait until tomorrow! Mind you, I betcha any money she doesn't show up tomorrow. Too fucking vain. She's gonna look like Marcia Brady after getting the football in the face! Beautiful! You fuckin' showed those bitches."

"So, you think that's the end of it?"

"Oh God, yeah. Definitely. Fucking cowards! I mean, you saw them limping away. '*Oh we have to help our poor little friend.*' Yeah right. Bullshit! None of them wanted to take you on. Believe me, you're laughing."

"Thanks, Mar. Really. Thank you."

"Hey, no probs. So, tell me, 'Chelle, what did you learn today? Eh? What did you learn from all this?"

I know what my sister is getting at. She wants me to talk about mob mentality, about breaking down the mob and stripping it of its collective power, but I'm thinking about something else entirely. I'm thinking about friends. I'm thinking about family. I'm thinking about the other important thing I learned from all this.

I finish my cig and crush it hard onto the pavement. Hop back into the giant Oldsmobile and head on home to rescue my sister.

—

When I get back to the house I find Marla and the fake mom playing Scrabble in the kitchen. Phony Freddy is asleep at their feet under the table. The father replicant is behind the counter, marinating the steaks in two large glass baking dishes. He's crushing garlic cloves into Worcestershire sauce, filling the kitchen with a pleasant stink.

"Hello, sweetheart. Welcome home!" says the father, with a vaguely Hungarian-like accent. I flash him a wry smile and begin unloading the booze.

"What took you so long?" asks Marla, staring at the board.

"I was starting to get worried!" says the fake mom, unconvincingly.

"Are you all right?" I ask my sister.

She glances up from the game. "Yeah. Are you?"

"Yeah." I pour myself a glass of the Irish and hold it up in the air. "Anyone else?"

"No, thanks," says the fake mom.

"Maybe later," says Marla, laying down a word on the board. "SHADOW, for one, seven, eight, ten, eleven, fourteen... times two is twenty-eight."

"Very good!" says the mom, jotting down the score.

Waste of an S, I think to myself.

Marla reaches into the sock for more letters. We always kept the letters in an old tube sock. I pour another drink.

"So, who's winning?" asks the father, a little late and with too much pep, as if he finally stumbled upon something to say and is thrilled and relieved by the discovery.

"I am," says Marla, self-consciously.

"Is that right?" I say, trying to catch her eye, but she won't look up from the game.

Nobody could beat our mother at Scrabble. Nobody. She was the best I've ever seen. And none of this scouring the *Scrabble Dictionary* or the OED for obscure words like *qilk* or *aap*. She knew how to really play the game. How to make six new words in one go. How to milk fifty-seven points out of a word like CAT. She had a special knack for clogging up the board so that nobody but she could figure out where the hell to lay a letter. She could get nothing but vowels the whole damned game and still score five hundred points. The real deal.

"So, you wanna go for a walk or something?"

My sister gives me a look. "I'm in the middle of a game, Michelle."

"Yeah. Well, when you're done. You're almost finished, aren't you?"

"Yeah, but—"

"OK, OK, I'm ready," says the fake mom, laying down CALM for a measly eight points. "Oh, that's it for letters!" She fishes the last remaining wooden chips out of the sock and dangles the thing upside down. Boingy-boingy.

"Well, it looks like I won this one," says Marla. "Which means we're supposed to play a tie-breaker."

"Oh, we don't have to, honey," says the fake mom. "Maybe Michelle would like to play."

"No, thanks."

"You love Scrabble!" pipes in the father, as if he just remembered the answer to an exam question.

"That's good for two points, Daddio." I pour myself another drink.

Marla frowns. "You'd better take it easy, Michelle."

"So, you don't want to go for a walk? I mean, I don't care, I just thought *you* might want to?"

My sister looks at me. I can't tell if she can tell that I'm trying to give her an out. Then suddenly it occurs to me that she can't tell if I can tell that she doesn't want one.

"Well, it's probably still really hot and sticky out there, but I guess if you really want me to..."

"No. It's what you want. I mean, I could walk or not. I could go lie down for a bit. I wouldn't mind a shower."

"Well... I wouldn't mind just hanging out for a while. I mean, it's so nice and cool in here."

Air conditioning, I think. *Freon and tubes.*

"OK," I say, grabbing my smokes and the Jameson. "I'll be upstairs if you want me."

"You're sure you don't want to play?" asks Marla.

"I'm sure. Sorry."

I go up to my room, lie down on the bed and attempt to comprehend this supremely surreal situation, attempt to come to grips with the apparently staggering depths of my sister's loneliness. I realize that I've never thought about Marla all the way through. Never really thought about her much at all. When I did think about her, I would always get a vague and rather abstract impression of the surface — swirling, chattering, clickety clattering. Manic motion. Aggressive. Explosive. Marla always seemed to have a million friends and a million parties to attend and a million movies to see and a million things to be and a million boy-toys to screw and a million things to do do do. It never occurred to me that there was something behind all that white noise and activity. Something soft and still at the centre of it all. Something tender and blue that needed to be warmed. Warmed by mother. Warmed by father.

Oh hell, maybe I'm getting it all wrong. Maybe she's just trying to make the best of a bad scene. Play along with the actors to please or appease Joel. A good report card when he finally shows up. Preparation for the big money payoff.

But no. It doesn't seem so. Marla did her duty while I was at the mall. She could have easily copped a walk after the first round of Scrabble. A little break from the fakes. A breath of fresh air. But no. She didn't want to go. And there was a peace in the kitchen when I first walked in. As I was coming through the hall I overheard Marla telling the fake mom about scoring 99 percent on a recent real estate exam.

"That's wonderful," said the mom, just before I busted in with the booze. "I'm so proud of you, honey!"

Maybe if I hadn't walked in just then the mom would have squeezed Marla's hand and brought it to her lips for a kiss. And maybe my sister would have smiled up at her and not have minded at all.

And maybe maybe the father would have congratulated my sis, and jokingly inquired about what happened to the other 1 percent. And they all would have chuckled about that as he came around to pat her on the back and kiss her on top of the head. And then perhaps everyone would have sampled the marinade the father was preparing and they would have decided that it was good. And maybe Freddy would have woken up and sampled some too and given a little yip of doggy joy. And they would have chuckled about that as well. And there'd be another game of Scrabble, and steaks on the barby, and chocolate pudding cup for dessert, and *oh I couldn't eat another bite*, and curl up on the family-room sofa, and Ed Sullivan on TV, and no bickering or accusations, and no screaming matches or crying, and no migraine headaches or cancer, and no Holocaust or suicide. Just Norman Freaking Rockwell descending on 5 Pinecrest Avenue, giving my sister what she needs.

Oh well oh well. Who the hell am I to judge? If a faux McCollum appeared in my room right this minute, would I say *Nice try, pal* and kick his ass out the door? Or would I lower the light and pull down the shades, shift my eyes to a squint and pretend for as long as I could that all was right with the world?

Who knows? I don't know. All I know is that it's going to be one hell of a long night. Glug glug glug.

—

"We're kind of like a family here," says the production manager, slopping ketchup and mayonnaise all over his chins. He puts the burger down and dabs his face with a stack of filthy napkins. "I'm sure Marla told you that."

"Yeah, she mentioned that," I lie. *Cult* was the word she actually used.

"Sorry about your father."

"Thanks."

"Wanna fry?"

"No, thanks." I look around the cramped office, at the framed Association of Multi Image awards lining the walls, at the boxes of product on the floor, at the myriad cheesy office toys, at the teetering towers of plastic slide trays in the corner, anywhere but at the fat, greasy fingers working the pile of soggy takeout that's obviously been sitting long and cold on the cluttered desk.

"We work hard, damned hard, but the atmo is casz. You can wear jeans, whatever. Do you like to work hard?"

"Oh yes."

"Good, because sometimes we work twenty-four hours or longer without sleep. Can you hack it?"

"Yeah. I'm pretty sure I could do that."

"Pretty sure or sure?"

"Sure."

"Good. Could you hack it with a cold? Could you work thirty-six hours straight with a cold?"

"Well, I've never tried, but I'm sure I could." *With a cold, on one foot, with a spike through my head...*

"Because a deadline is a deadline. No excuses. If a show is scheduled to run on Saturday at six, it runs on Saturday at six. We've never missed a deadline, though we've burned out a few people who couldn't hack it. Think you can hack it?"

"I can hack it," I say, thinking about my flight from Olde Country Donuts, about the three months' rent that I owe my landlord, about my need to move away from that haunted basement apartment.

"Good. There's a shower in Tom's office, there's a sofa in the coffee lounge and we supply cab slips if you work past 9 p.m."

"Sounds good."

"When can you start?"

"Whenever you like. Tomorrow morning."

"How about now?"

"Uh, sure. Now is great."

Bob, the production manager, leads me through the producers' area, past the camera rooms, through the art department and down a long hallway. It's eight o'clock at night and the joint is jumping.

"Put some pants on, you're givin' me a stiffy," says Bob to some guy who passes by wearing nothing but boxer shorts and running shoes.

"You get ventilation in the booth, I'll get pants on," says the guy.

"That's Roman. One of our programmers. He does the screenings. Ah, here we are, the production area."

We walk into a large turquoise room filled with glowing white tables — light tables, illuminated from inside by fluorescent tubes. The plastic tables are covered with dozens of clear acrylic pallets that hold thousands of 35-mm slides. A stocky twenty-something woman with burgundy hair is seated at one of the tables, smoking a White Owl cigar and listening to the Police on a portable cassette deck.

"Franny, this is Marla Schafer's sister, Michelle. A new slide rat."

"Hey! One takes a powder and another one comes along to fill the gap."

"Franny's the head rat, she'll show you the ropes."

"You want her to clean the tampon show?"

"Nah, start with some speaker support. She's never done this before."

"Gotcha."

"I'm gonna go finish my breakfast. Catch ya later."

"Breakfast! Oh jeez." Franny guffaws and flashes me an "isn't he incorrigible?!" look.

Then Franny gets down to beeswax and shows me the ropes. Shows me how to unload a tray of slides in order onto a plastic pallet. Shows me how to click open the plastic-and-glass slide mounts with a flick of the thumb, how to gently lift the piece of slide film aside while rubbing at the glass with a static-free cloth, how to blast the dust and dirt from the surface of the film with an air hose attached to a large industrial tank, how to poke the film sprockets back onto tiny plastic pegs and snap the mount shut without touching the cleaned surfaces, how to peer through a little magnifying device to make sure that the slide is clean, how to replace the slide in its proper position on the pallet and reload the slides upside down and backwards into the trays so that the images will project correctly. How to do it all while puffing on a White Owl and yammering incessantly about what an honour and a privilege it is to be a part of the team at AV Network, the biggest and best corporate communications house in Canada.

"So, you wanna give it a shot?" asks Franny. "You think you can do it?"

A child of four could do it. A dyslexic chimpanzee could pull it off. "I'll give it a shot!" I say, with as much pep as I can muster.

Franny hands me three trays of slides to clean. Speaker support slides for a presentation on dog biscuits. Snamburgers.

**IF YOUR DOG LIKES TO SNEAK
A SNACK, AND YOUR DOG
LIKES HAMBURGER...YOUR DOG
WILL LOVE SNAMBURGERS!**

announces one slide.

**40% OF QUEBECKERS SURVEYED
THINK OF SNAMBURGERS WHEN
DISCUSSING DOG BISCUITS**

says another.

Mind-boggling stuff. I imagine a bunch of francophones sitting around a café, absorbed in a heated discussion about dog biscuits. A researcher strides in, selects their table at random and says: *"Excuse me, were you by any chance discussing dog biscuits just now?"*

"Mais oui! Quelle coïncidence."

"And while you were discussing dog biscuits, did any of you happen to think of Snamburgers?"

"I did," says one of the five people at the table.

"So did I," says another.

By the time I've made it through two of the three trays I've learned that

**26% OF DOG OWNERS WISH
THEY COULD FIND THE TIME TO MAINTAIN
THEIR PET'S DENTAL HYGIENE
THROUGH BRUSHING!**

and that

**72% OF DOGS IN WESTERN CANADA
PREFER SNAMBURGERS TO
LIVER-FLAVOURED TINKY TREATS**

Information I would prefer to live without.

I've just realized that the speck of dirt I've been vainly trying to blow off the slide is in fact some kind of doggy mole on the jowl of a German shepherd, when a young woman runs into the production area and, fairly quivering with excitement, says: "Tom's latest is finished. We're screening in the boardroom in two minutes!" Then she scampers away.

"All-righta!" says Franny, hanging up her hose. "Break time."

The dimly lit boardroom is abuzz with anticipation, filled with mingling AV Network employees. Some are seated around the long wooden table, some are leaning up against the wall. Some are smoking cigarettes. Some are drinking coffee. All of them are wearing either blue jeans or sweatpants. All of them are under the age of thirty.

Bob the production manager sits at one end of the imposing table. At the other end, a cushy leather chair sits empty. A large panoramic screen stretches across one wall of the boardroom. It is lit up with a mishmash of overlapping grids that are being focused and shifted into alignment.

"That's the screening booth," says Franny, pointing to the opposite wall where a large glass rectangle separates the two rooms. On the left-hand side of the booth, Roman — still shirtless — is seated behind a computer. Filling the remaining space are five tall towers standing side by side, each one holding three slide projectors in a vertical stack. A shadowy figure is moving around behind the projectors, adjusting knobs on the sides of the towers, tweaking the grids into place.

"It's a fifteen-projector show," says Franny. "All the projectors have to be lined up perfectly. You'll see. It's amazing."

The screen goes dark and the lights in the boardroom begin to fade. A figure steals into the hushed room and slips into the leather chair. The people start to applaud.

"All right, Tom!" shouts one young man, with genuine zeal.

"Woo hoo!" yips another, with equal zip.

"Ahhh, my adoring public," breathes the man at the end of the table as he lights up a fat cigar. I catch a glimpse of the face in the glow of the flame. Even with the chubby cheeks and the dimples, I can see right away that it's one of the older faces in the crowd. In some other light it would likely be considered boyish or cocky, but lit from below it comes off as rather nasty. Devilish.

"Ladies and germs," says Bob, "I give you the latest masterpiece from our Creative Director extraordinaire!" Bob cues Roman and the lights dip all the way to darkness.

An uneasy second of silence... and the black room shudders and fills with an ominous rumbling that builds slowly in volume and intensity. The synthesized tone — all bass and throat — builds bigger and louder and bigger still, finally exploding into a torso-shaking blast of trumpets and horns. On cue, the screen flashes alive with a blinding panoramic close-up of an Olympic sprinter surging triumphant across the finish line, his gleaming muscled arms outstretched outstretched, his head thrown back from the sinewy vein-popping trunk of a neck, his giant teeth bared in a dazzling white clench. Now a voice-of-God narrator booms massive around the room:

> *Winning... Triumphing above all others! That's the challenge we face when we commit to the race!*

The music kicks into high gear — a driving, pumping, ass-kicking adrenalin rush of drums and drums and drums. Athletes from every Olympic sport flash fast and furious across the screen.

> *We welcome competition and we shower accolades upon those who take on the best... and win!*
>
> *Everybody loves a winner. Everybody wants to be a*

winner. Everybody wants to be number one. But there can only be one number one.

Try hard, you'll do well. Try harder, you'll do better. But you're never gonna make it to number one unless you try your absolute hardest. When you've given everything you've got to give, you can rest assured you've done your best.

But how many of us really do take it to the limit? How many of us even know how to reach down inside ourselves and tap into that extra reserve of power and determination that can thrust us into the lead and carry us across the finish line to victory?

These people know! They know the secret of winning. Sure, they have special skills and abilities which not all of us can hope to have. But they also make use of a dramatic strength within themselves which all of us have but few of us know how to utilize... THE STRENGTH OF THE WILL!

A powerful music crescendo and the screen dissolves to a *Strength of the Will* logo graphic. Red words emblazoned over three gold Olympic medallions.

Now the music changes dramatically, slows right down and transforms into a majestic and pompous march — vaguely military, immensely proud, an uplifting battle hymn of vast proportions. The images change too. The red words dissolve away, leaving the three Olympic medals stretched across the screen on a red background. Now the medallions disappear, leaving only the round shapes on the red background. The circles are instantly filled with photographs — poorly lit, vaguely greenish photographs of dumpy business people sitting at their desks, clutching boxes of Snamburgers. Now it dissolves to salesmen building Snamburgers displays in the aisles of grocery stores. Now it dissolves to factory workers on the Snamburgers line, wearing shower caps and latex gloves, smiling sheepishly at the camera.

The strength of the will is a source of immeasurable power that must be harnessed and put to work. It is the cornerstone upon which we must erect our dreams, desires and ambitions. The superior salesperson wills or desires to make the sale, never admits the possibility of defeat. It is up to you to have the desire to be number one. To be the best. To try your hardest, whatever it takes! If we truly have the will to be the best, if we constantly demand it of ourselves, then we will make the sale! We will be the winners. And nothing can stop us from being number one. Nothing can stop THE STRENGTH OF THE WILL!

They have got to be kidding, I think to myself, glancing around the room to see if anyone else is in shock. But no, all the sunflower faces are turned to the light of the screen in rapture. All but one. Tom, the cigar smoker, is also watching the faces. Watching with a smirk on his own plump visage.

Another musical bridge and the thing shifts seamlessly into a rousing, popular rock song. The screen is divided into three equal parts. In the centre we see pictures of Olympic athletes doing their thing. On either side we see Snamburger people and Snamburger product shots.

Champions make it happen. Champions are the best.
No time for losers or defeat, the champions never rest.
Forget about resistance, champions always go the distance.
As champions of the world we will rise to any test!

Massive musical climax and the *Strength of the Will* logo slide appears once more and then slowly fades away. The boardroom lights come up bright amidst a flurry of applause and hurrahs.

Clap, I say to myself, *for God's sake clap*, but my icy palms are polar opposites. I just can't do it. Should I toss back my head and chortle like a maniac? Should I sink to my knees and weep? Both seem equally appropriate. I have never felt so alone in all my life.

"Welly-well-well," says Tom around his cigar, "I do believe it's cocktail time. Beverages in my office for whoever's not on a deadline." A sea of AV Network employees parts as Tom leads the way out of the boardroom.

"Let's go, baby," says Franny, pinching the fold of dead skin at the tip of my elbow. "We're not really on a deadline."

I follow numbly along to the office, where Tom and a gaggle of women are making themselves comfortable. Tom unhooks a blood-red velvet jacket from the back of the office door and slips it on with a flourish. He ties the black satin sash around his waist, pushes a strand of blond hair behind one ear and glides towards a small wet bar in the corner. A rec-room model, upholstered in orange vinyl and studded with fat white buttons. Everyone seems extremely amused.

"Manhattans all around?" suggests Tom, waving a pair of metal tongs in the air.

Oh yes yes yes, say all the Network employees, and Tom gets to work with the ice and the rye.

Tom's office is a shrine to irony. There are lava lamps and bean-bag chairs, a *Lost in Space* lunch box and several vintage Partridge Family pin-ups. It all seems acutely incongruous after *The Strength of the Will*.

"Isn't he something?!" whispers Franny, below the din.

"Uh, yeah," I say. "Is he gay?"

"No, he's married."

"Oh, well then..."

"*And* he's screwed half the women in the office," says Franny, pressing her lips together defensively, and I can't quite construe which half she falls into.

"And who might you be?" asks Tom, floating a tray of cocktails in my direction.

"This is Marla Schafer's sister, Michelle," says Franny, grabbing for a drink. "A new slide rat."

"Marvellous," breathes Tom, eyeing me up and down and fixing me with a stare that he obviously intends to be penetrating. "Welcome aboard!"

I attempt the semblance of a smile, select the deepest drink from the tray and take a big swallow. It's sickly sweet with a bitter aftertaste. Not good.

Tom sweeps away to distribute the rest of the drinks. I begin to feel a little nauseous.

"Now then," says Tom to the general assembly, "now that we're all equipped with a strengthening libation, I'd like to go around the room and see what everyone thought of the show. Who wants to go first?"

"I do," squeals a pixie-cut blonde who looks alarmingly like Tweety Bird.

"By all means, lead the way."

"Well, I thought it was *really* powerful. And the images of the athletes were sooo *beautiful*!"

"Yeah," gushes the woman next to her. "That shot of the runner right at the top just totally blew me away. I thought the whole show was really, really motivating."

"I liked the use of the Olympic medals as a masking technique," remarks a brittle brunette. "I think that was extremely effective."

"And the music totally rocked," says Franny.

Oh yeah yeah yeah, the music the music, mumbles everyone present.

"And what did you think of it?" asks Tom, giving me the eye, already basking in the praise that I'm about to warm him with.

"Well..." I say, draining the awful draft and spitting a lemon seed into my mug. "I've never really been too enamoured of the Champions of the World."

"You mean the song?" asks Tom, puffing hard on his cigar in the suddenly quiet office.

"No, not the song," I say, and I feel a big sicko smile spreading unbidden across my face.

"Does your sister work here?" snips the brittle brunette with furrowed brow.

"Uh, she used to," I say. "Marla Schafer."

"Oh, *she's* great," chirps Tweety Bird. "Tell her Jan says hello."

"Sure."

"And um...sorry about your dad," says Tweety.

Oh yeah yeah sorry, murmurs everyone, and I sense a slight change in room temperature.

"Well, who would like to see the show again?" asks Tom, with a big smile, scanning the assembly but avoiding my eye.

Oh me me me! says the group, and they all troop away en happy masse towards the boardroom.

I wander off in search of the bathroom, feeling nauseous and a teeny bit dizzy. The layout of AV Network is like a labyrinth; it takes me a solid five minutes before I locate a can. I stare at myself in the wall-to-wall mirror and wash my hands again and again. My skin looks bad in this new light. I am pale. There are grey circles under my eyes.

"Hello," I say, and my voice bounces hollow around the empty room. "Hello…" I hit the metal button on the hand dryer, rub my hands on my jeans and turn the nozzle up towards my face. Feel the air blowing hot against my skin, against my forehead and eyelids. I think about the absurdity of the last few hours. I think about McCollum gone, and no one to tell. *How am I going to make it through without anyone to tell?*

"I can't hack it," I say to the girl in the mirror. "I can't hack it," she whispers back to me.

But I do. I make it through eleven entire months. I make it through the first seventeen weeks without a single day off. I make it through *The Strength of the Will* and *Success Is the Best!* and *The Strong Get Stronger!* and *The Way of the Winner!* I make it through the dancing cigarette show, the 3-D vacuum-cleaner show and the skin-cream show set to Bob Dylan's "Forever Young." I make it through *Shaping Our Future!*, *Eyes Towards the Future!* and *The Future Is Today!* I make it through the upbeat nine-projector show about a new pharmaceutical that chemically shrinks the testicles off of cancerous men. I make it through a series of empty, cold-hearted fucks on the floor of Tom's late-night office. I make it through the client from Calgary demanding that Alberta and BC appear as large as Ontario and Quebec on his speaker support map. I make it through the AV Network's Annual Fun Day at Marineland and Game Farm. I make it through George and Ira Gershwin's "Nice Work If You Can Get It" reworded and rerecorded for a chicken chain's franchise recruitment show. I make it through countless letters to McCollum c/o the U of T's entomology department, unopened and Returned to Sender. I make it through panic attack at the Eaton Centre on my first day off in months. I make it through health spiralling out of control, an unspoken brush-off by Tom, no time to move out of my haunted apartment, few words from Marla and fewer still from Joel, every free moment spent in hospital emergency wards, raging headaches, jackhammer palpitations, nausea, dizziness, sleeplessness, diarrhea. I make it through Dr. Shore's incisive stare, a CAT scan that tells me I'm perfectly well, and a ridiculous promise to go see a Dr. Eric Ramu at the Clarke Institute. I make it through eleven months at the AV Network...without anyone to tell.

Now it's three o'clock in the morning and I've just eaten the last diazepam handed to me by the angel of mercy at Women's College Hospital. I have been hanging around the office with my insomnia and my stomach ache, recleaning clean slides, hoping to score a ride home and possibly one more fuck-fest out of Tom. He's a narcissistic prick and not much of a lay, but he doesn't try to be my boyfriend. Good.

I go to his office to see if he's almost ready to hit the road, but the door is shut tight and the lava lamps are on and someone's in there giggling. The new assistant in the art department or the owner's bored wife.

Fuck it. I grab a dented box of Pot of Gold chocolates left over from a product shoot and call for a taxi. Go down to the lobby to wait and smoke. I'm on my second when the thing pulls up. It's some new guy I've never had before. Some guy who looks alarmingly like one of the villains out of *Dick Tracy*. The poor slob has an immense head that resembles a halfway morph between James Cagney and a keg of draft. I butt out, slide in and tell him where to go. We haven't even rounded the corner before he opens up on me.

"So, what's a young gal like you doing out so late?"

"Working," I say, tersely. I'm not in the mood for taxi chat.

"Working? Really?" He sounds as if he's never heard of the thing before.

No, actually, I spent the early part of the evening running up and down the hallways playing stickball. When I tired of that I broke into the executive washroom and spent eleven glorious hours looking at my own asshole in the mirror. I don't say that. What I say is: "Would I lie to you?" Then I yawn meretriciously and resort to that old chestnut — fake sleep. I close my eyes and commence drooling. Before long, the diazepam kicks in and I actually go under. That's why I don't see her coming. No time to even lock the doors.

"Mind if I ride along?"

I open my eyes, but the image of a six-foot-tall blonde hooker sliding in beside me just doesn't compute.

"What?" I ask, jolting upright and looking around. We've stopped at a red light at Church and King. There are no other cars in sight. She — I'm pretty sure it's a she — pulls the door shut.

"Can I ride with you for a bit?" she asks brightly, reaching her hand into an old-fashioned beaded purse and holding it there. She sounds casual, but there is something tense and menacing in her posture. The smile is stretched tight and the eyes weren't going along with it at all.

"All right, dear," says the driver, "outta the cab."

"It's OK," I say, staring at her hand in the bag. The last thing I need is a mace nightcap or a face full of Swiss Army knife. "Go ahead, it's all right."

Cagney sneers into the rear-view and drives on. The hooker settles back into the seat and winks at me. "Thanks, hon, you're a peach."

She removes a high-heeled shoe and begins massaging her foot. I try to check her out as casually as possible, not wanting to seem like some goggle-eyed greenhorn who has never seen a prostitute before. But I haven't really; not at close range.

I glance quickly at her neck, then look away. No Adam's apple. She is definitely a she — an extremely large she who looks a little like Vanessa Redgrave. Or more like Miss Redgrave reflected in one of those funhouse mirrors, plus a poodle-like perm, a far too generous helping of shiny beige foundation, a cheesy rabbit-skin jacket and a skin-tight spandex mini-dress cut just below the pudendum. Her stockings are fishnet, the colour of Mountain Dew soda and exactly like a vintage pair I picked up in Kensington Market a few weeks back. Weird. Mind you, I wear mine with army boots, not six-inch spiked pumps.

The hooker catches me looking and smiles. "This one's John," she says, pointing a long lacquered nail at one of two swollen bumps on the side of her foot. "And this one is Paul."

"Beatles?" I say, waiting for her to whip off the other shoe and introduce me to George and Ringo.

"No, silly!" she laughs. "Bunions! Paul Bunion and John Bunion!"

The driver snorts and turns on the radio. Jazz instrumental. Loud.

The hooker raises her voice. "*Grace Abounding to the Chief of Sinners*. John Bunyan wrote that. In prison. Ever heard of him?"

I shake my head no.

"How about *Pilgrim's Progress?*"

The driver cranks up the music.

The hooker presses her lips together and then smirks at me. "Oooh, I love this song!" she squeals, and begins to croon, "*When the band starts to play, it brings back a night... of music so sweet and starlight sublime... we swayed with the palms, rhapsodic, suspended in time... when the band starts to play it brings back the night—*"

The driver turns the radio off. The hooker keeps going. She has a surprisingly sweet voice.

"*Perfection in time, a memory so green, then rain came and washed away the delight we had tasted. And now when I hear others curse a chance that was wasted I know very well what they mean...*" She clears her throat, reaches into her purse and pulls out a pack of smokes. Large, regular Player's Extra Light. My brand. She lights up and puts the pack away without offering me one.

"Hey," barks the driver, "this is a non-smoking cab!"

She looks at me with a cool expression of collusion. "Do you mind if I smoke?"

"It's not up to *her*, honeybuns, it's up to me. And *I've* got asthma and *I* said get rid of it!"

"My name's not honeybuns," she says, raising one eyebrow, "... it's cookie-buns." Then she blows a smoke ring at his head and starts to laugh.

"Okey-dokey," says the driver, slamming on the brakes. The donut of smoke caroms off the side of his monstrous neck and breaks apart. He jumps out and storms around to the hooker's door, yanking it open with such force that it hits the spring mechanism and slams shut.

The hooker stops laughing.

When the driver whips the door open again, she flicks the cigarette past him. "There," she says, trying to look bored about the whole thing.

"Get out of the cab," he growls. He's not tall, not nearly as tall as her, but he's stocky and mean-looking and mad.

"It's gone, OK. Chill out, buddy."

"Did you hear what I said?" he yells, grabbing at her arm and, I notice, also at her breast.

"Don't you fuckin' touch me, asshole!"

"Then get the fuck out!"

"Screw you. She said I could have a ride!"

"That's it, bitch!" He reaches into the cab, takes her by the belt and the hair and starts pulling. She flails and kicks and screams, but he has her out within seconds. Then he grabs her purse from the back seat and heaves it as far as he can down the road.

As the driver turns to get back into the car, she lets him have it, pounding her enormous fist into the centre of his back. The eyes bug and he lets loose a hideous wheeze-squeal. He swings around and punches her hard in the face. Speechless, I watch her fall to the ground, blood trickling down from above the eye. Now the driver looks scared.

"I'm outta here," he says, hurrying back to the car.

"Fuck you, pencil dick!" she screeches, and with the amazing strength of pure fury she lurches into the front seat, rips the stainless steel meter from its mount and flings it crashing into the middle of Richmond Street. Then, with her face full of tears and blood, she leans into the back of the cab, snatches the box of Pot of Gold from my lap and says, "Thanks a lot, bitch."

As the cab drives off I watch her limping along a dead stretch of factory road with the dented box of candy crushed against her chest.

When we finally arrive at Grace Street, the driver cracks the thick silence. "Listen," he says, "since that cow wrecked my meter, I don't know how much to charge you. Whattya say we make it an even fifteen bucks?"

Now, finally, something comes out of my mouth.

"Fuck you, pencil dick," I say softly, wadding up the cab slip and bouncing it off his pony-keg head. I get out of the cab and head towards the house.

"All the same," he yells into the night as I traverse the narrow path to the backyard. "All a bunch of freakin' whores!"

I go inside, take a long shower and fall dead into bed, the cabbie's words reverberating in my head.

Two weeks later I return to the AV Network to pick up the last of my golden-handcuff cheques.

—

I am unemployed, but I am rich. I have close to eighteen thousand AV Network dollars lolling fat in my bank account. I say goodbye to the brown basement and take an apartment in the Annex. The main floor of a Victorian house on Major Street. Near the University of Toronto. With windows.

I start seeing Dr. Eric Ramu at the Clarke Institute. I like his ill-fitting polyester slacks and his ugly-ass sweaters. I like his no-nonsense approach and his big prescription pad. We both find it very interesting that since quitting my gig in corporate communications my health has improved immeasurably. The stomach aches, nausea, diarrhea and chest pains have all gone bye-bye. Now it's mostly just headaches and palpitations. And only when I leave my apartment. But I force myself to go out.

The streets around me are electric. Charged with the potential presence of McCollum. I never walk out the door without first sprucing up. My eyes are in continuous scan mode. Sweep left. Sweep right. Connect with every window of every building. For all I know he could live next door or across the street or in an apartment above a store on Bloor or Bathurst.

During the week, when the streets aren't too clogged with humans, I wander around the neighbourhood, bundled in my parka. Sometimes I stroll through the university campus or linger near the entrance to the giant cement peacock that is Robarts Library. I pretend that I'm just taking a smoke break. I manage to blend in. Sometimes I hang out in the park on Albany Avenue or I go up and down Philosopher's Walk. I dine almost every night in one of the Hungarian restaurants on Bloor Street. The Continental has the best chicken paprikas, Country Style has the best cabbage rolls, but the Korona has the most amusing music — an unconnected array of bizarre tunes on a continuous tape-loop. None of them even attempting Hungarianness. My favourite is the one with the lusty all-male choir singing *Going down to Washington to shake hands with President Nixon!* but there are a lot of gems. This is the kind of place McCollum would dig. Sometimes I come in for my morning coffee and a piece of poppyseed strudel. Sometimes I just come in, look around and then leave.

The pills Dr. Ramu gave me have helped a lot. I'm sleeping now. Ten or eleven hours a night. It feels good. I still can't ride public transit or go into a mall, crowds are a big no-no and I don't really feel comfortable leaving the Annex, but I can function in the neighbourhood with relative ease, interact with people, go in and out of the shops on Bloor. Except for Honest Ed's, that colossal bargain barn/battlefield where students, the recently immigrated and impecunious types stampede for lost leaders and wage tug-of-wars over the shmatte tables.

Dr. Ramu encourages me to look for work. Eventually I take a part-time job at the local bookstore. Book World. The pay is awful, but I don't mind the drill. It's a quiet job. And no shame. Best of all, I've discovered two crucial authors: Knut Hamsun and John Fante. I fall in love with the dead.

Once in a while I borrow a magazine from the Book World racks and go for a frozen yogourt at the Have It Your Way Café. It's not likely that McCollum would show up here, but it's possible. They play Ella Fitzgerald and Billie Holiday and you can monopolize a table for several hours for the price of a cup of coffee. Of course, the place is lousy with caffeinated artists pumped up on refills — sculptors and painters, playing chess and chaining Gitanes, faded kaffiyehs draped dramatically around their necks, black berets angled jauntily over their eyes. There are writers too, scads of them, scribbling in notebooks, trying to appear thoughtful, their dog-eared volumes of Dostoevsky and Dylan Thomas conspicuously displayed, their precious poetry voices rising above the din as they recite their latest mope to some dewy-eyed first-year poly-sci student who is being mentally undressed with great precision as the anemic words leak out.

I've slept with a few of these boys. Once with the curly-haired installation artist from Paraguay. Several times with the big-dicked jewellery maker from Kapuskasing. Twice with the welfare performance-poet who sold stolen cases of imported pantyhose somewhere down around Queen and Spadina. I soon learned that their art was the most interesting thing about them, and the art wasn't very interesting at all. Sex — what a goddamned pain! Of course, I never stayed the night, and I was smart enough to never bring them to my place. The last thing I need is some virtuoso nesting in my apartment like an unwanted raccoon. Besides, I left my forwarding address with my landlord on Grace. McCollum could show up at any time.

If only he would.

Where the hell is he hiding? I am everywhere and he is nowhere. I've done everything but audit his classes. I can't bring myself to do that. I won't do that. I don't want to hunt him down. I want us to find each other. Again. I still believe in Magic, especially when it comes to McCollum, and I have a powerful feeling that we are supposed to be together, that we are going to be together. I can see us old. I can see us old together. Not a fantasy. A premonition. Day after day, night after night, I wander the neighbourhood, up and down Bloor Street, up and down the side streets, putting myself into the middle of it all because I know he is supposed to find me. I know it. I can feel it. Blood. Bones. Belly.

Uch! What a load of romantic crap! Too many movies. Too much Gilbert Blythe. Hell, it's been almost two years since McCollum pulled a Houdini. He's with someone by now. McCollum is way over it. I am an anecdote in bed at night. Chuckle chuckle chuckle. The crazy girl from the hospital. The evil first girlfriend. Well, maybe I really am crazy. It's hard to tell. Sanity is a tightrope walk. Easy to falter and plunge.

But things had been going well before he left. Better than well. McCollum had really started to relax and get comfortable. We took baths together. Bubble baths. McCollum valiantly taking the end with the dripping taps. All scrunched in — six feet four inches — with the cold water trickling down his neck and chest, his knees rising white out of the water like titanic icebergs. We'd stay in there for ages. Adding more and more hot.

"What's the most powerful word in the English language?" McCollum asked one Sunday in mid-soak.

I mulled it over for a while, trying a few out: *Death, War, God, We*... but nothing settled sharp in my mind.

"I don't know," I said. "What do you think?"

"I'm not sure," said McCollum, adding more hot. "Let's think about it and get back to each other."

The baths were good. The showers were good too. Long ones full of soap and song, our voices ringing sweet off the tile and sounding to us just exactly like the Guess Who, the Monkees, the Supremes, the Flirtations.

The sex took some easing into. It wasn't all instantly OK. McCollum was extremely nervous and self-conscious. The first time we tried intercourse he came right away. Ditto the next night. And the night after that. I didn't care, but McCollum got all paranoid about it. I told him it was because it was all new. And not to worry. I was happy. Happier than I've ever been with anyone anytime. Happier than I've ever ever been. And so we went on. And McCollum ditched the sweatpants and started sleeping naked beside me.

The day he disappeared was cold. Minus two with the wind chill. And snowy. I was at the donut shop, taking my break — fifteen minutes to smoke and drink hot chocolate and jot notes on a napkin for my next Selectric epistle — when my mom walked in. Wow. A visit. This was something other. As she smiled and came towards me, I knew that something terrible had happened. I offered up sugar donuts and tea, but she wanted to go outside and sit in the car. I thought: *Maybe something has happened to my father. Maybe something has happened to Joel or Marla.*

"I was at the doctor today," she said, looking straight ahead at the street through the windshield.

Oh no. Oh no.

"I have cancer. Liver cancer." The eyes turned to me, looking for the reaction.

"What?!"

"I have cancer. And I'm going to die." She said this with a strange resolve, bordering on determination.

"No — but how do they know? Maybe it's something else?"

"No. That's what it is. I'm sorry, Michelle."

"But you have to get a second opinion! Maybe they're wrong."

"No, honey. I've done all the tests. There is no other opinion."

"How do you know?!"

"Because I know. I've been pursuing this for a while. I didn't want to say anything until..."

"Oh God, it's freezing in here, can you turn up the heat?!"

"It's all the way up. Do you want to go inside?"

"No! So... so what do we do now?"

"Well, I start chemotherapy tomorrow. But it's really only a matter of time."

"How can you say that?! Maybe the chemotherapy will work!"

"Maybe... But I just want you to understand, bubelah. I want you to be prepared."

"Oh God, I'm sick of being prepared! I don't want to be prepared."

"I know..." said my mom, and she put her cold hands on top of my cold hands.

We sat there for I don't know how long, then my mother said, "Marla and Joel cried. So did your father."

"...I'm freezing," I said eventually, through chattering teeth.

Her green eyes looked into my green eyes. "You'd better get back," she said.

"No."

"Yes. I'm tired. I have to go."

"Can I come with you tomorrow?"

"We'll see. Go on now."

I didn't say anything and I didn't move.

"Go on. I'll call you tomorrow. Maybe you'll come with me."

I got out of the car without saying goodbye and watched her drive off. Small behind the wheel, awkward in traffic.

I stood in the snow for a minute or two, then I walked to the nearest bar and sat down at a small brown table. For the first time in my life I wasn't asked for ID. They brought the whiskey and they kept bringing it.

I drank and I didn't feel anything. My feet were wet and uncomfortable and that was about it. *My mother has cancer*, I kept reminding myself, but I just sat there empty. Blinking and eating peanuts.

When the money ran out I left. I walked carefully down Bloor Street towards Grace. Everything looked very white and unreal. People seemed to be looking at me. I tried to step sober. Turned down Grace, where a station wagon sat stuck in the snow, spinning its wheels in the ice. Two or three passersby were pushing the car from behind, rocking it back and forth. I walked on.

I was thinking about the caloric content of peanuts when I noticed a chain of humans coming towards me. Wide across the sidewalk, holding hands. An old woman in a dark blue coat, a young woman in yellow, and a little girl balanced evenly between them, in a pea green jacket and matching tam. I stepped off the sidewalk to let them pass, and as I did I felt a terrible twist of sadness rise up from my chest and lodge in my throat. My heart started pounding and my head was full of pressure and ringing. I started to run. Run run run. Fast down the street. My hands were in my pockets, and when I wiped out there was nothing to cushion the impact. I went straight down. Hard into the snow. Face down into the snow.

"Hey! Hey, are you OK?!"

I felt a hand on my back. A hand on my shoulder. The hands rolled me over and I saw the guy from across the street, Camaro Guy, leaning over me. He brushed the slush from my face. "Are you OK?" he said softly.

"Yeah..." I answered, and then I started to sob.

"It's OK," he said. "Come on..." And he pulled me to my feet. "Are you all right now?"

"...Yeah." But I couldn't stop sobbing.

"Come on, I'll take you home." He put his arm around me and led me gently across the street and down the path to the backyard. "Where are your keys?" he asked, but I couldn't find them in my pockets. "Hold on," he said, and he ran out of the backyard. A few seconds or an hour later I heard him coming back down the path. "I found 'em," he called out, and then he appeared, dangling the slush-covered keys. "They must have fallen out." He opened the door and we went inside.

I stood drunk and dumb in the middle of the apartment, wiping the tears from my face. He handed me the cold keys.

"Here," he said. "You OK now?"

"Yeah. Thanks."

"OK," he said, and he stood there looking at me. We just stood there for a couple of seconds and then he said, "OK, I'm gonna go." He gave me a quick, friendly hug and then he stepped back and looked into my face. And something in my face said *kiss me*, and so he did.

He kissed me strong and hard. He tasted like cigarettes and he smelled like snow and sweat. I thought about him across the street with his shirt off and his jeans slung low, working on that car. All summer long, half naked with the jeans hanging low below the navel, strutting tough with the thick arms and the powerful chest warm and golden in the sun.

I tugged at the zipper of his ski jacket. He took it off and threw it on the floor, started working on the laces of his Kodiak boots. I got out of my parka, my wet shoes and socks, peeled off the Olde Country smock, and started in on the buttons of his red flannel shirt. He stepped back and pulled the thing up over his head. God, he was beautiful with the arms up over the head! I moved in and kissed the chest, bit the biceps, licked the belly. I got down and found the stiff cock through the jeans, kissed the cock hard through the jeans. He unzipped and pulled it out. Beautiful. Thick and hard like the rest of him. He grabbed me by the hair and shoved the cock in my face, shoved it stiff into my mouth. All that good male stiff in my mouth. I looked up at the solid flesh, the thick neck, the chiselled face in need of a shave. He was watching me as I sucked, watching me with half-closed eyes and the hint of a sneer on his open mouth.

"Jesus..." he breathed, and he pulled away. He yanked me to my feet and pushed me onto the bed, pulled the bra down and squeezed my tits. I undid my jeans and he pulled them down and off. I started to remove my panties.

"No," he said, stepping out of his clothes, "turn over."

I turned onto my stomach. An arm slid under my waist and pulled me to the edge of the bed, pulled me to my hands and knees. He moved the panties aside and stuck his cock hot against me. Then he held it there in a tease.

"Come on..." I whispered, and he let me have it. Worked it in slowly and pushed it deep inside. Started fucking me from behind. It was brutal. Exciting. I had never had sex that way before. He pulled my head back by the hair and grabbed my tits with his other hand. *Yeah*...he said, *oh yeah, yeah*...When he was about to come he stopped and pulled out, turned me over and got in between my legs. Then he sank it in and started fucking me again. Slowly. And then not so slowly. I closed my eyes and ran my hands over his wide back, down the perfect smooth vee of his back towards the ass. Such new flesh. So strange. Strong. He started pumping. Hard. He reached back with one hand and grabbed my leg around the ankle. Oh yeah...That hand around the ankle put me over the edge. I started to come. And then he started to come. And it was a perfect four seconds of no thought and all good...during which McCollum walked in early from a class that must have been cancelled.

"Oh God!" I cried, pushing the body off me.

McCollum's face was dead white and covered in pain.

"Shit!" said the Camaro Guy, covering himself with his hands. "Oh shit."

A terrible moment of blazing silence, then McCollum turned and walked out. He didn't say a thing. He just turned and walked away.

"Jesus," muttered Camaro Guy. "Sorry about that..."

I jumped up and made a quick grab for some clothes. Found my pants and got them on, then the parka and the wet shoes.

"You should put on a shirt," he called out after me, "...and socks. It's freezing out there!"

As I moved through the cold room I felt a gush of semen seep warm into my jeans. I zipped the parka up to my neck and ran sober into the yard, around the side to the front of the house. McCollum was nowhere in sight. I jogged up to Bloor Street and scanned in all directions. Nothing! I stood on the corner, turning, panicking... Finally, I picked east. Started walking fast towards the university.

Words in my head began tumbling unbidden from my mouth. "*Fuck!*" I said. "*Stupid fucking idiot!*" People and dogs got out of my way.

My feet were freezing. A satisfying pain. I flashed upon my father, twelve years old, being marched through the streets of Budapest in the middle of the night. Marching barefoot through the snow from the orphanage to the ghetto. "*Once you were in the ghetto, there was only one way out...*" I kept walking. I walked to the university and all around the campus. Young men and women were moving around the grounds, evenly spaced, like in an architect's rendering. I thought about going into one of the buildings for a minute. My jeans were frozen stiff around my shoes and halfway up my shins. *No, you idiot. Keep walking!*

I walked down to College Street and stood on the corner. It was starting to get dark. Everything was a deep blue. I had a strong and sudden vision of incandescent light, of McCollum returning to the apartment. No money for a cab. I started to jog west.

Jog, walk, jog, walk, all the way home through the snow. *Please please please*... I thought, as I hustled down the path to the backyard, as I jumped down the cement steps and quickly turned the frozen doorknob. But the place was dark. And no music. I moved through the cold room and flicked on the overhead. The apartment was deserted. But McCollum had been there.

"Shit!" I said, staring at the small brown dresser. The drawers were out and empty — gaping MACtac mouths. Some books were gone too. Ditto the toothbrush and the acne medicine. McCollum had left his keys on the table next to the Selectric. A piece of paper had been rolled into the typewriter, but there were no words on the page. I stared at the thing and thought it over. With anybody else this could have meant a number of things:

1. That they had resolved to say something but then abruptly changed their mind.
2. That they couldn't think of how to say what they wanted to say.
3. That they were too angry to say it.
4. That they were waiting for some kind of explanation.

With anybody else it could have meant any one of those things. But not with McCollum. I knew what he was trying to tell me, just as clearly as if he had written it in capital letters across the page: THERE IS NOTHING TO SAY.

It is irrevocable.

I took a shower. Washed the dried semen out of my pubic hairs. Washed the sweat of a stranger off my body. *There is something to say*, I thought. *There is a lot to say*. I wrapped myself in a towel and went to the Selectric. I removed the blank sheet of paper from the typewriter and folded it carefully into my underwear drawer. Then I rolled a new sheet into the machine and started typing. I told McCollum about my mother. About the cancer of the liver. I told him about going to the bar and five or six whiskeys. About the family on the sidewalk and falling down into the snow. I told about being helped back to the apartment. And being drunk and not thinking. Not thinking. Not thinking. I told him that it was the first time that I'd done anything like that. And that I would never do anything like that again. I told him that I didn't give a shit about the guy, and that it was all about forgetting. It was all about forgetting and it had nothing to do with him. NOTHING WHATSOEVER TO DO WITH HIM! I told him that I loved everything about him. Every every thing. And that I was sorry. More than sorry. And that he had to believe me... blah blah blah.

I typed endlessly. On and on. Finally, there was nothing to say. And no more cigarettes. I made an envelope out of paper and Scotch tape and addressed the letter to McCollum care of the entomology department at the U of T. I would drop it off in the morning. Maybe I would be lucky enough to run into him.

I found a decent-sized butt and smoked it in front of the mirror. I had a bruised bump on the left side of my forehead. My tongue was coated white. I got into bed, but I couldn't sleep. I stared at the telephone. Concentrating. Invoking my powers and willing it to ring. But it just sat there looking calm and peaceful. Buddha phone.

Eventually there were footsteps above me and it was morning. I had Taster's Choice instant coffee and cereal with water; the milk had gone sour. I called my mom and arranged to meet her at the hospital for the first chemotherapy. Then I called the donut shop and told them I was sick. Much too sick to function.

—

Three weeks later I come home after work and find a manila envelope in the mailbox, addressed to me in McCollum's handwriting. I press the ballpoint words to my lips and sniff the envelope. It smells like paper. Nothing else. I hurry inside and tear into the thing. Find my taped-up missive returned unopened (a punch to the solar plexus). The first of many.

I change, wash down a can of sardines with some Bushmills and head to Mount Sinai. My mother has been admitted.

I am not even close to being prepared.

—

The disease moved through fast. Appallingly fast. My mother was transferred to the palliative care wing at the Princess Margaret Hospital. The Cancer Ghetto. Only one way out.

"Don't remember me this way," she would say, but the bedsores and the bile — dark green in silver receptacle — burned and sloshed hot in my brain.

I hated the nurses. So brusque. So matter-of-fact. Singsong voices pasted over their roughness. *Where are the hearts?* I wondered, observing their abrupt hands and their stern weariness. *All frozen over. Dead of exposure.*

Before long there was little hope and much morphine. One evening, father watching CFTO news on the tiny TV with the sound off; mother drifting in and out of consciousness on the narrow white bed. I am leaning into the window, looking at the street lights diffused and magic through the foggy patches of my hot breath on the icy pane. Marla and Joel arrive with a bag of Harvey's takeout. Onion rings, well done. An old favourite of my mother's. She hasn't been touching the hospital food. Only mouse bites of the macrobiotic meals my father ordered from the weird hippy lady who brought them in especially. He is trying to believe in the kale and the brown rice. He wants desperately to believe in the carrots and the steamed kelp.

An argument erupts:

Your mother can't eat that crap! Get it out of here.

She has to eat ***something****! This is better than nothing.*

I said get it out of here! Father lunges furious at the paper bag in Joel's hands.

Stop it! screams Marla.

My mother opens her eyes. She looks bewildered and upset. This is not what anyone wants. They huff it out into the hallway. I can hear them going full volume outside the door.

"Tell Freddy to get down from there!" says my mom, stabbing through the bubble of the morphine world.

"Freddy," I say, "c'mere boy. Come on down. That's a good boy... OK," I tell my mother, "he came down."

No response. Just breathing and a slightly furrowed brow.

...what the hell difference does it make?!!

Shut up, you... Just shut the hell up!!!

I go into the hallway. *We can hear you from inside!*

Joel throws the Harvey's bag at my father and storms away.

Happy now? hisses Marla.

My father's eyes bulge. His face turns red and rumbles volcanic.

Insane. Ready to pop. He grabs my sister by the arm and pulls her violently down the corridor. Away from my mother's door.

I pick the crushed bag up off the floor and go back into the room. My mother opens her eyes.

"Is everything OK?" she asks, confused.

"Yeah. Everything's fine."

She looks up at me and then closes her eyes.

"That's Michelle," she says to someone I can't see. "She's the most like me..."

—

I am surprised and impressed by my father's sudden attentiveness. He is at the hospital all the time, doing whatever he can to make my mother as comfortable as possible, keeping a hawk eye on the IV bag, chasing down the nurses when painkillers, extra blankets or a clean bedpan is required. More juice from the kitchenette, take the robe home and wash it, fluff the pillows, crank the bed up, crank the bed down. Practical action. Of this, he proves extremely capable.

Marla is there all the time too. Joel, most of the time. I am the worst. The most negligent. The ratbag. I continue to report to my shitty job each day. I tell myself that I need to go to work. And I do. But not for the obvious reasons.

I head to the hospital each evening, but sometimes on the way I nip into the bar around the corner and have two or three quick hits. One night I stay for four or five, possibly six, then stumble drunk and late, reeking of smoke and whiskey, into my mother's room.

She is unusually lucid. And angry.

"Where were you?"

"Um, work. Sorry. The new girl didn't show up and my boss forced me to work late."

"You have to take a few days off," she says, her green eyes bright and fierce. "Not for me... for you."

"OK," I agree, refusing to process what I know she means. "Man, it's pretty warm out. You can really smell spring in the air. In a couple of weeks we'll be able to take you outside for some fresh air and sunshine."

Yeah! pipe in Marla and Joel and father. *Sunshine, Sunshine! Fresh Air and Sunshine!*

"Fine," says my mom, rolling laboriously onto her side, turning her back to my face. "Just take a few days off, Michelle."

Two days later, pneumonia.

We don't leave the hospital at all now. There are masks every three hours. Day and night. To help the breathing. The breathing is everything. It is terrible and torturous. Exhale... Now wait and watch and listen for the inhale. Wait and wait too long too long... Then, just as you're about to leap from your chair, it comes in a short gasp. A quick thick wheeze. And then the exhale. And the waiting and watching and listening again.

We each have a chair. Orange vinyl or black vinyl. We sleep covered in our coats. Take turns dozing off. Take turns dashing out for provisions. There is nothing for my mother except morphine and the mask. A restless morphine coma and every three hours the mask. Tight around the skull. Covering up the face. One of the nurses brings it in and we take it from there, thank you very much. After seventy-eight hours of pneumonia we are experts with the mask. We know how to do it right. How to lift the heavy head gently, and careful careful with the strap. And watch the plastic reservoir until the medicine has vaporized and there's just a couple of milky white droplets clinging and vibrating against the plastic. Get it off the face as soon as possible. Careful with the strap. Seven a.m. and 10 a.m. and 1 p.m. and 4. Seven p.m. and 10 p.m. and 1 a.m. and 4. Now again it's 7 a.m. and it's my turn with the mask. I lift the sleeping head gently and slip the elastic in behind. I am about to lower the blue plastic slowly over the small face when a hand lashes tight around my wrist, yanking it away with sharp, ferocious strength. The green eyes flash open. Blazing. Intent. For the first time ever, my mother raises her voice.

"I WANT THIS TO STOP!" she says.

And, of course, it does.

—

The more I drink the less surprising things become. Not that anything is terribly surprising any more. Years and years ago I was surprised when I heard about my father's death. Suicide after all that *surviving*. I remember being surprised when I saw a she-male for the first time. Breasts and a penis. That was surprising. Watergate was surprising. So was John Lennon's death. When the shuttle exploded with the schoolteacher on board, the world stared with disbelief and surprise at the fiery chunks plummeting from the sky. The end of the Cold War was more than a relief, it was a surprise. Canadians were surprised when Ben Johnson tested positive for steroids. When Lorena Bobbitt lopped off her husband's shmeckie and chucked it out the window of a moving automobile, people were surprised. Then a woman in Thailand did the same thing, minus the automobile portion. Then a man in Georgia did it to himself with the top of a tin can. O.J.'s arrest was surprising. Not so much his acquittal, right?

These days there are few surprises left. Unexpected events, yes. But few new surprises. *Surprise: This test-tube baby has a baboon heart!* Yeah? That's nice. Best of luck to him. *Surprise: This sitcom starlet prefers pussy to dick!* So what. It's just prime time and laugh track. *Surprise: President Clinton stuck his cigar in an intern!* More people giggled than gasped, and the approval rating soared. *Surprise: The priest buggered the altar boy and the hockey coach fondled the goaltender!* Nobody is surprised by that any more. Saddened but not surprised. *Surprise: Fred Astaire's back from the dead and he's dancing with a vacuum cleaner!* It's all done with computers. You ain't seen nothin' yet. *Surprise: I used to be a man and now I'm sleeping with the babysitter!* Not a surprise, just another mildly titillating talk-show topic. *Surprise: Howard Stern called the French peckerheads!* French Canadians were pissed off but hardly surprised. *Surprise: A flesh-eating super virus gobbled my extremities!* Oh dear, must remember to pick up some hydrogen peroxide and tend to our paper cuts. *Surprise: We've cloned a sheep and a cow!* Well, that's just plum wrong, say the human beings, but they don't seem terribly surprised. In fact they're now waiting for the not-so-surprising news of the next logical step.

We're running out. We're running out of surprises.

Maybe that's what this is all about. Maybe Joel has run out of surprises in his movies, so he's moved on to real life. Both of his last two films tanked at the box office. That in itself was something of a surprise. Joel was consistent. Surefire for the longest time. The highest-paid screenwriter in the world. A wunderkind. Famous for receiving million-dollar development deals for single-paragraph synopses. A player. A character. One of the only Hollywood hacks to warrant a five-page feature in *Vanity Fair*. Complete with photos. Glossy and slick.

No B-list stars for Joel's pictures. He attracted the best. Hollywood royalty. And the stars trusted the scripts and did what they were told. Stab a baby in the heart with a knitting needle... Expose your less-than-extraordinary hard-on to the world... Sodomize a sixteen-year-old girl with a pepper mill... It can't be bad for your career: it's a Joel Schafer picture. These are the scenes that everyone talks about. These are the scenes people remember, for heaven's sake. *Oh, oh, remember that scene with the knitting needle! Oh God, that scene with the pepper mill! No, no, the scene with the famous actor's erect dick!* There was always a must-see moment in each of Joel's movies. Something shocking and gossiped about. Something that would quickly enter the *Zeitgeist* and become fodder for late-night talk-show monologues. Joel was clever. No doubt about it. The movies were always hits and always essentially the same — heavy-handed morality plays in the guise of taut thrillers. A taut courtroom thriller, a taut medical thriller, a taut detective thriller, a taut psychological thriller. Always a taut thriller studded with snappy, relatively intelligent dialogue, plenty of twists and turns, one shockingly memorable scene and a surprise ending. Always a surprise ending. Joel was the first one to come up with the undead villain. A cliché now, but a stunner in its time. We all know the drill: at the end of the picture the hero or heroine has finally dispatched the villain in a climactic flurry of scary-ass music, flashing cleavers and bloody cudgels. The hero/heroine slumps as their ordeal comes to an exhausting end, the music calms, the audience settles back into their seats and resumes popcorn and Twizzler consumption. But wait! The villain, stabbed forty times, beaten about the head and floating face down in the swimming pool, isn't dead yet! Up with the scary-ass music, another two minutes of *look out behind you* capital-A Action before the Rasputin of anti-heroes is finally ass-kicked beyond resurrection. Beautiful.

Joel's last two pictures, a taut political thriller and a taut domestic thriller, had all the elements — celebrity snatch, newfangled violence, a key sensational scene and the big surprise ending — but they just didn't fly with audiences. The audiences were expecting it all. They were bored. Jaded. Not surprised.

And I'm not surprised when I glance up at the ceiling fixture in my old bedroom and notice that the white plastic screw-top thingy that holds the milky white square of etched glass over the two light bulbs has been replaced with something black and shiny and high-tech-looking. I'm curious, but not surprised, as I push the night table into the centre of the room and, half cut on Jameson's, clamber on top and discover that the black and glass button is some kind of lens, some kind of surveillance device. I'm perturbed, but not surprised, as I realize that Joel has been monitoring — perhaps even filming — our activities since we arrived at number 5 Pinecrest. Perturbed, yes, but not really surprised. Maybe it's the booze.

I flash the tiny bubble of glass my best snide smile. Then I give it the finger. Very cool. Then, as I reach up to unscrew the thing, I lose my balance and tumble backwards off the night table. Flat on my ass on the amber carpet. Yeah, very cool, Michelle. Way to go. I grab for the Irish, raise it in a toast to the ceiling and take a good hit. Marla finds me sprawled on the shag, giggling like a maniac, with whiskey trickling down my chin.

"What in the fuck is going on?"

"I've fallen and I can't get up."

"Jesus Christ, Michelle, are you pissed or what? I mean, what's with the little miss booze-hound routine? Since when are you a drinker?"

"I'm not drunk," I say, straightening up. "I lost my balance."

"Yeah right!"

"Yes, it is right. You see that thing on the light fixture, that little glass nub in the middle there?"

"Yeah... what is that?"

"That is a lens, some kind of surveillance device. Little Brother is watching. Probably recording too."

"*What?*"

"Check it out. I was attempting to remove it when I lost my footing."

Marla looks hard at the ceiling, then charges out of my room, across the hall into her room. "There's one in here too! Fucking bastard!"

"Uh uh uh, Joel is listening..."

"I don't care. This is — this is too fucking much!"

I follow Marla into Joel's room. There's one in there too. Nothing in our bathroom, a small nod to privacy and decorum. But there's one in my parents' bathroom, that viciously clean chamber of horrors with its gleaming lavender tiles — replaced and regrouted — and the brand-new vintage wallpaper with the patterned reproductions of nineteenth-century ads for hair-growth tonics, laudanum restoratives and licorice pastilles. And look, there's one over the bed in the master bedroom. And, yes, here's another one in the hall.

"Maybe you were right," says my sister. "Maybe we should just change our tickets and blow this pop stand. Get the hell out!"

"I think that might be wise. I'm kind of glad you feel that way."

Marla comes up close beside me, cups her hands over my ear and whispers soft and staccato into the side of my head. "Obviously, this is just some kind of sicko peep show. Some kind of weird experiment starring you and me as lab rats. I mean, Joel is probably stretched out on his massage table in Ojai, eating bonbons and watching the video wall. Probably taking notes for his next piece-of-shit blockbuster or something."

I step back and scrub the tickly breath from my ear. "Maybe, but you know what's more likely?"

"What?"

"My guess is that Joel—"

"Whisper it!" says Marla.

I direct my hot whiskey breath into her ear. "My guess is that Joel—"

"Helloooo? Anybody home, perchance?" My brother's stentorian voice rises from the deep of the downstairs hallway.

Marla looks into my smirking face. "What were you going to say?" she asks.

"I was going to say that Joel is probably closer than you think — in a van around the corner or a house across the street — and that he's probably on his way over this minute to prevent us from leaving, now that his little video game has been busted."

"And now here he is," says Marla.

"Yeah," I say. "Surprise surprise."

—

One day the feeling disappeared. The feeling that McCollum was out there somewhere. Overnight, the neighbourhood went from feeling shaky electric to empty and dead. It was August, two and a half years after McCollum walked out the door. Mother dead. Father dead. Joel in LA. Marla in Vancouver.

There was activity in the neighbourhood. Stained futons and splayed velour couches and broken Ikea on the curbs. Students moving out. Students coming in. Overnight, the jangly feeling of expectation was snuffed out. Extinguished. Every cell in my body sensed that McCollum had gone away. Out of the Annex. Out of Toronto. It was like the city flatlined. Shifted from Technicolor to sepia.

At first I felt hollow. Cast off and deserted. Much better to leave than be left behind. The one who leaves moves forward. Tallyho. The one left behind gets frozen in the past. Locked into a narrow sliver of time. For a while I slouched around with stomach full of sad and mouth full of mope. But eventually it was a relief. Like sleep after a long and jittery caffeine buzz. Anticipation...abandonment...and finally, acceptance. Time to move on. *Yeah right.* Move on!

And so there was George. Curiously nervous George, the sous-chef who wanted to be a writer and who wanted to go to bed with someone. Ultimately, that someone became me. I could tell by his increasing edginess each time he came into Book World. He was a nervous type to begin with. Painfully self-conscious and overly analytical. He moved as if he were being watched. Watched by a bevy of critical, gum-popping cheerleaders. No flow. Herky-jerky. There was something definitely askew in his wiring. A delay in the impulses. You could literally see him thinking about each action before he attempted it. Every action, no matter how trivial. An arm would never just reach out for something. No. First there would be the impulse to reach out, then the split-second delay while he thought it over: *I want to reach out. Should I? Is now a good time? Is anybody looking? Shall I reach out slowly? Yes, that would probably be best. OK, easy does it. Here goes...* And then the reach, which would inevitably end up wrong. Spastic. Awkward. Lurching out and knocking over the glass. Or the book. Or the ashtray. Or the wine bottle. Too much thought. Not enough flow. Somewhere down the line something or someone had interrupted the flow. Dammed it up with Scorn/Criticism/Laughter/Derision. Was it a single indelibly traumatic embarrassment, or a childhood peppered with harping and nitpicking?

It was the same with speech. No flow between the brain and the vocal chords. He could barely speak. All stutter and sputter. All stammer and spurt. Stiff little utterances punctuated by bitter little laughs. You could see the lines forming, forming beautifully and eloquently behind the eyes, but the words didn't correspond. They came out all wrong. Tumbling off the gangplank of his tongue as if they had been pushed. And you could also see that as soon as the words tumbled out, the brain would flinch with embarrassment and instantly realize what should have been said, and then throb with shame because it was too late to say it. The brain and the mouth just couldn't get it together. So the mouth cut its losses and stayed shut as much as possible.

The first time he came into Book World he picked up a hardcover tome entitled *Chess Is My Life*.

"*Chess Is My Life*," I said, ringing it through.

"Well, ha, you know... heh, heh, not really. Ahem—"

"I just finished *Tiddlywinks Is My Life*. It improved my game immeasurably."

"Oh yeah? Heh, heh... well, um, thanks. See ya." He grabbed the bagged book and lurched towards the door, lips pressed tight together as the perfect comeback, the snappy little retort formed too late behind the blue blue eyes and the serious black brow.

He came in more and more. Almost daily. Knocking over displays, bumping into other customers, dropping change all over the floor. Once or twice he left the store without taking his purchase and I had to chase him halfway down the street. He was impossible not to like. He would careen towards the cash with his selection and blurt out some rigid rehearsed line. It was embarrassing. And endearing. He bought a lot of Russian novelists. He was big into the Russians. He told me that he was teaching himself to speak Russian so that he could read *Crime and Punishment* in its original state. He sputtered something about rhythm and the futility of translation, and then he dropped a hardcover copy of *War and Peace* on my foot. Once, in an attempt to initiate any semblance of conversation, he asked me to recommend a novel. I told him to try *Women in Love*. I figured D.H. Lawrence would be perfect for the guy. All that acute below-the-surface analysis, the shrewd multi-page dissections of the most casual, apparently meaningless gestures. It was a good choice. George went gaga over

D.H. Bought everything he could get his hands on. Including the poems. As his esteem for D.H. increased, so too did his interest in me. The conversations were as stilted and offhand as ever, but I could see in his eyes that some kind of vicarious connection had been made.

Once when he came in, I was perusing a collection of Purdy poetry. He didn't say anything about it, but the next evening he showed up at the store with a black binder, a three-ring vinyl binder that he left behind on the counter after he made his purchase. This time I didn't chase him down the street. I could see by his movements that he meant to leave it behind. He left it behind for me to look through. I flipped the thing open and saw page after page of typewritten poems, gummed up with crusty blobs of whiteout. Uh oh, I thought, this is going to get ugly. The guy can barely formulate a sentence and he's attempting poetry? Not a good idea. Now, what am I supposed to say? I lugged the thing home to my apartment, dread quashing the tiniest quark of curiosity.

But the poems were good. Better than good. Radiant and clean and full of flow. Passionate not florid. Sweet but never schmaltzy. If anything they were a teeny bit earnest. But just a teeny bit. George was good on the page. Very good on the page.

A full four days without any sign of him, and then:

"Oh, um, hi. How's it going? Look, I think I left my... the last time I was here—"

I fished the binder out from behind the counter and handed it to George. His pale, angular face was flushed red. He wouldn't look me in the eye. "Thanks. Sorry about that. Uh, see ya later." He bolted from the store before I had a chance to say anything. But I had suspected that discussion would be difficult if not impossible, so I had taken precautions and slipped a little note in the binder. Just a few words to thank him for the good poems. A few words in an easier language:

black binder, mind bender
brainwave patterns of the lender
exposed
in dark poetic splendour
who ever would have guessed
so tender?

Clearly, I wasn't as good on the page as George, but he obviously appreciated my clunky rhyme. A large and corny bouquet of obscenely red roses arrived at Book World with a cleverly worded note attached. A note inviting me over to his place for coffee and a game of chess. Chess. Being part Hungarian, I, of course, knew how to work the board, how the players moved and even a few classic openings, but I was never very good at the game. Chess requires logic — reasoning and sound judgment. I am almost completely bereft of logic. I decided to go for the coffee.

Tuesday night. A severe apartment with hardwood floors, a few hard-back chairs, a grey metal desk and a long wooden coffee table. Bookshelves lined with hardcover books. Erect and alphabetized. A bare light bulb dangling from the ceiling. A manual typewriter. A black and white onyx chess set. A chess clock. A wall clock. Ticking…ticking…Several glass ashtrays. A window painted shut. A Mason jar full of pointy pencils. And a telephone. No sofa. No pillows. No rugs. No curtains. Nothing soft or breezy or pliable in sight. No plants. No photographs. No pictures on the walls. And no music. Not even a radio.

We left our shoes on. Big shoes in a small apartment. We faced each other across the coffee table. George on hard-back pine. Me on hard-back oak.

"So, how long have you lived here?" I asked, my voice clanging hard around the room. I had been trying to kick-start some dialogue for close to an hour. Nothing took. The words echoed, decayed and disappeared under the tick of the clock and the faint high-pitched scream of 120 watts.

"Um…uh, about two — no, I guess by now, um — ha, you'd think I would know. I guess about twenty-eight months. Uh, twenty-eight and a half months. Ha, not that I need to be quite that specific, right?" George stuck the wrong end of a cigarette in his mouth and lit the filter on fire with trembling hands.

"Wrong end," I said, laughing a little.

George leapt to his feet and plunged the flaming cigarette into his coffee cup. He looked mortified. Deeply ashamed.

"I do that all the time," I lied, banishing the laugh from my lips. The room smelled like burnt plastic.

"Brilliant. What a — Jesus! I can't believe — ha. What a goof."

I downed the cold remnants of my second Nescafé and stood up.

"I guess you have to go," said George, bitterly.

"Yeah, it's the coffee," I said. "Where's the bathroom?"

George blushed terribly, laughed far too loud and pointed to the hall.

I sat on the john and listened to the sound of the fluorescent tube blinking above the medicine cabinet. Like moths bumping into porch light. Clink, clink, clink. I didn't even have to take a piss. I just needed to get away for a minute. The bathroom was stained but scrubbed. No shower. A claw foot tub with a beige and calcified Shower Massage hanging limp from the faucet. One threadbare navy blue bath towel. A deeply cracked sliver of Ivory soap on the side of the sink. And a toothbrush, bristles splayed and curled back from overuse. I opened the medicine cabinet. One Remington electric shaver. One jumbo bottle of Tums. Nothing else. No bubble bath, of course.

After an appropriate interval I flushed the toilet, washed my hands and returned to the living room, overcoming my urge to sneak down the hall and peek into the bedroom. Could George possibly own a bed? Or did he sleep on a wooden plank? No, too harsh. He probably curled up on a thin tatami mat. And covered himself with tinfoil for warmth.

"Would you — would you like some more coffee?"

"I think I'm OK for now." I lit a cigarette and checked the clock. Two hours would be acceptable. I had just under an hour to go.

"So," I said, smiling at George and fumbling for topic, "I guess since you cook at work all the time, you probably don't feel much like cooking at home, eh?"

"Uh . . . yeah. That's true. Very true. I don't really — you know, but sometimes — I mean, there's a lot of good restaurants around here. So, no. Not really."

Flinch. Sigh. Fidget.

Tick tick tick.

"So . . . how about that game of chess?"

"Really? I thought — I mean, if you don't want to . . ."

"No, I changed my mind. I'd like to try a game."

"We don't have to. Are you sure?"

"Yes," I said, glancing at the clock. "I'm sure."

George trounced me twice in short order. Single-minded. No mercy. He wanted to go again, but I gave him the gotta-get-up-and-work-tomorrow spiel. He followed me to the door, running his hands manically through his wiry black hair. As I was thanking him for having me over, he suddenly pitched forward and clanked his mouth against mine. Teeth on teeth. More of a head-butt than a kiss. I checked for blood. There was none.

"I should go," I said, slipping quickly into the hall and pulling the door shut behind me. The last thing I saw was George's pained face, his mouth half open, waiting for the words.

I slunk home and tried not to think about McCollum.

By the time I arrived at Book World the next morning, George had been there. He left a shiny tangerine and a three-page single-spaced letter. A wonderful letter about our not-so-wonderful evening. It was funny and self-deprecating and insightful. Full of warmth and flow. Seductive. I read it several times, trying to connect the man in the apartment with the characters on the page.

Poor George is trapped, I pronounced gravely to myself, and the saviour in me reared its noble head. I will be the one to lead him from bondage. I will be the one to set George free! Like an archaeologist I will patiently sift away a century of sand, penetrate a lifetime of crust and, with the gentle stroke of a tiny brush, bring the priceless treasure to the surface. Into the sun. My tools will be soft music and kind words, alcohol and candlelight, good food and marijuana, magic mushrooms and oil massage, bubble baths and old movies, steamy sex and cozy in bed.

The challenge has been issued and accepted. George will be my second great love. Eyes Towards The Future. Tallyho ho ho!

After two months my patience began to wane significantly. It was always the same: a pitifully strained and painful encounter, punctuated by mishap or misunderstanding, followed by a five-, ten-, fifteen-page letter. A wonderful letter or a perfect little poem. George was great on the page. Great on the page and deficient in every other area. A real writer.

George didn't care much for music; he could easily go without.

Alcohol had little effect on him. Marijuana just made him paranoid. George was a vegetarian. He didn't particularly enjoy food. Rice cake and lasagna were one and the same: sustenance. Necessary. Sometimes he forgot to eat. He didn't care for cake or sweets. George was allergic to perfume and preferred showers to baths. Warm showers. Hot water gave him a rash. The Marx Brothers weren't very funny and the Three Stooges weren't funny at all. Jane Austen was a regular laugh riot, but the Three Stooges were puerile. George awoke every morning at 6:45 a.m. He never slept more than six hours. He wrote passionately about sexual desire, but most of the time he was impotent. And he took his vegetarianism to bed — he refused to eat anything with a face.

Eventually I had to face facts. George was not my lover, George was my pen pal. More importantly, George was always going to be George. No matter how much I dug I was never going to unearth McCollum.

And so I gave up and broke it off. And of course, the letters came fast and furious. Beautiful, desperate, rhapsodic letters. Intense. Moving. Remarkably well written. But I didn't respond. And eventually the letters stopped coming. An empty mailbox for several months and then one last perfectly penned missive. From Moscow of all places. George had emigrated to the Soviet Union. He was working in the kitchen of a large hotel and had taken a wife who could speak his language, but not English. Everything had worked out for the best. He was as happy as a clammed-up clam. He advised me to have a good life and thanked me for giving him the impetus to skedaddle. Dos Vidaniya. Catch ya later.

After George, I realized the futility of pursuing a real relationship. I was like one of those movie widowers with the six-foot-tall portrait of the dead spouse hanging huge above the fireplace. Frank McCollum loomed large and life-sized. Accept no substitutes.

I figured I could go it alone. I was good at it. I enjoyed being alone. Once every year or two, either Marla or Joel would breeze into Toronto for a short visit. I was always glad to see them arrive and equally glad when they left. McCollum was the only human I'd ever encountered whom I could tolerate indefinitely. After twenty-four hours with any other human I felt a powerful need to get away, to retreat to my cave for a prolonged recovery period. Solitude was a restorative. As necessary as sleep. And solitude was freedom. Never *what do you wanna do?* Always *what do I want to do?* What movie, what restaurant, what concert, what cassette? Want to stare slack-jawed at the boob tube until four in the morning? Sure, why not? Fish sticks for breakfast? Okey-dokey. How about dinner every night in bed at eleven, toss the empty plates on the floor, brush the crumbs from the sheets, masturbate and pass out without brushing your teeth? That's all right too. Want to neglect your laundry duties for several months until one day you find yourself trudging to the Coin-o-Mat, wearing Lederhosen, a *Kiss Me I'm Ukrainian* T-shirt and a couple of Food City bags for socks? It's fine. Perfectly fine.

I would be fine. As long as there was music and movies and food and art and whiskey and weather and bubble baths and books. As long as there was Louis Armstrong and Charles Bukowski, Adolph Marx and Henri Matisse. As long as there was *Harold and Maude, Love and Death, Adam's Rib* and Stanley Shapiro. As long as there was *Pet Sounds, Pillow Talk, The Glass Menagerie* and Jean Dubuffet. *Mary Poppins*, coconut milk, George S. Kaufman and lemon meringue pie. Emma Peel, the Riddler, Johnny LaRue, the Monkees. *Raise High the Roof Beam, Carpenters* and *Mockingbird Wish Me Luck. Court and Spark, Blonde on Blonde, The Hissing of Summer Lawns.* As long as there was lobster bisque and Apple Jacks, poppyseed cake and hot banana peppers. Fresh figs, purple plums, Pablo Picasso, "The Reverend" Al Green. As long as there was sunshine, the smell of snow, white tulips or any kind of tulips. *Madama Butterfly*, monarch butterfly, basset hound and French poodle. Orange cats, *Cat Ballou, Cat on a Hot Tin Roof.* As long as there was heat wave and thunderstorm and hail the size of golf balls. Pralines and cream, chicken soup, black pepper and black coffee. *Guys and Dolls, Hello, Dolly!, The Secret Life of Walter Mitty.* Frédéric Chopin, Lucy Maud Montgomery, the Beethoven Violin Concerto. Cumulus clouds, fresh-cut grass, the Four Freshmen, the Five Stairsteps. As long as there was full moon, nighthawk and the mad mouth music of Tom Waits. Dubble Bubble, Cool Whip, Pop-Tarts and Pop Rocks. As long as there was autumn and woodsmoke, dead leaves and icicles. Henry Miller, Henry Moore, James Taylor, Freddie Scott. Tikki lounge, discotech, jack-o'-lanterns and Dr. Seuss. As long as the Mr. Softee truck tinkled down my street on a couple of summer evenings. As long as the knife-sharpener man came around ringing his bell. As long as people still gathered to gawk at something as useless and expensive as fireworks big in the sky. As long as I could thrill to the unique vocal stylings of the Velvet Fog. As long as Marla and Joel were alive and well and accessible via Bell long distance. As long as there was Klonopin, Irish whiskey and IBM Selectric. As long as there was all of this light flickering audaciously in the blackness, as long as I had these pretty good friends all around me all the time, I would be fine.

Just fine.

And I was. I didn't feel the need to "share" my life with anyone. Except McCollum. If something struck me as especially amusing or demented, fascinating or absurd, if something absolutely had to be expressed, I would put it in a letter. If I was proud of Joel or worried about Marla, if I missed my mom or felt guilty-sad about my father, I would put it in a letter. If I stumbled upon a great movie, book, album or poem, I would put it in a letter to McCollum and send it express post to the yellow nylon Midas Muffler bag in the back of my bedroom closet. Every year when the new phone book came out, I would scan the F. McCollums for new entries and dial them up. *Sorry, wrong number* when the voice wasn't right. I called directory assistance in every major city across Canada, looking for the right F. McCollum. Luckily for me it wasn't a popular name. The country was lousy with McCallums, but McCollums were rare. I would wait a couple of months and then call again for the new listings.

The owner of the bookstore promoted me to manager. I cut my hair short and bought a new couch. I joined a health club and went twice. I got a colour TV and a video cassette recorder. I started drinking herbal tea. I was fine fine fine. Until the desire for sex punctured the routine. Sex. I had crossed it off the list. Frisbeed the Triphasil into the trash. But here it was again, complicating my life. Certain to cause problems.

Against my marginally better judgment I began to seriously consider the various opportunities that presented themselves. There was the new tenant who moved into the apartment upstairs. Friendly, good-looking but too close for comfort. There was the amicable drink-meister who worked the bar at Major-Roberts. A little too chatty, a little too nosy. There was the painter who hung around Have It Your Way Café who told me that my hair was "undeniably Titian." A windbag to be sure, not to mention the goatee. I tried to hold off. I tried to hold off, but I went back on the pill. I went back on the pill and I bought some new underwear.

Eventually I took a chance with a married man. Happily married to a wonderful woman. Two beautiful children and a golden retriever. Simon Shropshire. Thirty-seven years old. I met him at the bar. A jingle producer who owned a small recording studio. Moderately successful. Moderately interesting. Moderately attractive. Moderately diverting. It turned out to be perfect for both of us. A friendly fuck once a week. My apartment. No public appearances. In and out and then out the door. I never asked him to stay. He never wanted to stay. He would never leave his wife and I would never want him to leave his wife. A moderately passionate fuck once a week, someone to chat with, someone to bathe with. He was completely self-absorbed and quite guarded about his personal life. This suited me just fine. I didn't want to know his particular bleat and woe, and I had no desire for him to explore mine. It was surface chat mostly, about work or the news of the day. Sometimes I would critique a jingle he was working on. Occasionally I'd help him pen a couple. That was good. I liked that part. The whole deal was easygoing and easy to maintain.

We carried on for a long long time. He had another son and started to lose his hair. He moved into a bigger house and bought a myna bird and a hot tub. I didn't miss him over the holidays or when he went away on vacation, but I was always glad to see him when he came back. In the nine years that we were (often) together it had never once occurred to me to telephone him. He called me when he wanted to and when he could.

Only once in nine years did I telephone him at work. It was a Tuesday morning. I had been sucking coffee and reading the *Globe and Mail*. In a nod to regional reporting, Toronto's National Newspaper had included a short article from Winnipeg. The city's trees were under attack in the Wolseley area. For the second consecutive year, city environmental workers had found evidence of the elm bark beetle, a tiny insect that spreads the fungus that causes Dutch elm disease. An expert from the University of Montana who had been called in to help quell a similar outbreak that had claimed ten thousand trees in Great Falls was on hand to advise on the situation. This professor was in the process of researching a new, environmentally friendly approach to disease management that focused entirely on the biology of the insect vectors. The entomologist in shining armour was Dr. Frank McCollum of Missoula, Montana. There was a quote: "There is no cure for DED once the infection reaches the trunk and roots. The alternative method of control that we're looking at is not a panacea. It is designed to work in tandem with sanitation, the severing of root grafts and the planting of replacement trees. The beauty of this new method is that it may one day reduce or even eliminate the need for potentially harmful fungicides and insecticides." The article went on to describe the usual program of control and the types of chemicals used. It ended with a quote: "'The main thing is to act quickly,' said McCollum. 'We don't want to look back and say we could have, we should have, we would have.'"

I telephoned Simon at the studio. He was understandably surprised to hear from me.

"Hi. What's going on? Are you OK?"

"Is this cool? Can you talk?"

"Yeah, for a minute. What's going on?"

"Nothing. Sorry to call you at work, I just wanted to let you know that I can't see you tonight. I'm going out of town for a few days."

"You're going out of town? You never go out of town."

"I know, I just figured it's time to take a little vacation."

"Oh... What a concept. So you're going to LA?"

"Winnipeg."

"*Winnipeg?* Who goes to Winnipeg? That's not a vacation, babe, that's a mandatory sentence."

"Yeah, well, an old school friend of mine just had a baby, so I'm gonna go visit for a couple of days."

"Hmm..."

"What?"

"Nothing... you just sound funny."

"Funny ha-ha or funny strange?"

"No, seriously..."

"What?"

"It just strikes me as odd, is all."

"Why?"

"Well, a couple of months ago your brother invites you to Los Angeles, all expenses paid, you know, swimming pools, movie stars, the whole nine yards, and you don't want to leave Toronto. Now some woman you haven't seen for twenty years or something cucks out a kid and suddenly you're shuffling off to Saskatchewan."

"Manitoba."

"Whatever."

"Just for a couple of days. You want me to call when I get back?"

"So this isn't a brush-off? You haven't met someone, have you?"

"Yeah right."

"When do you get back?"

"I'm not sure. Probably Sunday."

"Give me your friend's number. I'll try and give you a call."

"Actually, I think I'm gonna stay at a hotel."

"Uh, yeah...that should be fine. Tell Havoc that we're mixing this afternoon and I'll give him a call later."

"Someone just walked in?"

"Yeah, OK. Sounds good. Talk to you soon!"

Click.

I called a travel agent and booked the next flight to Winnipeg. It felt good to book the next flight to anywhere. It felt free and sophisticated and jet-setty. I packed in a hurry, waterlogged my philodendron, fished out the Midas Muffler bag from the back of the closet, and called for a taxi. I waited on the front porch, listening to my Walkman. It was a big and beautiful day. Sunshine everywhere — on my face, on my shoes — a huge and yellow day. I didn't feel afraid to leave. I didn't feel nervous or panicked. I didn't even feel like popping a Klonopin. For the first time in about a decade I felt giddy. Giddy and giggly! I bopped happy around the white porch, swinging my arms and wriggling my toes to the euphonious pop-o-matic warblings of Edison Lighthouse. I was singing: *she talks kinda lazy, people say she's crazy, and her life's a mystereeee. Oh but love grows where my Rosemary goes and nobody knows like meee.*

I was thinking: Fuck the elms, bring on the bugs! Go, bark beetles, go!

—

"Come out come out wherever you are," Joel's voice booms rich and resonant from the downstairs hallway. Basso profundo.

Marla flashes me a quick look. It says: we're in this together, two against one. I follow her slowly down the carpeted stairs. Joel is standing in the hallway, next to a small, expensive-looking suitcase, fanning himself with a panama hat. He is wearing a fashionably wrinkled off-white linen suit, a white shirt and an off-white cravat striped in a colour that is probably called "cappuccino" or "sand." Very theatrical. It takes a millisecond for my eyes to adjust. My brother no longer looks like a kid, or even a "guy." My brother has morphed into a man — a prematurely middle-aged-looking man with a serious weight problem and an equally serious tan problem. His puffy face has acquired an unearthly tanning-bed tint, "butternut" or perhaps "adobe."

"Salutations, sisters!"

"Hey you!" Marla disappears into Joel's vast linen embrace. He closes his eyes and holds tight, holds on at least a second too long, and when he releases my sister his eyes are shiny and moist.

"Michelle! How are ya?" The arms open to me. I move in for the hug.

"All right, Mr. Capote, where's Joel, what have you done with him?" My brother smells strongly of cologne with a faint bottom note of pomade. No trace of jet fuel or airplane about him.

"Mr. Capote! What, you don't like the suit?"

I pry myself out of the wrestler grip and survey the attire. "Yeah, the suit's all right…"

"But I'd lose the scarf," says Marla, capping my opinion.

"Lose the scarf," says Joel with a sarcastic grin. "'Lose the scarf,' she says. You know how much this farshtinkener foulard cost me?"

We all laugh. A triangle of happy. Warm and reconnected.

Joel coughs, a thick phlegmy cough, then he reaches into his jacket pocket and pulls out a cigarette case.

"You're smoking?" says Marla with a censorious frown.

"Obviously. Wish I'd never stopped. That's how I gained the weight. Very polite of you not to mention the fact that I've doubled in dimension, although I prefer to think of it as magnitude." Joel offers us the case. Marla and I each select one of the handsome brown cigarettes. "Nobody smokes in LA, of course. Except cigars. Big fat turdy Cubans. You're a fucking pariah if you smoke cigarettes. A leper, an untouchable. Call me Ishmael," says Joel, firing up with a shiny gold lighter. "You like the lighter?" he asks, passing it to me.

"It's nice," I say, feeling the dead weight of it in my hand.

"Twenty-four karat," he says, with a strangely mirthless grin.

Marla surveys her cigarette. "What are these?" she asks.

"Nat Shermans. One hundred percent natural tobacco. No additives."

"They're good for you," I offer.

"Yeah," says Joel. "Strengthens the lungs."

"None of us should be smoking," says Marla, lighting up.

"Yeah, well I quit for about a year. 'Try sunflower seeds,' said my quack doctor. What a fucking quack. I went through about ten pounds of the bastards a day. I was like a frenzied squirrel, I couldn't stop cracking. The shells were all over the place, in my keyboard, all over the floors, I'd wake up with them in my eyebrows, I'd find them stuck to my ass in the morning — I kid you not — dropping off my bare ass into the toilet. I had to switch to unsalted because my lips were disintegrating, shrivelling up, turning grey. Fattening little suckers, too. I gained eighty-three pounds in six months. Very healthy."

Joel holds up his cigarette, making the international sign for "ash-tray." We follow him into the kitchen. I see the fake parents through the window. They're lying on lounge chairs in the backyard, talking. The fake father checks his watch and looks up at the kitchen window. I move away.

"Then the quack recommended a diet. I did Weight Watchers, Jenny Craig, Fit For Life, The Zone. I tried the Rotation Diet, the T-Factor Diet, the Tri-Color Diet. I did the McDougall Program for Maximum Weight Loss, Dr. Abravanel's Body Type Diet... hmm, what other ones?"

"Jesus," says Marla, "didn't any of those work?"

"What does it look like? Oh yeah, then I did ten days on the 20 Day Rejuvenation Diet, and another ten on the 5-Day Miracle Diet, with miraculously poor results. I think I gave the Living Heart Diet a whirl. Tried the New Beverly Hills Diet, the Hilton Head Diet. I temporarily took part in Dr. Atkins' Diet Revolution and even went back in time and gave Pritikin a go. And then Scarsdale, remember that one? No wonder somebody shot the man — three ounces of shaved turkey and a bread stick for dinner — the pecker deserved to get plugged. Wish I'd shot him. I gained another twenty with the farshtinkener diets." Joel laughs.

"But did you exercise?" asks Marla.

"Exercise! The new religion? No, thanks. I've witnessed the opacity of the masses after a step class. I've seen what your exercise can do, and I reject it. Every muscle acquired is an IQ point lost. No pain, no gain and, before you know it, no brain."

"Oh, come on," says Marla.

"I'm serious. Endorphins are a dangerous thing. High impact. Every woman in Beverly Hills considers it a profound accomplishment to be able to open a beer bottle with her ass — a non-alcoholic light beer, of course. Buns of steel. Tits of titanium. Kegel Snatch of Death. You know that personal trainers screeching beside treadmills earn five times as much as schoolteachers? I kid you not. Sit and spin now refers to a trendy cycling technique. Ab Crunch, Butt Crunch — the breakfast of champions. The body is a temple, the mind a mere pimple. You should see these people, rolling around on giant rubber balls, taking the elevator to the StairMaster."

"Sounds like LA," I say.

"Oh, this was a good one: In a bid for 'better definition' my personal assistant had calf implants — silicone pseudo-muscles inserted into his legs. One of them got loose and migrated up to his thigh. Had to push it back into place with a butter knife. Very nice." Joel cough-laughs and stamps out his cigarette. "No, thanks. I believed once, but I've seen the cellu-lite of day. I don't require a washboard stomach; I've grown accustomed to my washing machine stomach. I do have a home gym, of course."

"Of course," says Marla.

"But you guys look great," says Joel.

"I look old," fishes Marla.

"No you don't. Not at all. You both look very youthful. Positively California slim."

"Well, the camera puts on ten pounds," I say. "In person we must appear comparatively svelte."

"Yeah," snips Marla, "what the fuck is that all about?!"

"What is what all about?" Joel's slight smile betrays his guilt.

"The little cameras all over the house? The camera on my bedroom ceiling! I mean, what the fuck? Have you been spying on us this whole time from a van around the corner or some house across the street?"

"Spying on you? Oh man!" Joel starts laughing, a phony chuckly kind of heh-heh-heh. "I thought *I* was the one who had seen too many movies. Spying on you! Yeah, I need to spy on my sisters. What am I, the Man Called Insipid? Joel Ovstrofsky — By Way of Dementia?"

"So what's with the surveillance cameras all over the house?" I ask.

"Jesus H. Christ! They're not 'surveillance cameras,' they happen to be video cameras, OK? I thought we might want a home movie of our weekend together. I didn't feel like schlepping a camera around, so I had the house rigged up in case we wanted to tape something. I did it for you. I thought you might want a souvenir."

"Yeah right," says Marla.

"Oy vey! Already you're taking my kishkas out?" thunders Joel. "The fuckin' things haven't even been on yet! Jesus Christ. I just got here, didn't I? You see, this is what happens when you try to do something nice for people."

Uh oh. Here we go.

"Oh really?" snaps Marla, flushing red. "Are you referring to anything in particular?!"

"Yes, I'm referring to what just transpired. What the fuck do you think I'm referring to?"

"I don't know. Maybe you're trying to tell me something!"

"Oh boy, oh boy. You have problems, you know that? Are you aware of that simple fact?"

"Oh, *I* have problems? *I* have fucking problems!" Marla goes shrill and approaches full volume. "He's taping his sisters *naked* in their bedrooms and *I* have fucking problems?!"

Joel's brown eyes bulge with rage — my father's eyes, a familiar mad cow expression. He tears the cravat from his neck and flings it onto the kitchen counter. A corner of it lands in the steak pan. The silk sucks up the marinade like a paper towel. I watch it spread. "Are you nuts?! Are you insane?!" Joel's right hand is trembling in the air, fingers stretched to maximum span, the palm shiny and shaking. "I'd rather stick hot pins in my eyes! I'd rather pluck my own orbs out and crush them flat under my boot heels! You're crazy, you know that?! You need help! Is she crazy? Is she crazy, or what?"

"Yeah, Michelle, am I crazy?! Tell him who's fucking crazy, why don't you!" Flecks of white spittle form at the corners of my sister's hot mouth.

"Yeah, Michelle, look at her and you tell me who's fucking crazy!"

I lift the silk scarf out of the marinade and hold it over the glass pan. "I am," I say quietly, feeling an old familiar itch along my forearms, watching the reddish brown liquid drip drip onto the raw meat.

A nanosecond of stupefied silence, and then an eruption of laughter — from Marla and Joel simultaneously.

"So much for your foulard," says Marla.

"Guess I'll have to 'lose the scarf' after all," says Joel.

"Secret ingredient."

"Extra flavour." Joel springs the cigarette case. Friends again. We all light up and blow smoke.

"Believe me," says Joel, the rich voice carefully modulated and awash in sincerity, "I wasn't spying on you. I was just… just trying to do something nice for my sisters. A home video. A small souvenir."

Marla looks at me to see if I believe him. Joel catches the look and its meaning. "You believe me, don't you, Michelle?"

"Yes, I believe you," I say, but I know better. I lie for peace.

"So they haven't even been on yet?" asks Marla sceptically.

"How could they? I just got here, didn't I? The remote is in my suitcase. I have to switch them on to work."

"Can I see your airline ticket?" asks Marla.

Uh oh.

"Again with the 'van around the corner' bullshit? I wouldn't crawl into the back of a van if you paid me. Not in this suit! I'd piss up Gaddafi's ass before I'd climb into the back of a stinking van."

"So then let me see your ticket," says Marla.

"I don't have a freakin' ticket!"

"I see."

"No, you don't see, actually! You don't see anything. I happen to have flown here in a private jet. I did not require a ticket!" The voice booms kettledrum around the kitchen.

"You have a jet," snaps Marla, crossing her arms.

"Noooo. I did not say that. It was Shlomo Caro's jet."

"Shlomo Caro," says Marla, smiling in spite of herself.

"Yes, Shlomo Caro. Perhaps you've heard of him?"

"Shlomo Caro," I say, trying out the sound.

"Yes, Shlomo Caro."

"O Mio Babbino Shlomo," says Marla.

Joel clears his throat and begins to sing: "O Mio babbino Shlomooo, You've got a chromey dome-oooo…"

We laugh and stamp out our cigarettes. Crisis averted. Marla seems convinced. I don't buy it, but I'm not going to get into it.

Joel checks his watch and glances out the kitchen window. "You like the watch?" he asks, shaking his wrist.

"Is that a Cartier?" asks Marla.

Joel pops the watch off his wrist and hands it to her.

"It's stunning," says Marla, turning it over in her hands and then passing it to me.

"It's a watch," I say, handing it back to Joel.

"Damned right," says my brother, putting it back on. "Sixty-three Gs for that baby."

"Holy shit," says Marla. "It's really stunning."

"That reminds me, I brought you guys something." Joel points to the hall. "In my suitcase, in a small red bag. You can get it if you want, but don't touch anything else in there!" Marla rolls her eyes and goes for the package. Joel says: "I can see that you don't believe me, Michelle, but I swear on my life I wasn't crouching in some van or hiding out in some house across the street."

"OK," I say. "So what's with the locked basement door?"

Joel smiles at me through smoke. Marla comes back with the red bag.

"Is this it?"

"Yeah, open it up."

"What are those pills in your suitcase?" asks Marla.

"Jesus H. Christ, I told you not to touch anything else!"

"I didn't touch anything! They were sitting right on top!"

"They're just mild sleeping pills, OK? Are you gonna open it or not?"

Marla opens the bag and peeks inside. "Oh my God..." She pours the contents — two slinky bracelets — into the palm of her hand. Chunky diamond bracelets shiny in her hand. "Oh my God, they're gorgeous. Thank you!!" Marla kisses Joel's puffy cheek and hands me one of the bracelets. "Here, 'Chelle, aren't they stunning? My God, these are incredible diamonds! I've never seen diamonds this big on a tennis bracelet."

"Very pretty," I say. "Thank you very much."

"Do you even wear jewellery?" asks Marla, putting hers on.

"Not usually."

"I've never seen you wear jewellery."

"So sell it," says Joel, checking his watch. "Buy yourself a record store."

Now the old familiar sound of doggy toenails on the wrought iron side porch. Now the fake parents and the fake Freddy bust in on the reunion at what I assume is the agreed-upon time. A flurry of greetings followed by a shuffly couple of moments during which only the dog seems to know exactly how to behave. Finally, Joel says: "Isn't this great? All of us together again?"

Not all of us, I think, but he seems to really mean it, so I don't say anything. I decide to hang back and just observe for a while.

"It's been a long time," offers the fake mom.

"Too long," says Joel, smiling at Marla and me, trying to coax us into the thing.

"It is nice," says Marla, giving me a look. The look says, *Come on, Michelle. Play along for one night.*

"So...would anyone like a drink?" says the phony father, grasping this appropriate nugget of subject matter. *Oh yes, yes please. A drink a drink.* He busies himself with the ice and the glasses, relieved to have something to do. I watch him work, slowing the action, milking the activity for as long as possible. I don't think he's an actor. Too nervous.

Too confused. I think he's probably just some poor schmuck who happens to look like my father. Probably got scouted in a mall or restaurant by one of Joel's minions. Seduced by the cash but didn't fully grasp the concept. He seems utterly confounded. Wonders what he's doing here. Misses his family. Wishes the whole thing was over already.

He pours himself a healthy double and it's single malt all around, except for the fake mom, who is definitely experienced (dinner theatre, at the very least) and who looks extremely thirsty but has obviously been instructed not to partake. She opts for a Fresca just like Mom used to do. Joel instructs us to take our correct places at the kitchen table. I am directed to my old spot by the window. We drink and we smile at each other.

"So," says the fake mom to Joel, "did you know that Marla is a real estate agent now?"

"Is that right?" says Joel, affecting an expression of interest. "How long have you been doing that?"

"Just a couple of weeks. Guess whose house I just listed?"

"Who?"

"Remember Cary Silver? He lived over on Rockwood?"

"Hmm..."

"Dad made a fur coat for his wife, remember?"

"Did they have a Yorkshire terrier named Mitzy?"

"Yeah! They split up a few years ago. She's still in Toronto."

"And he looked like that actress, what the hell is her name? Fay...Kay Lenz! He looked like Kay Lenz with a beard."

"What?! He did not."

"Yeah, he did," I say, agreeing with Joel. "He looked exactly like Kay Lenz with facial hair."

"You guys are crazy," says Marla, laughing.

"He was a creep. Didn't he make a pass at you at Dad's shiva?"

Marla looks at me. "I can't believe you remember that! He was eating egg salad. He was trying to pick me up with a mouth full of egg salad. Ucch!"

"Ahem," says Joel, indicating that shiva talk is not permitted. Father is right here at the table, for Christ's sake. Clearly, there was no suicide. Obviously, there was no egg salad.

"Well," says the phony father, draining his drink, "I should probably get those steaks on." He glances at my brother to see if that's all right.

"I'm pretty hungry," says Joel, patting his paunch. "Are you guys getting hungry?"

Yes yes yes, we're all terribly hungry. The phony father makes his getaway with a couple of pans of raw meat.

"Maybe I should give Dad a hand?" offers the fake mom.

"He'll be OK," says Joel, going for more Scotch.

The fake mom sips her Fresca and sits tight. Joel pours another round and we empty the cigarette case.

"So, what's going on with work?" asks Marla. "Are you working on a new movie?"

"As a matter of fact I recently completed the final revisions on the final draft of my final script," says Joel, rubbing smoke out of his right eye.

"What do you mean 'final'?"

"Final, as in last. The last screenplay that I will ever write." Joel flicks his ash with a flourish. "I've decided to take early retirement."

The fake mom emits a tiny animal sound. Dismay. Disappointment. Obviously, she's been banking big on this connection — dreaming of a future filled with supporting roles in Joel Schafer's pictures.

"Are you serious?" asks Marla.

"Perfectly. Unequivocally."

"Why? Just because your last movie didn't make a gazillion dollars like all the other ones?"

"Last *two* movies, actually. Though they adored them in Malaysia."

"Well, I don't know what's wrong with those critics," sniffs the fake mom with fake maternal pride. "I thought they were both very very good." *And there's still one screenplay to go. All it takes is one breakthrough role*...

"So did I," says Marla. "Although that scene in *Opposites Attract*—"

"With the Braun Multipractic?"

"Ucch! Disgusting! That was totally twisted."

"Of course, you were spared that," says Joel, smiling at me. "Have you even seen any of my work?"

"I've seen all of your movies," I say, taken aback.

"Really?"

"Of course. I've seen every single one of your movies, including the last two."

"Hm, go figure. I didn't think you bookish types went in for that sort of low entertainment."

"I'm not bookish. I happen to love movies."

"Really? But not my movies, right? No, you love quirky independent films, preferably foreign and subtitled, preferably black-and-white and playing down at the multiplex on a screen no bigger than your average headboard, not the prurient divertissement that are my movies, right?"

"I wouldn't say that."

"You love Canadian movies, publicly funded and carefully crafted — like chilled white pie crusts, pinched and perfect. Brechtian epics, cold and detached, devoid of fat, sugar or meat, all wry and dry, all bloodless and white-boned, clicking a bony subconscious Morse code message about isolation, dissociation, miscommunication. You love movies, right? But not the mind-achingly formulaic mainstream boner-chow that I vomit onto the big screen on a regular basis."

"Wow. It sounds like you don't like your movies all that much."

"They have their moments, I suppose — the odd turn of phrase here and there — but overall I'd have to say that I've spent most of my life churning out crap. Crap from the crapulous," says Joel, burping discreetly and pouring himself another Scotch.

"I think you're being too hard on yourself," says Marla. "You're just bummed because the last two movies didn't do so well. I mean, you didn't feel this way after *Habeas Corpus*, did you? That was two thumbs up and made a ton of dough, right?"

"I suppose you're partially right, there is satisfaction in success. And a period of failure is inevitably a period of reflection and clarity. But long before *Habeas Corpus* I had stopped confusing popularity and prosperity with happiness. Long before *Habeas Corpus*, as a matter of fact." Joel sighs. A moment of silence, all eyes on my brother.

"I know how you feel," says Marla, "and I know that when your latest screenplay comes out and becomes a big hit, which it will —

you just had a small slump, everyone has slumps — you're gonna feel better. You're gonna feel like writing again. And you're gonna laugh your ass off at the thought of hanging up your pen."

"Holy commission cheque, Batman, you sound just like my agent! Kind, bolstery, ultimately well-meaning words, but way off the mark, I'm afraid. My latest screenplay will never come out, never become a big hit, and I will never write another one. Here's to cobwebs on the hard drive from here on in!" Joel raises his glass and drinks.

"Well, that's your prerogative," says Marla. "Luckily, you have the resources to retire if that's what you want to do. You certainly don't have to work if you don't feel like it."

"So what are you going to do?" I ask him.

Joel smiles — a strange mischievous smile, the mouth full of secrets, the eyebrows twitching suggestively. "Well," he says, "that remains to be seen. One of two things. I can't say just yet."

His words hang heavy in the air, fat with hidden intent. Marla takes it all in and then checks my expression. Hers is one of uneasiness. Joel measures his effect, watching the exchange between my sister and me. Finally, the fake mom pierces the inaudible din of sibling communication.

"Well," she says, her voice dripping with honey-feigned archness, "maybe you'll finally get married and have a family. Maybe you'll finally make me a buby."

Marla bristles and stamps out her smoke. She looks hard into my eyes, and I suddenly flash on something. The family. The family on the street the day my mom announced her impending disappearance. I return my sister's hard gaze. A quiet commiseration across the expanse of Formica. Joel just laughs.

"*Make me a buby, big boy!* Don't hold your breath, Ma. Unless, of course, Marla and Michelle decide to go that route. Either of you planning to breed a brood, spring into offspring, descend into descendants?"

"I have a philodendron," I say. "That's more than enough responsibility."

"Well, you never struck me as the nurturing type," says Joel. "Didn't you barbecue your Barbies once upon a time?"

"No, I believe that was your handiwork," I say. "And it was Midge, not Barbie." As if that made any difference.

"Well, in any event, I would have thought that *you* would have produced progeny by now, Marla."

"Really? Well, it's not bloody likely since I've had a hysterectomy," says my sister matter-of-factly, as if it were a pedicure or a fluoride treatment.

"What?! You did not," I say.

"Yes, I did. Just over a year ago. I had fibroids that needed to be removed, so I told them to just take everything away. And they did. They took it all away and they incinerated it. I have the scars to prove it if you don't believe me."

"I believe you," I say. I don't need to see the scars.

"And I suppose you've gone and had a vasectomy?" says the fake mom in a tsk-tsky tone of voice.

"No, Ma, nothing that drastic," says Joel, looking at Marla. "Just a simple get-her-offa-me. Very effective. And virtually painless."

"So you're not seeing anyone?" I say.

"No, I'm not 'seeing anyone.' I've seen enough. Didn't particularly like what I espied."

"What happened to that woman in the article?" asks Marla.

"Which woman, which article? Which month, which issue?"

"The one in *Vanity Fair*?"

"Oh, her. She didn't last long. Just one in a steady stream of large-breasted vampires that regularly descend on my estate. Where the ghouls are, someone waits for me."

"Very nice!" says Marla.

"What?"

"That's how you view women? As large-breasted vampires?"

"Nooo. That's not how I view women. Now you're gonna turn this into some feminist diatribe?"

"Oh, that's rich! I simply draw attention to the fact that you have a warped perspective — which you obviously do — and it's my problem. *My* fucking problem! I'm a militant feminist because I don't happen to think that women are monsters with irresistible titties who just want to suck poor Joel dry!"

Uh oh. Here we go.

"Are you nuts? Are you insane? Do you have some sick compelling need to pounce on every word I utter and twist it into something hideous and toxic?"

"Yeah, that's me! That's what I do! I was put on this earth to fuck you up. Just another vampire, I guess. Just another monster female put on this earth to suck out your precious soul and your precious cash. Maybe you should ram a stake into my heart! Is that how you handle the steady stream of vampires that descend on your sprawling estate?!"

"Oh my fucking God! I don't fucking believe this!" Fist slams on table. Bottle teeters. Ice cubes rattle. "Am I nuts? Am I fucking crazy? I say one simple thing and suddenly I'm a monster. A killer! A cold-blooded killer of innocent women!!!" Joel grabs wild at his hair. Wrenches at the hair in his manic skull.

"That's not what I meant and you fucking well know it!" screams Marla, flashing on the past. The broken condom in the belly. The hash oil in the tender young belly.

"You don't give me a chance to speak! You jump down my throat and you claw at my freakin' kishkas! I'll tell ya, it's no wonder, Marla. It is no fucking wonder..."

"No wonder *what*?!" shrieks Marla, jumping up from the table. "No wonder *what*?! No wonder that I'm not married? No wonder that I don't have a man? Is that what you were gonna say?!"

"Again with this bullshit business? Putting words in my fucking mouth!!!"

"I don't need this shit!" screams Marla. "I don't need this fucking shit!"

I don't need it either, I think. I take my drink and slip away from the bray. Nobody seems to notice. Just like old times. The battle rages fierce and hot in my wake. No scuds in this army. All direct and lethal hits. I go AWOL. Up to my amber room. Close the beautiful door and fumble for the Walkman. Jam the headphones deep into my ears and wait for some kind of peace to break out. A metallic taste in my mouth. Metal filings shifting through my body, in my gut, in my veins, haphazard and sharp, spiny piles of filings jagged in my hands, shifting heavy in my brain.

I go full volume on the nocturnes. Good, very good. The melody rolls over me like a wave. A giant and powerful magnetic wave, moving from my head to my toes, pulling all the metal filings into one smooth and steady direction. Smoothing. Soothing. I stare at the photo mural on the wall beside my bed. An empty expanse of pristine beach. Slick white sand. No footprints. No boats. Just gentle palms curving gracefully to high yellow. Just big sky and shiny coconut bobbing quietly in the surf.

I slip out of my clothes and walk into the water. Cool and blue. I go under. Swim down and down to the bottom of the sea. Pass slowly through a cloud of billowing pink. Jellyfish. Delicate. Now a stingray moves overhead and my fingertips graze the belly. Down down to the bottom, where the sand is the softest. Skim evenly across the surface, where the sand is like silk. Roll over onto the back and sink into the muck. A fat starfish in each palm to weigh me down and hold me under. My hair floats up and undulates anemone. My eyes are wide open, bright with filtered sunlight. A mass of fine fish flit by overhead. A twinkling spasm of brilliant purple.

I can finally breathe.

—

I ask the cab driver to recommend a hotel. He suggests the Fort Garry for its proximity to The Forks — a fresh-food marketplace with restaurants, bars and boutiques at the forks of the Red and Assiniboine rivers. He also touts the Crowne Plaza Holiday Inn — spitting distance to Winnipeg's famous Warehouse District. I tell him that I want to be as close as possible to the Wolseley area. I don't tell him that I want to be as close as possible to the fungus-spreading bark beetles. About two minutes after scooping me from the airport he drops me at the Baron Dort Hotel on Portage Avenue. A down-in-the-mouth Ramada sort of affair.

"So why is this hotel called the Baron Dort?"

The front-desk clerk peers at me through a pair of taped-up Lenscrafters. He has the same rocker hairdo as the cab driver: short and spiky in the front, long and straggly in the back. "I'm not sure exactly. I think the guy who owns it is from England. I guess he must have been a baron or something."

"And his name is Dort?"

"Yeah. Baron Dort."

Something of a misnomer, I think as I survey my room. It's clean and serviceable but not exactly regal. The Serf Dort Hotel would have been closer to the mark. Or maybe the Sir Dort Hotel if you held your nose and squinted a little. I crank the AC and take a hot bath.

I have never been in another province. Or even in another city. My body looks different in another city. My feet look different in another bathtub. Everything seems unusually vivid and ultra-real. Is it the presence of McCollum out there somewhere among the elms? Or just the newness of my surroundings? It could be the light. I noticed the light as soon as I stepped out of the airport. It's different in Winnipeg. Hard-edged and clear. Prairie light. Direct.

I air-dry on the quilted floral bedspread and try to figure out a plan of attack. Whom do I call? Where do I go? I can't just skulk around diseased elms hoping to run into McCollum. I need a strategy. I have to figure this thing out. I suppose I could probably track McCollum down through official channels — the Ministry of Natural Resources, the Department of Something or Other — but I hate official channels. They make me nervous. What would I say? *Oh hi, I'm trying to get in touch with Frank McCollum. I'm an old friend of his, Michelle Schafer*... How many layers or levels would I have to go through? I'd probably have to leave messages all over the place. With government workers! What if McCollum never got my messages? I didn't fly all the way out here for that, thank you very much. What if he got my message — *Michelle at Baron Dort* — on a little slip of pink and it seemed too pathetic and ridiculous to even justify a response?

No. There's got to be a better way. Maybe I'll call the official channels and pretend that I'm a journalist, pretend that I want to interview him. That way I can find out where he's staying. Or better yet, I'll skip the official channels completely and just call all the hotels in Winnipeg. How many can there be? I grab the Yellow Pages and flip to hotels. The list is longer than I expected but definitely manageable. It suddenly occurs to me that McCollum could be staying right here at the Baron Dort. For all I know he could be on the same floor or in the next room, on the other side of the stucco.

With shaky fingers I call up the front desk and ask them to put me through to Frank McCollum's room. No go. No guest by that name registered at the Baron Dort. I try the Fort Garry next. Then the Crowne Plaza Holiday Inn. Bingo! Should have listened to the rocker cab driver! I slam the phone down before the front-desk clerk has a chance to connect me. I didn't hear a ring. I'm pretty sure it didn't go through.

I light a smoke and pace pace around the room. My heart is pounding hard. I can't think. I can't think. OK, OK, just chill out. Chill out! It's two o'clock Winnipeg time. McCollum is probably not at the hotel. McCollum is probably out doing something official, saving trees or attending some kind of bug persons' luncheon. Should I leave a message for him to call me? No, definitely not. Should I go over to his hotel and watch for him? Yes. No. Yes. Maybe. What am I going to do, sit in the lobby for ten hours waiting for him to appear? Would they let me sit in the lobby for ten hours? With my luck I'd get wrestled to the door by hotel security and tossed out on my ass just as McCollum was walking in. Perfect. Great. Forget it. Just forget it. Maybe what I should do is leave some kind of phony-baloney message with my number here, then when McCollum calls I'll know that he's back at his hotel and I can zip over. *Oh God oh God. Is it at all possible that this is some other entomologist-type person named Frank McCollum and not my Frank McCollum?* No, it's not possible. It's him. I can feel it. In my chromosomes and cells. In my hair, nails and teeth. OK, OK, maybe what I should do is call back. Maybe McCollum is there after all. If he answers I can hang up and then head over. OK. Good. But what if someone else answers? What if a woman answers? His wife? No! What if a little kid answers?! No no no! Just chill out. Chill out chill out.

I crush out my cigarette and light another cigarette. I call the Holiday Inn and ask for Frank McCollum's room. The receptionist puts me through. I clamp my right hand firmly over the mouthpiece of the telephone. *What, like he's going to recognize my breathing after thirteen years?* Just keep that hand clamped tight, you never know with McCollum. One ring, two rings... three rings — he's not there — four rings, and suddenly, to my astonishment, a recorded message in McCollum's own voice. The voice. His voice. The same perfect voice.

"Hi, this is Frank McCollum. I'm not here right now, but you can leave a message for me and I'll call you back. If this is Edie, I'll probably be out for most of the day. Some of the faculty members want to take me out for dinner after my lecture, so I probably won't be back here until nine or ten. Anyway, give me a call later on if you feel like it." BEEP.

Edie? Who the fuck is Edie? I knew there was probably an Edie. There had to be an Edie. But it hurts to hear it spoken so warm and private. A punch to the heart. Bruised valves, dangling ventricles. I call back to listen. I call again and again, alternately drinking in the voice and dissecting it, trying to discern the importance of Edie by the tone and the meter. Maybe Edie is a personal assistant. Spectacles and lab coat. Halitosis and phlebitis socks. Hair in a knot at the top of the tight head. Corns and bunions. Sensible shoes. I listen again. Edie is not an assistant. Edie is definitely a confidante. Maybe a close personal friend. A colleague, a buddy. A house-sitter, a plant-waterer. A squash partner, a car-pooler. Minivan and three beautiful children. A bad Montana haircut. A burgundy dye job. I listen again. Edie is not a buddy. Edie is most definitely a wife or a girlfriend. Yes. Edie is comfort and magic. Loyal and trustworthy. Smart and beautiful. Sexy and sophisticated. Edie is funny and talented. Earthy and sweet. Clever and witty. Graceful and athletic. Edie is first violinist, renowned psychiatrist, rocket scientist, multilingual sculptor. Edie is kind to animals and good with small children. Edie is nothing less than perfect. Edie recycles.

I call the official channels and find out where and when McCollum's going to be lecturing. I call the front desk and find out how long it takes to get to the University of Winnipeg. I have three hours to kill. Fuck Edie. Fuck perfect.

Something about being in a hotel room makes me want to telephone people. I call my sister and my brother. They seem inordinately surprised to hear from me. I realize that I'm usually on the receiving end of the calls, and make a mental note to dial them up more frequently. Both invite me to continue west, to visit for a while. Filled with a strange feeling of optimism and goodwill, I tell them that I'll consider it, depending on what happens with McCollum. They wish me luck. They tell me to bring him along if I want to. Blab and gab for as long as they'll let me, then I go for a walk in search of something to eat.

I like what I see of Winnipeg. It's not trying too hard. It doesn't seem to be trying at all. No desperate attempts at world-class status. No fully engorged phallus towering proud in the clouds. No Pei-in-the-sky monuments to prosperity and success. Zero flash, zero glam. No condo or cell phone. It's like the eighties never happened here — except for acid-washed denim, a repugnant and alarmingly popular holdout. If it wasn't for the preponderance of acid wash I'd swear this town skipped from the seventies directly into the nineties. I spy a veritable convoy of rust-bucket Chevys but not a single BMW. I pass a grocery store with a handwritten sign promoting *Appetizing Canned Goods*. No mention of arugula. No five-dollar seven-grain bread. I notice that an inordinate number of individuals are sporting old sweatpants out in public. And faded T-shirts with outdated slogans. It's like being at home in public. Wandering the streets in your pyjamas.

I pop half a Klonny and slide into the old-shoe comfort of Winnipeg. Locate a greasy spoon and grab a clubhouse sandwich with a side of fries and a chef's salad. French dressing and black coffee. No offer of latte or cappuccino. This town is regular or Sanka.

I make it back to the Baron Dort with plenty of time to spare and prepare. I shower and shave, blow-dry and gel, moisturize and deodorize, perfume and preen. Put my hair up, take it down again. Put it up again. Take it down again. Smear some beige goo under my eyes, try to blend away the years. A touch of lipstick, nothing drastic, and the slightest hint of blush. The long green dress. Then the short black dress. Jeans and a white blouse. Then tank top and jeans. Sandals with a heel. Sandals without a heel. The short black dress and the sandals with a heel. The long green dress and the sandals without a heel. OK, screw this noise, I gotta go. Peel off the green dress and toss it on the floor, jump back into my jeans and pull on the tank top. Put my hair up again and let it down again. Put it up again and call for a taxi, grab the Midas Muffler bag full of letters and hightail it to the lobby. I'm a little nerved out. A little nauseous. A tad dizzy. Maybe the green dress would have been better. I pop another half a Klonny.

I arrive a couple of minutes early, expecting to have to navigate through a vast labyrinth-like campus, but the Eckhardt-Gramatté lecture hall is surprisingly easy to locate. Through the front doors, up the escalator, through another set of doors and there it is. A couple of students are lingering around the entranceway. I slip past them into the small, dimly lit auditorium. About seventy people have gathered to take in McCollum's lecture. I select a seat near the corner in the top row of the theatre, as far away from the lectern as possible and squarely behind two tallish students so that I can observe unobserved. There is an overhead projector on a table next to the lectern, a cardboard box, a jug of water and a disposable cup. I slump down in my seat, try to blend in and calm down.

A minute or an hour later a professor type emerges from a passageway at the bottom right-hand corner of the theatre, and McCollum appears following close behind. A powerful jolt of electricity wows throughout my body. A surge so mighty I can barely focus or breathe. The professor type steps up to the lectern to make the introduction, but I don't process a word he says. My head is full of heart-pound and blood-rush and flashing migraine light. The ticker is pumping fast and jumping irregular. I feel like I'm in real danger of passing out. I close my eyes and try to pull it together. Deep breaths through the nose and out through the mouth. In through the nose and out through the mouth. Cool clear water... Cool clear water... McCollum is three minutes into his lecture before I can open my eyes and risk retina burn/cardiac arrest.

"I know that a lot of the people who came out today are members of the Wolseley community who want to know more about DED and what can be done to protect the elms, and I realize that many of you don't have a background in entomology or arboriculture, so I'm not going to get too technical. I'm going to present you with an overview of the situation and describe various methods of control that are currently being used as well as some new alternative methods that may be implemented in the future. For those of you who are studying entomology, conservation biology and environmental bioremediation, come back tomorrow morning at 9 a.m. and we'll delve into the really meaty bits."

The crowd titters. McCollum switches on the overhead and fumbles through his slides. He looks taller and skinnier than ever. And pale. Extremely pale. The acne has healed up. No more oozing boils, just an agreeably bumpy surface. And he's grown a fuzzy beard and moustache that cover a lot of the scarring. But the face looks drawn and sallow. Tired. Unhealthy.

"Dutch elm disease was discovered in Holland in 1919 and was introduced to the United States around 1930 via infected wood. Since then it has spread rapidly from the east coast to the Rocky Mountains and north into Canada. DED has devastated elm populations across North America. In Great Falls, Montana, DED claimed ten thousand trees — half of the city's elm population — over the course of seven years, although that was largely a matter of too little too late, a good example of what can happen if you ignore the warning signs. The situation isn't quite as dire in Manitoba, thanks to a rigorous control program and quarantine directives. Nevertheless, DED will kill hundreds of elms every year in this province. Clearly, more needs to be done. So, what exactly is Dutch elm disease?"

I sink down into my seat and peer at McCollum between the heads of the people in front of me. It looks as if he has been ill. Or could it just be fatigue? Hopefully, jet lag or the flu. Maybe just the passage of time.

"...basically a vascular disease caused by the fungus *Ophiostoma novo-ulmi*. The tiny spores or seeds of this fungus germinate in the water-conducting tissues of the tree. As the fungus grows it causes the tree to form gums that plug the transport vessels, causing the tree to wilt and eventually die."

McCollum changes the overhead. A beetle specimen appears on the screen. "The disease is spread principally by this little sucker: *Scolytus multistriatus* a.k.a. the smaller European elm bark beetle. These beetles are attracted to dead, dying or recently cut elm wood, where they breed and winter as larvae under the bark. In the spring, adults emerge and...um..."

McCollum pauses in mid-sentence and looks up into the audience. I duck down deep in my seat as he scans the faces in the crowd. It's as if he suddenly sensed an alien presence or picked up an unusual signal on invisible feelers. I pretend to fiddle with something on the floor while I wait for him to resume.

"Excuse me...um...Adults emerge in the spring and carry fungal spores from egg galleries in the infected trees to healthy trees on which they feed. The spores are introduced to the healthy elms via feeding wounds. As you can see, the beetle is dark reddish brown in colour and about three millimetres long. The underside of the posterior end of the body is concave and features a prominent spine." McCollum changes the image. "This is another, slightly less aggressive culprit, the native elm bark beetle — *Hylurgopinus rufipes* — dull grey-brown in colour, under three millimetres long and without the concave underside of the posterior abdomen and without the prominent spine."

McCollum changes the overhead image and continues with his lecture, but he appears slightly distracted. He keeps glancing out into the audience, vaguely unfocused, a little thrown off. I keep well out of sight, hunched low in my chair, carefully sneaking the odd peek here and there.

Eventually, McCollum's concentration returns when he gets to the part about alternative methods of disease control. He's all pumped and enthusiastic about trap trees and chemical ecology. He's all flushed and excited about pheromone lures and the various field studies he's conducted. He's especially geared up about the pheromones, a variety of substances secreted by animals including the elm bark beetle, an invisible stimulus that can be used to attract and disorient. "As far as I'm concerned," says McCollum, wrapping up the lecture, "pheromones are the key."

As he switches off the overhead projector, the professor type stands and leads the audience in a polite round of applause. I can't resist the urge to clap as loud as possible, cupping my hands for maximum reverb. I resist the urge to whistle and cheer and stamp my feet. I resist the urge to jump on my chair and hold a lighter flame high to the sky. McCollum picks up the jug of water and begins pouring himself a drink. Suddenly, his head lifts and he finds me in the crowd. Eyes lock for one terrible thrilling moment, then I dive for cover behind the students, sink out of sight behind the heads. A wave of heat shivers across my face and down the back of my neck. I feel like a fool hiding out behind the heads. Ridiculous. Pathetic. Ten years old.

"OK," says the professor type, checking his watch, "we're going to have a very quick Q & A, so if anybody has any questions for Professor McCollum . . . ?"

Hands shoot up in the audience. I take a deep breath and sit up straight, expecting McCollum to be looking in my direction. But he isn't.

"Yes?"

"I just want to know," says an oldish man in a Tilley hat, "what are the earliest signs that an elm has been infected?" The audience groans. McCollum has already covered that part. With pictures.

"Well," says McCollum, with a slightly strained and shaky voice, "the first signs appear in the leaves, but the symptoms depend on when the tree has been infected. Um...from June to mid-July the leaves on one or more of the branches in the crown will begin to wilt and turn brown. Uh, usually in about ten days. Some of the leaves might fall off, but most will stay on. If the tree is infected later in the summer the leaves will turn yellow and usually fall off before the autumn drop." McCollum takes a sip of water and composes himself. He sounds serious and authoritative. Almost borderline angry. "Sometimes trees will leaf out in the spring with small or dwarfed leaves, which means that the tree has been infected in late fall of the previous year. If you suspect that an elm has been infected, the best thing to do is to immediately notify the City of Winnipeg Forestry Department or the Forestry Branch of Manitoba Natural Resources. They'll be able to determine whether or not it's DED and proceed accordingly."

McCollum scans the audience for the next question, avoiding the upper right-hand corner of the auditorium.

"Yes, sir?"

"Yeah, I'd like to know, I can't remember if you said, once a tree shows the symptoms of infection, is there anything you can do to save it or is it too late at that point?"

"On rare occasions the infection can be pruned out. But you have to catch it in its earliest stages." Now McCollum looks hard into my eyes and speaks directly to me in a strange and steely voice. "Usually by the time the damage has been noted, the infection has spread to the trunk and roots and it's too late. Too late to save the tree." McCollum clears his throat and takes a long drink of water.

I don't hear any of the other questions or answers. I feel dizzy sick and deeply ashamed. Soon there is a smattering of applause. I watch McCollum pack up his cardboard box as the audience rises and begins to file out. I wait for him to look up to see if I'm still here. How could he not look up to see if I'm still here? I know he will. He has to. But he doesn't. He picks up the cardboard box full of beetles and disease and, staring straight ahead, follows the professor type briskly out of the Eckhardt-Gramatté auditorium.

After all this time no hope for forgiveness. No glance or chance after all these years.

I wait in the dim theatre until everybody has left. Then I wait ten minutes more. Stumble out of the university into the cruel prairie light. Find a taxi that will whisk me quickly to The Forks. To the river. To the water. Muddy and deep. Zombie past the people and down to the walkway. Down along the river walk away from other humans. Past the statues and the families, past the memorial plaques and the dog walkers, past the benches and the couples, past the furtive dope-smoking teenagers. Underneath the train tracks and on and on and on. Nobody in front of me now and nobody behind me. Walk to the edge of the river and stare down into the water. Check in either direction to make sure nobody is coming, then take a deep breath and drown all my words in the river. Down down they go. No bob or glide, no maiden waiting downstream to fish them out and raise them up. The Midas Muffler bag sinks fast into the muddy Red River. A gurgle of yellow. Air bubbles burst and disappear.

I go on a bender. Slip quickly into a murky haze of booze and Klonopin. Winnipeg is good for this. The bars stay open until 3 a.m. I go from bar to bar, looking for one without music. Music has started to hurt. I've had it with music. I find a cocktail lounge tucked away in the back of an old steak house. Red and dead. Red carpets, red chairs, red vinyl bar, red velvet wallpaper. No tunes. Few customers. Plastic swords. Shrivelled peanuts. Stale waitress. Cheap whiskey. I select a table under a burnt-out light bulb and settle in.

On day three it occurs to me that things could have been worse. Infinitely worse. McCollum could have been friendly and genial and completely unaffected. All breezy and easygoing. *Hey, great to see ya! Look me up if you're ever in Montana!* A matchbook exchange of addresses. A Christmas card every December. A merry, cheery, offhanded death sentence. What happened was better. Much better. I am grateful for the snub. I thank God for the snub. At least

McCollum still felt strongly. At least McCollum still felt something. Unforgiven but not forgotten. One way or another I still exist. Wound, tumour, maggot, radiation. One way or another I'm still in there. Still alive. A sick seed of hope sprouts anew in my brain. Always this hope. Malignant. Imperishable. I douse it with whiskey. Try to kill it before it cauliflowers.

Eventually there are messages at the hotel. From my sister and brother. From Simon in Toronto. From my boss at Book World. More and more messages, then the red light stops blinking. One afternoon I am awakened by a rapping on the door, a nervous rat-a-tat-tat brimming with energy and impatience. My hangover and I sit up slowly, slouch gingerly to the door and squint into the peephole. It's a porter. Smiling and biting his nails. Wide-angle warped.

"Yes?"

"I have a special delivery for Michelle Schafer."

"Oh…um, hang on a minute." Fish the green dress out of a heap on the floor and slip it on. Tortoise back to the door and open up a crack.

"Michelle Schafer?"

"Yeah."

"I have a special delivery from a Mr. Joel Schafer!" The porter dangles a set of car keys in the air. He's all smiley and excited, shaking the shiny metal in my face, waiting for me to giggle and grab like a dazzled baby, waiting for some kind of *Price Is Right* reaction.

"Oh," I say, pinching the keys in mid-air to stop the jiggling, which is making me dizzy. I hold the things steady and examine the handsome leather key tag.

"It's a car!" he says impatiently. "It's downstairs. Right outside!"

"Oh…um, OK. Hang on a minute." I move thick through the room, looking for some cash. Find a crumpled fiver in my jeans pocket and hand it to the porter. "Here. Thanks a lot."

"It's a Jaguar," says the porter. "Brand new. A convertible!"

"OK," I say, closing the door in his mystified face.

"Fully loaded!" he calls out as the door clicks shut.

I drop the car keys in a clean ashtray and crawl back into bed. Scissors beat paper. Hangover beats automobile.

Later I will order room service and eat a large and insipid meal.

I will clean myself up, get dressed and go sit in the Jaguar. I will find a missive from Joel in the gleaming walnut glovebox. The missive will say: *Now you can drive home in style, sis!* I will write him a letter on Baron Dort stationery. Thank him for thinking of me and thank thank him for the car. I will unload the Jaguar for as much as I can get.

I have decided to stay in Winnipeg with the beetles and the disease.

—

All is forgiven.

Marla and Joel have patched things up. Pals again. They call me down for dinner.

I find it difficult to watch my brother eat. Short breaths and a sheen of perspiration on the deeply tanned forehead as he packs in forkfuls of sour cream and butter and glistening hunks of marbled beef with a rapid, ferocious hunger. I think about his heart. I can't help wondering about his heart. Every time he dabs at the sweat with a paper napkin Marla casts me a sombre glance. She is thinking about it too, while she nibbles on a plain cob of corn, meticulously gnawing off every last kernel.

Steak, baked potatoes, fine red wine. If this was a real family dinner the father would have found it necessary by now to launch into his favourite mealtime allocution. The one about his wartime hunger and his mother killing and cooking the family pet. *And those were the good times, you understand. That was before things got bad. I don't have to tell you that I couldn't eat it. My brothers ate, but I couldn't do it.* He'd slide effortlessly into the one about the orphanage, the eleven children dividing up the banana peel — *not the banana, mind you, the peel!* Eventually he'd drive it home by moving on to present-day famine: starving Ethiopian children with distended bellies — *that's not food inside, that's air* — young mothers unable to nurse, their breasts withered and dusty dry. He'd finish with how lucky, and why aren't you eating, don't you dare waste that, and what the hell is the matter with you? But the faux father is totally unobtrusive, keeping the mouth busy with the good food, seemingly oblivious to our ill-deserved good fortune.

Marla sucks the juice out of the cleanly gnawed cob of corn and sets it neatly on her plate. She is done. Finito. California slim. Practically Auschwitz thin. Joel keeps going, eating as much and as fast as he can.

"Dee-lish," says Joel, reconsidering a discarded, partially chewed chunk of meat fat and forking it into his mouth. "It's been a long time since I've had this kind of food." He swallows, dabs his forehead with a napkin and, without missing a beat, reaches for a cigarette and lights up. "What's for dessert?"

"Ice cream," says the fake mom, getting up from the table. "Does anyone want coffee or tea?" She retrieves an ashtray from the counter and sets it down beside Joel's plate.

"Why don't we take a little break," says Marla, trying to sound casual, but the undertone screams *Stop it! Stop eating, for God's sake!* The fake mom waits for her cue.

"Sure, we can wait a bit. We'll digest for a while." Joel smiles at Marla. The fake mom takes her seat at the table. "This is nice," says Joel. "Isn't this nice, you guys? I can't remember the last time we had dinner together as a family."

Takeout in my mother's hospital room. Not so nice.

"I could get used to this," says Joel. "Couldn't you guys get used to this?"

"It is nice," says Marla.

"Food was great," I say. "Thank you very much."

"The steaks were all right?" asks the faux father, even though we've been through that already. And it's *yes yes yes*, all around, again.

Joel grinds out his cigarette and lights another one. "You guys remember that time we went to the House of Chan?"

"Oh, that was great!" says Marla.

"We had lobster," I say. I kept the shells, the head and the claws. My father rinsed them for me in the bathroom sink. I took them for show-and-tell the next day.

"What were we celebrating again?" asks Joel.

"Dad had sold two coats in one week and Mom wanted to splurge," says Marla. "Chinchilla, 'member, 'Chelle?"

"Yeah." Chinchilla was the softest fur. Softer even than baby seal. I remember the smell of the pelts in the basement. Chinchilla, mink, rabbit, raccoon. My father would make rabbit-foot key chains for us and dye the fur pink or green or baby blue. He would let us take the discarded mink faces to school to give to our friends. Shrivelled suede slits where the eyes used to be, tiny dried-up noses and the whiskers still intact. He made a chinchilla hat for my mom. I used to take it into the bathroom sometimes, lock the door and rub the fur against my bare skin.

"I don't remember the coat part," says Joel. "I just remember we were celebrating something and we had to drive downtown and everything was very fancy and candlelit and we all had our own lobster."

"And Dad ordered a Bloody Caesar and let me have it," says Marla. "And I got totally smashed."

"Oh yes," says the fake mom, tittering.

"You know," says Joel, "I've had many a fine meal in my time — Spago, Morton's, you name it — but that dinner at the House of Chan was the best I ever had. By far the best!"

"That was a good night," I say. And it was. No bickering, no brawls, no lectures, no guilt, a rare night full of laughs and warmth. Even in the car. We sang all the way home. About lobsters. We took popular songs and changed the lyrics: *My lobster flies over the ocean, my lobster flies over the sea... Catch a falling lobster, put it in your pocket, save it for a rainy day... Lobster, O happy lobster, I know this lobster will last all my life...*

"I have an idea," says Joel. "Let's go there for dinner tomorrow night. My treat!"

The phony parents exchange a quick, covert glance. "But you kids won't be here tomorrow night," says the fake mom with a forced smile. She gets up and starts clearing the dishes from the table. Clinking ceramic. Short sharp moves.

"You're flying home tomorrow, aren't you?" says the faux father, a tad too insistently.

"Yes," I say.

"Theoretically," says Marla.

"Screw that, we can change the tickets. Arrangements can always be made," says Joel, hawk-eyeing the fake parents. "Come on, people, all the lobster you can eat! Three-pounders, four-pounders!"

"I should really get back," I say.

"We can see a movie first. Or a play. Maybe one of the mega-musicals? Whatever you guys want."

"Why do you have to go back?" asks Marla.

"Well…I have the bookstore. I have food in the fridge."

"It'll be fine for one more day. And you can fly home on Monday."

"Yeah, but the store's gonna be closed all weekend. I should really open on Monday."

"Take an early flight and open a little late. The time change is in your favour. Or get someone to open for you."

"I can't. I don't have anyone."

"You don't have any employees?"

"No. I run it myself."

"So keep the damned thing closed," says Joel angrily. "Winnipeg can't survive one day without your bookstore? It's not the only bookstore in town, is it?"

"No. But that's not the point."

"What, you're worried about the food? I'll give you money for the food. I'll take care of it, don't worry about it."

"I'm not worried about the food…I just might feel like going home—"

"Hey! We could go shopping tomorrow during the day. Get some furniture for the living room! Hey, Ma, you wanna go to the Art Shoppe and pick out a dining-room set?"

"Oh…I don't know," says the fake mom with a big strained smile.

"Why would we do that?" asks Marla.

"Because it would be fun," says Joel. "Because it's about time we got some furniture in there."

"But why?"

"Because it's a waste of space and I'd like to make it more comfortable. We could get rid of that dinky piano and get a nice baby grand or something!"

Nobody says anything for a couple of seconds. Silence as we ponder his nonsensical suggestion. I try to feel my way around the forced cheerfulness of his tone; there's something underlying, something strangely unsettling. Marla gets up and starts clearing away the food. Joel scowls and heads for the hallway.

"Well, I think I'll take Freddy for a walk," says the faux father, glumly.

"Has anyone fed him?" asks Marla.

"I did," says the fake mom, scraping the plates. Metal on ceramic. Scrape scrape scrape.

I go into the hall to talk to Joel. I find him next to his open suitcase, snapping the lid back on a small prescription bottle.

"I thought you said those were sleeping pills."

"Don't worry about it."

"You're not going to sleep now, are you?"

"I said don't worry about it, OK?" Joel drops the bottle in his pocket and closes the suitcase.

"You've had quite a bit to drink. If those are sleeping pills you shouldn't be mixing them with alcohol."

"Oy vey! You're gonna start with me?!" Joel's voice bounces big around the hall.

The faux father comes by with Freddy on a leash. "I'm just gonna take the dog for a walk," he says sheepishly.

"Fine," says Joel. "Take the dog for a walk."

I sit down on the stairs and wait for the front door to close behind them. "I'm not trying to give you a hard time," I say quietly. "I'm just worried about you, that's all."

"Oh, all of a sudden you're worried about me?" says Joel bitterly. "Just keep worrying about yourself, Michelle. I'm a big boy. You just keep worrying about yourself." The words resonate in the hallway. Joel leans against the wall, glowering.

"You think I only worry about myself?"

"What do you think? What does the evidence suggest?"

"Because I might want to go home tomorrow?"

"Well, yes. That's part of it. That's your MO for sure."

"What do you mean by that?"

"I mean you do what's right for you and you don't worry about anyone else. You run off to your own little world and you don't give a shit about who or what you leave behind. That's what you do. That's what you've always done. That's your MO."

"What are you talking about?"

"You know what I'm talking about. That's what you've always done. Think about it, Michelle."

I flash on my father's shiva. That day in the bedroom. The three of us hiding out in my parents' room, stretched out on the bed amongst the piles of coats. The ensuite bathroom door shut tight, challenging me to enter, staring me down. Marla and Joel on my father's side of the bed. A confrontation. A proposition. Marla and Joel wanting to keep the house. A business plan. How it can be done. Between Joel's drug profits and Marla's AV Network job we could probably swing it. We could definitely swing it. Marla could get a job for me at the AV Network too! All I'd have to do is move back in. That's all I'd have to do. Just move back in. Leave downtown and return to the suburbs. Leave the brown apartment where McCollum once slept, where McCollum once breathed. Leave my quiet existence and go back to the family. *I'll think about it*, I say. Within hours I refuse. I continue to refuse. Stone. Ice. Intractable. The house gets sold — a tough market (and tainted with death). A few thousand dollars each. Joel packs his bags and his guitar and, without a word of goodbye to me, flies alone to LA. Marla puts everything in storage and follows her boyfriend of the moment to Vancouver. A teary farewell and promises to keep in touch.

"You're talking about selling the house? About me not wanting to move back?"

"Well, yeah. That's part of it. A continuation of the pattern."

"What pattern?"

"My God, are you really that dense?"

"Are you talking about me moving out of here when I was little?"

Joel doesn't say anything. He just gives me that strange mirthless grin.

"Are you talking about when I moved out with Frank McCollum?!"

"What do you think I'm talking about?"

"I don't know. But if that's what you're talking about, it seems a little odd. I mean, no one seemed too worried about it at the time. It wasn't like anyone tried to stop me, or even noticed for that matter."

"Oh, that's rich!" says Joel. "That's really rich!"

"I think I would have remembered, Joel."

"You only remember what you want to remember."

"Oh yeah?"

"Yeah. You think nobody noticed when you moved out? Allow me to let you in on a little secret, Michelle. Everything was peachy-keen until you moved out. Everything went rapidly to shit in a handcart when you moved out."

"What? What are you talking about?"

"You don't think your disappearing act had any effect on this family?"

"Not particularly, no."

"Oh my God," says Joel, laughing to himself. "She's totally delusional. Totally self-absorbed."

"Maybe, but I still don't know what you're going on about."

"Hello! Earth to Michelle! I'm talking about Mom. I'm talking about Mom freaking out when you left. I'm talking about Mom blaming herself and all of us for driving poor delicate Michelle away. Poor mentally fragile Michelle. Don't push her over the edge. She might just cut up her arms with razor blades or mainline heroin or jump in front of a train. Yeah right! I'm talking about Mom freaking out and getting sick almost right after you left. I'm talking about all the shit that went down after you flew the coop with your loony boy toy."

"Oh my God…"

"What, this is news to you?"

"I don't believe this. Are you saying that I'm responsible for Mom getting sick? You think it's my fault that Mom got cancer?!"

Joel stares into my stricken face. He crosses his arms over his chest and coughs. "I'm just saying that everything was fine up until that point."

I try to absorb and sort through this spectacular revelation. Is this what my brother thinks of me? That I single-handedly demolished all that was warm and good? Does Marla think that? And more importantly, is it true? I ruined it with McCollum; maybe I ruined it for my family too. Was everything clam happy and Rockwell until I moved out of the house? Am I destruction? I feel my face grow hot; I can't focus; I need to think.

"You know, if Mom hadn't got sick, then Dad wouldn't have…well, what's the point?" mutters Joel.

I stand up and start moving up the stairs.

"Oh, very good. Run away, Michelle. Just run fucking away!"

I stop and sit down. A challenge. A staring contest.

"What's going on?" asks Marla, coming into the hall, piercing the moment.

"Nothing," says Joel, looking away.

"What about Marla?" I say, my thoughts all hot and jumbled. "Marla went to Vancouver."

"What are you guys talking about?!"

"Marla went *after*. Marla was there when *that cunt* Suzy Fish took a powder. Marla was there when Dad got all depressed and... lost it."

"Why are you guys talking about this?!"

"And Marla picks up the phone to call me once in a while. Marla picks up the phone once a month to tell me what's going on. And you know what else? Marla actually comes to see me when I invite her. Marla has actually been to my house!"

"All right, it's enough," says my sister, looking at me.

"And another funny thing," says Joel. "Marla doesn't hawk every gift that I give her. Can you believe that? I know it must be difficult for you to fathom."

"All right already! Jesus H. Christ!"

"Am I talking to you?! I don't think I was talking to you!"

Uh oh. Here we go.

"What the hell are you doing, Joel? What is the point of this, exactly?"

"Nothing! I just want everyone to stay, that's all." Joel lowers his voice, he sounds pouty, almost as if he's going to cry. "I don't see why she has to run away and wreck everything. I mean, why can't she stay just one more day?"

Suddenly Joel is baby boy and Marla is big sister. She moves across the hall for a great big hug. She'll make everything all better.

"You went to a hell of a lot of trouble," says Marla softly. "I'm sure Michelle can stay. Right, Michelle?" She looks hard into my eyes. The look says: Do it, for Christ's sake. Can't you see that our little brother is on the verge of a nervous breakdown?

"Yeah, sure," I say, bristling at the thought of it. "I can stay for another day."

The front door opens and the faux father enters with the phony Freddy.

"Hey, Freddy! C'mere boy! You're a good boy, aren't you? Yes, yes you are. You're the best best boy!" My brother pat-pats the dog, all smiley and happy. "Did he go?" asks Joel.

"Yup," says the father.

"Then let's have some ice cream! Who's ready for ice cream?!"

—

Marla slips into my room after everyone has gone to bed. "Oh my God, I am sooo tired. I have never been this tired! Ucch, I feel sick from all the food. It was gross. I shouldn't have had dessert." She sits down on the end of the bed, sighs and massages her temples. I don't say anything. After a few seconds she looks over at me. "What's the matter with you?"

"Nothing."

"You sure?"

"Yeah."

"Something's wrong."

"No."

"What? What Joel was saying before?"

No answer.

"He's just really, really stressed, that's all."

"And angry," I say.

"Well, angry is nothing new."

"Really? It's kind of new to me."

"Oh come on!" My sister looks incredulous. She knows something I don't know.

"I guess you guys talk more often."

Marla laughs. "Yeah, I guess."

The laugh unnerves me. I picture frequent confabulations and the laying of blame; I'm on the outside, the target of their wrath.

"I mean, I had no idea that he hated me so much."

"Oh please! He doesn't *hate* you, Michelle."

"No?"

"You just frustrate him, that's all."

"I frustrate him?"

"Yeah. He expects you to be a certain way and you're just not that way."

"Oh yeah, what way am I?"

"You're like Mom."

"What does that mean?"

"Well, you know, sort of off in your own universe kind of thing. I mean, you're a lot like Mom if you think about it."

I don't want to think about it. I'm tired of thinking. A dull ache forming behind the forehead. The need for sleep. I lie back, sigh and pull the covers up around me, but my sister doesn't get the hint. She crosses one leg over her knee, lifts up her foot and inspects the heel. "Fuck!"

"What?"

"I thought I got rid of this, but I think it's growing back."

"What is it?"

"A plantar wart. Have you ever had one? I had it frozen off, but it looks like it's still there."

"Lemme see."

She swivels on the bed and sticks her foot in the air.

"Hmm, I can't tell. It just looks like missing skin."

She swivels back and peers at it again. "No, I think it's still there. I'll have to go and get it zapped again. Great, this is all I need." Marla looks up at the ceiling fixture. "You took down your thingy, eh?"

"Yeah."

"Me too. I was gonna flush it, but I decided to just stick it in a drawer."

"Hmm."

"So, 'Chelle..."

"What?"

"What do you think?"

"About what?"

"About this weekend? About Joel?"

"I don't know. Maybe the pills have something to do with it. I caught Joel popping them after dinner. If they're sleeping pills, that's a bad sign."

"I don't know what the hell they are. I looked at the label quickly when I got the bracelets, but the directions and everything were in another language. Spanish, I think."

"Spanish?"

"Yeah. Maybe it's someone else's prescription."

"Actually, I seem to remember reading about Americans going across the border to Mexico to get prescriptions filled."

"Why would they do that?"

"For drugs that have been banned in the U.S., or if their doctors have cut them off because of an addiction or something. Apparently you can get whatever you want. A veritable pinata full of pills as long as you have the cash to play."

"Shit, you're kidding."

"No. I think I read it in the *Globe*, or maybe the *Free Press*. No, it must have been the *Globe*."

"Well, that could definitely be exacerbating everything. But frankly, I suspect it's mostly about work."

"You do?"

"Yeah. Think about it. Joel has always been successful. Always. It's his whole identity, you know. Money, fame, the big house, the Cartier watch. I think he's totally stressed because of the last two flops. Maybe he's not such a big macher in Hollywood any more. Maybe he can't really cope with that."

"I don't know. I don't think that's it. I think it goes beyond that. Way beyond that."

"Yeah, but that's what I'm saying. I think Joel needed to get away. To get back to something that is the antithesis of his life in California. Something real."

"Real?!"

"You know what I mean. The whole family thing. I can understand, you know. I mean, it's kind of been nice, don't you think?"

"You think so?"

"Kind of. Some good, some bad." My sister flops back on the bed, her arms behind her head.

"Mar?"

"What?"

"Nothing. Never mind."

"What?"

"No, no, nothing..."

Marla sits up and stares at me. "What? Just tell me!"

"Um...do you ever think about why Mom got sick?"

"What are you talking about?"

"I mean, why do you think she got sick?"

"What do you mean, why did she get sick? Why does anybody get sick? It just happens. Bad genes. Bad luck."

"Hmm."

"Why do *you* think she got sick?"

"I don't know. I was just wondering."

"That's a weird question, Michelle."

"Hmm."

"Michelle!"

"What?"

"People get sick. There's nothing you can do."

"Yeah."

"We did everything we could."

"I know. Whatever." I sit up and reach for a cigarette. Light it. Blow smoke. "So anyway...do you still think this is some kind of test or something? I mean, I thought you thought Joel was planning to pull something Maple Leaf Gardens–like?"

"Ucch, I don't know. I'm too tired to know." Marla gets up and moves towards the door. "All I know is that Joel appears to be genuine, so we might as well give him the benefit of the doubt. I think we should just try to make this time as happy as possible for him. I mean, one more day isn't gonna kill us, right?"

"I guess you're right."

"Sweet dreams."

"Sleep tight."

—

The following day is jam-packed with non-stop activity. Joel leads the way. The beaming master of ceremonies, ushering us through it all. First, breakfast at the Pickle Barrel, then home to walk Freddy. Then over to the Art Shoppe and a flurry of pointless and exorbitant purchases. Then downtown to Bay and Cumberland to pick out two plush rugs. Then a detour to Holt Renfrew to shop for clothes and shoes, sunglasses and perfume. Then a bite in the café on the second floor of the store. Then down the street to Remenyi to select a proper piano. The whole thing is absurd and obscene. My brother is hemorrhaging cash. To what end? To keep us happy for one day? Everyone seems to be happy. We're all flushed with the excitement of buying whatever we desire, giddy with the thrill of ordering from the left-hand side of the menu. No one asks Joel what he's going to do with all these objects. No one seems to care where that baby grand piano is going to end up. We roll merrily along with the fantasy. We're on a spree. A slap-happy spree!

Eventually it's back to the house to drop off our purchases, tend to Freddy and get showered and changed for dinner. I'm ready first. New sandals. New top. New Armani shades. I feed the dog and take him for a walk to the park. A few blissful minutes away from other people. A chance to recover after a full day of trooping around in a gang.

It's a beautiful park, but not as beautiful as it once was. The Don River used to run through here, a thin stream gurgling along at the bottom of the hill, trickling towards the trees and into the ravine. You could hear the frogs at night. A rich and calming sound. But the river is gone, filled in with soil and covered up with sod. I follow the groove in the grass at the bottom of the hill over to the mouth of the ravine — the ravine I used to walk through to get to the OH Complex, the ravine I used to flee to just to smoke or walk or think. There have been alterations here too. The small dirt path has been widened and covered with wood chips. Hideous and phony-looking. And there's a big sign: WELCOME TO THE WESTVIEW FITNESS TRAIL. About five metres down the path sits an exercise station, an iron bar mounted between two thick pieces of pressure-treated wood. Greenish. Ugly. Another sign with a giant number 1, and a two-part diagram showing a trim male figure doing chin-ups. I decide not to go in. I turn around and head home.

When I get back to the house I find Joel sitting on the front porch, a little slumped, with his eyes closed. He's wearing a different linen suit. Pale green and freshly pressed. Unlikely that it came out of his small suitcase.

"Hey."

"Oh, hi there." Joel looks up, dazed, as if I just woke him from a deep sleep.

"You OK?"

"Yeah, I'm great. Just a little tired, that's all." He looks drowsy, almost drunk. The lids hanging heavy over the eyes. "Did he go?"

"Yeah." I let the dog into the house and toss the leash into the vestibule.

"Cigarette?" says Joel, offering me the case. I take one. Joel fishes in his pockets and hands me his lighter.

"Thanks." I light up and try to pass the thing back.

"No, it's OK. You keep it."

"Joel, I don't want it."

"It's OK, really. I want you to have it." He smiles up at me — a big, buzzed-out mile of mild. I wouldn't be surprised if he flashed me a peace sign to go along with it.

"Here," I say, holding the lighter out to him.

"I'm not takin' it." He folds his arms across his chest.

"Fine, I'll give it to you later."

"Don't give it to me later. Just say thanks, OK?"

"Fine. Thank you very much." I slip the lighter into my pocket, resolving to return it to him later. I don't want Joel's gold lighter. The whole gift-giving thing is making me uneasy already.

"The shoes look good."

"Thanks." I sit down on the front step and look at my new sandals.

"This was a good day, eh?"

"Yeah. It was fun."

"You're glad you stayed, right?"

"Yeah, it was a good day."

"I told you you'd be glad you stayed." Joel smiles and the eyelids droop just a little bit lower. Neither one of us wants to revisit the conversation of the previous day.

We sit quietly and take in the sounds of the street. Distant dog bark, kids laughing, skipping rope slapping driveway, sprinkler on foliage. The air smells like barbecue and freshly mown grass.

"Can I ask you something?" I say after a while.

"What?"

"You know that thing you held at Maple Leaf Gardens. Was that all true or what?"

"Uch..."

"Is that a yes or a no?"

"I'm sick to death of talking about it already. I wish to God it never happened." Joel takes out a cigarette and fumbles for fire, patting at his pockets. He's already forgotten.

"So it was true, eh?" I hand the lighter back.

"More or less. Certain elements were exaggerated."

"Oh yeah? Which elements?"

"It's certainly not what I intended."

"What do you mean?"

"I mean that I never intended to humiliate anyone."

"Oh come on. How can you say that, given the circumstances? I mean, it's not like you held a gun to their heads or anything, but please, don't tell me that wasn't designed for maximum degradation."

"Wrong, Michelle. You have no idea. You don't know what occurred."

"That's why I'm asking. I want to know."

"Look," says Joel, sitting up and launching into the thing as if he's been through it countless times before. "I have a reputation in LA and, I'm pretty sure, beyond for being... well, let's say 'theatrical.' I happen to enjoy practical jokes and divertissement of that nature. The more elaborate the better, generally speaking. It amuses me to concoct beguiling little scenarios and engaging little episodes."

"Yeah, I know that. So?"

"So I wanted to have a get-together with the old gang, but I wanted to make it interesting, you know?"

"Yeah, well, that's pretty interesting all right. That's downright engrossing. Not to mention gross."

"You fail to comprehend, I'm afraid. You're pole-vaulting to conclusions, Michelle. Like I said before, I never intended to humiliate anybody. My intention was merely to freak the boys out a little. Live up to the reputation. Knock 'em for a bit of a loop. The whole thing was a joke, a shtick, a caper. A painfully obvious burlesque, if you ask me. I didn't think for one second that they would take me seriously or even consider going through with it."

"Is that true?"

"Honest to God. I assumed they would either laugh their asses off or tell me to take a fucking hike and storm out of the joint en masse. That's what I would do! I had my people waiting outside, waiting to haul them back in so I could tell them it was all a big yoke. You know, I was planning all along to slip each of 'em some cashola — not what I ended up laying out, mind you, but a handsome chunk of change nonetheless. Thanks for the memories, buy yourself a Buick or something."

"All right, so assuming that's true — "

"It's true."

"Fine, it's true. But why didn't you intervene? I mean, you could have intervened, right?"

"Yes. I suppose so. But think about it, Michelle. Think about how riveting it would be to watch it all happen."

"I think it would be rather nauseating and very depressing."

"I'm not talking about the distasteful end result — pardon the pun. I'm talking about the actions that led up to that point, the unravelling, so to speak. Trust me, you would have found it extremely compelling. I was far too intrigued to put a stop to it, I'm afraid."

"But what was so captivating about it? What exactly happened?"

Joel smiles at me with half-closed eyes. "You want to know, don't you?"

"Obviously."

"You don't want me to stop the story right now, correct?"

"I see the point you're trying to make, but it doesn't translate. Yes, I'm very curious, but I don't have the power to alter the results. You telling me what happened isn't going to have an effect on anyone. You were there, you had a choice. I don't have any kind of a choice to make."

"Bullshit. You can choose not to know."

"Fine. Don't tell me."

"Fine. I won't. Tick-a-lock." Joel mock locks his lips and throws away the key.

An interminably long forty-five-second silence. Then: "All right, just fucking tell me already." We both laugh.

"Well, it's hard to describe. At first it was what I expected: shock, followed by nervous laughter, followed by disbelief, followed by revulsion. That's when I thought the boys would take a powder — say 'screw this' and march out. But they didn't march out. I suppose I had underestimated their desire for the cash, which in itself isn't all that interesting. I've seen countless people peddle their integrity and dignity for less dough, believe me. What was interesting to me was that, with the exception of Jason, when faced with this disgusting proposition none of the guys seemed to want to decide for themselves what to do. Instead, they immediately looked to each other for reaction. Stephen looked to Randall to see how he would react. Randall was looking to Howard to see how he was taking it. Howard was looking to Grant who was looking to Mark who was looking to Stephen, you know what I mean?"

"Yeah."

"Suddenly I could see this unspoken agreement ripple through the assembly. They had decided collectively to treat the thing as nothing more than a lark. Each individual wanted the cash and, at the same time, each individual wanted to maintain his dignity. The solution was to band together and act as a group. The group is dignity. The group can't be wrong. If the group agrees that it's a lark, then clearly it's a lark. If the group says it's the right thing to do, then it's the right thing to do. Eat shit, shoot up a village in My Lai, hack a Tutsi to death with a machete... Sure, why not? Majority rules. The majority knows best. When you act alone you have to take full responsibility. With the group there's room to shift it around. Hot potato. You know what I mean?"

"Yeah."

"The only dissenter was Jason, and he quickly became the outcast, the loser, the freak — the designated driver who didn't know how to cut loose and have fun. Relatively speaking, it was his behaviour that became unimaginable. By the time they actually got down to the deed they were all laughing and clapping each other on the back and acting as if nothing much was out of the ordinary. Just another day in the life. I'll tell you, it was fascinating to watch. A revelation of sorts."

"How so?"

"It gave me tremendous insight into extreme behaviour and how it can quickly become quite run-of-the-mill and acceptable."

"Hmm."

"So I let my old friends go through with it. What can I tell you? I was intrigued. Utterly compelled."

"Well, I can see what you're saying, but I wonder, is curiosity — you being all compelled and intrigued — justification for not intervening. I mean, Mengele was curious too, right?"

"Oh please! Now I'm Mengele? Like you said: 'It's not as if I held a gun to their heads.' They were free to leave at any time. And my initial intentions were good. We've been over that part already."

"I suppose."

"But speaking of curiosity and unethical experimentation, you know what I think about from time to time?"

"What?"

"Well, I always thought it would be interesting to raise a child from birth to adulthood in complete isolation."

"Why?"

"Say, in a huge white chamber — no doors, no windows, nothing inside at all — a total sensory vacuum."

"Impossible. What about food and water? What about hygiene and elimination?"

"This is hypothetical. Let's just assume you didn't require any of those elements to function. Obviously, if you had to put food in the chamber and take the remnants away, the subject would develop an inkling of 'beyond,' of being enclosed, of something or someone else existing outside. So let's just pretend you could function without those things."

"So we're stripping away anatomical or physiological requirements. Are we also stripping away emotional needs? Because if we're not, Subject X would likely expire long before reaching adulthood."

"Fine, whatever. I'm not interested in the emotional state of the person. Strip that away too."

"OK... So what are you looking for, then?"

"What I'd want to know — and I don't know how you would find this out, maybe slowly expose the person to stimuli, teach them to communicate and then question them about their life before — but what I'd want to know is whether or not they would have an inkling of the existence of anything else. Would they think that their little world was the entire world? Or would they look at the walls and wonder what was on the other side? Would the concept of 'side' or 'beyond' even be there? If the chamber was lit all the time, would they have a sense of darkness?"

"When they closed their eyes."

"OK, say the chamber is dark all the time. Would they have a sense of light? What about colour? Pink, blue, green, violet? What about fire or water? What about shape and size? Octagon, mountain, molecule, star?"

"Hmm... Why don't you just ask a blind person if they can sense colour?"

"That wouldn't work. Too many associations with the other senses. 'White as snow,' 'red hot,' 'green with envy,' 'blue in the face,' 'yellow-bellied,' 'in the pink,' etc., etc. White could be associated with snow, cold and wet. A sense of red could be a sense of heat or warmth. Green is jealousy, blue is exasperation, pink is health, yellow is cowardice. It gets too muddled, if you see what I mean."

"Maybe. I'm not sure."

"And this part bugs me: what would Subject X dream? Think about it. I can't figure out what he would dream."

"I don't know. It's an interesting question. What you want to know is if humans are born as totally blank slates or if they come with some built-in memory. Like instinct, but not instinct. Are we just hardware or do we come loaded with an operating system and some kind of stock image file? Isn't that what Jung referred to as the collective unconscious? A kind of inherent memory of universal themes and symbols."

"I don't know. What I'm really wondering about are the limitations of perception. I guess what I think about the most is whether or not we're all Subject X, you know, sensing something 'beyond' but being hopelessly restricted by what we can actually perceive."

"By 'beyond' do you mean some larger world? Some alternate reality?"

"Not really. I was thinking more specifically about God."

"Do you believe in God?"

"Does Subject X believe in blue?"

"I don't know."

"And what would happen if you suddenly collapsed all the walls of the chamber? Would it be heart attack and retina burn? Or monumental recognition, overwhelming relief, freedom, peace, joy?"

"The former, no doubt."

"You'd have to be gradual, eh? Like God with Moses." Joel laughs, lights another smoke and checks his watch. "What's taking them so long?"

"Hungry?"

"Starving. You?"

"I could eat."

Joel closes his eyes and drags deeply on his cigarette. I realize that this may be my last chance to talk to him one-on-one before we leave. "So, Joel?"

"Yeah?"

"This weekend...you know, the whole family-reunion thing?"

"Uh huh?"

"This wouldn't by any chance be one of your so-called 'beguiling little scenarios'? I mean, is this event some kind of a test, some kind of elaborate experiment being conducted on me and Marla, a.k.a. Subjects Y and Z?"

"Hardly!"

"Are you as surprised by our reactions as you were by your buddies' at the Gardens? Are you 'intrigued and compelled' right now?"

"What are you talking about? This is totally different. This isn't a joke. This is not a joke, Michelle!"

"OK, so it's not a joke, but it is a little peculiar, don't you think? I mean, what's really going on here? Are you gathering material for your final screenplay, or what?"

"I told you, I finished that. I'm done. Finito. Kaput. History."

"All right, fine, whatever. Just tell me this then: what's in the basement?"

Joel stands up and flicks his cigarette into the garden. He doesn't answer me. He stares off towards the park.

"You were here first, weren't you? Watching us with those surveillance cameras."

"Oy vey, not this again."

"It's funny, because at one point on the night I arrived I had a feeling that I was being watched, that I wasn't alone. And that music in the middle of the night, the nocturnes — that was real, wasn't it? Piped in or something. I didn't dream it, did I?"

Joel wipes sweat from his forehead and looks at me with a wounded puppy expression. "Is it so weird, Michelle, is it so peculiar for me to just want to be with my family? Is that crazy? Is there anything especially crazy about that?"

"I don't know. But this isn't our family, is it? I mean, come on, Joel, what's the deal with the parent types?"

"Mom and Dad? What about them?"

"Oh come on!"

"What?!"

As if on cue, the fake parents emerge from the house, all pressed and dressed for dinner.

"Don't worry," whispers Joel. "All will be revealed." Then he turns his attention to the parents and how fresh and nice and dapper they look.

—

Dinner is good but vaguely uncomfortable. We drink cocktails and wine and eat great big lobsters. "Cockroaches of the sea," Joel calls them. He selects the biggest beast in the tank for himself. Almost five pounds. Customers at other tables gesture and stare, watch with titillation as he tears into the behemoth, the massive shell cracking.

Joel keeps ordering up the wine, trying to keep it all loose and light, trying to recapture the giddy goodness of our long-lost supper. Trying and trying too hard too hard. When the tension becomes appreciable or the conversation falters, he launches into tales from Hollywood, entertains us with amusing little anecdotes and secrets of the stars. Whose tits are real. Who's a pain in the ass to work with. Which ones have hair plugs. Which ones are gay. Who bought their wife an entire town in Oregon. Which ones are members of an international cult. He drunkenly details his last trip to Cannes. Who threw the best parties. Who threw up at the best parties. What he had to pay for a lousy cup of coffee, and how many porn stars parading at the beach. How bad the service, and how fine the wine. The pickpocket in the lobby, and what a difference a bidet makes! He is witty and drunk, pilled up and exuberant. He doesn't seem to notice that no one else at the table is really participating. He is flushed red and excited, magnanimous with the wait staff. *We'll be back!* he tells them as we waddle out of the restaurant. *Same table next Sunday! We'll be back. We'll be back.*

In the car Joel's soliloquy lapses into silence. The sound of old engine and a growing aura of apprehension. Marla, the faux father and me in the back. The fake mom driving, Joel quiet in the passenger seat. Quiet but not calm. He is biting his nails. I can hear the little clicks as he chews his way down.

When we get back to the house Joel asks us to take the dog for a walk. All of us. All four. A short walk. Fifteen minutes. The fake parents acquiesce and get the dog ready to go. Marla and I are suspicious, demanding to know why.

"I just want to set the table for dessert. Nothing major, you guys. Just give me ten or fifteen minutes."

"But why?" asks Marla. "Why can't we just wait upstairs? I want to pack, maybe grab a quick shower. I promise, we won't come down until you're ready."

"Uch, do you have to give me a hard time with this? Did we not have a perfect day? Why do you want to start?"

"I'm not starting!"

"Then give me ten minutes to set the freakin' table, is that too much to ask?!"

"I just don't understand why, that's all."

"Who says you have to understand everything? Why can't you just trust me for ten minutes? I told you, I want to set the table for dessert. Is that a crime? I mean, what the fuck do you think I'm gonna do here?"

"I don't know." Marla checks my expression. She looks scared and anxious.

"Come on, girls," says the fake mom, earning her pay. "It's a lovely night. Let's get a bit of fresh air."

"Yes," pipes in the faux father. "A bit of fresh air!"

Marla sighs and considers. She chews the inside of her cheek. She scrutinizes my brother's face.

"Go ahead," says Joel. "Once around the block."

"You better not do anything stupid," snips Marla, angry with an undertone of deep concern. She's thinking about our father. The loud goodbye.

"I'll be here when you get back," says Joel, picking up on the old fear. The big one. Unfading.

"Fine. We'll be back in fifteen minutes." Marla moves towards Joel, squeezes his arm hard and kisses his cheek.

"I said I'd be here! Just go already, OK?"

We go. Reluctantly. Hot silence. Thoughts boiling. A top note of stress-sweat acrid in my nostrils. We are now beyond the realm of speculative chatter. Marla clutches my hand the whole way around. Anxiety and solidarity surging through the palms pressed tight tight together. Fourteen minutes exactly. I pull my sister aside and hang back at the porch, make sure the parents go in first.

The sound of greetings, Joel's voice casual in the kitchen. Marla bursts into tears and crumples into my arms.

"It's OK," I say, holding tight, rubbing the centre of the back. "Shaaa, shaaa... it's OK, shaaa..."

Marla steps back, laughs, and wipes her eyes and nose. "Oy, I don't know what's the matter with me. I think I must be premenstrual or something."

"It's been pretty stressful," I say.

"I don't know, I just had this awful feeling. I thought... uch, never mind."

"I know."

"Oh well, whatever mishegoss Joel has in store, I can definitely handle now."

"Good."

"Ready?"

"Yeah. You?"

"Yeah."

The kitchen table is laid out with bonbons and champagne. Rich and powdery Belgian truffles, fancy chocolate centres nestled in dainty gold boxes, cunning marzipan candies sculpted like tiny pieces of fruit — peach, pear, banana, pineapple — a magnum of Cristal chilling in a silver ice bucket, and five hand-blown champagne flutes festooned with delicate golden ivy curling up and around the slender stems.

"Hey! How was the walk?" asks Joel, popping a marzipan banana into his mouth.

"Don't ask," says Marla. She lights a cig, inhales deeply and lets the smoke out with a weary sigh.

"Doesn't this look fabulous?" asks the fake mom, eyeing the giant bottle of champagne. She takes a seat at the table and pulls her glass close towards her.

"Very pretty," I say. "Where did all this stuff come from?"

"Secret stash," says Joel, winking at me. "Come on, you guys, sit down, dig in."

"Well, you don't have to ask me twice," says the faux father, settling in. "You know my weakness is sweets." He selects one of the fat truffles and fills his mouth with dark chocolate.

I take my usual seat by the window and scan the candies on the table. For some reason the thought occurs to me that they've all been poisoned. I watch the phony father licking truffle goo off his fingers. I think about the scene with the grapes at the end of that movie, *Montenegro*.

Joel lifts the champagne, heavy and dripping, out of the ice.

"Here," says Marla, "put a dishcloth over the top."

"What the hell for?"

"So the cork doesn't take out somebody's eye!"

"Yeah right!" Joel aims the bottle at the family room and pops the top. My sister quakes at the sound of the cork releasing.

"Jesus, Joel!"

My brother laughs and tongues the froth bubbling up and out of the bottle. The fake mom claps her hands with glee.

"All right, here we go..." Joel fills the five glasses and sets the bottle back in the bucket.

"Whose gonna make a toast?" asks the phony father, pinching another truffle.

"I am," says Joel. "I'm going to make the toast."

We raise our glasses and wait for it. Joel looks slowly around the table at each of us. He holds his glass high, clears his throat and pauses. Then he looks directly at me and in a grave, stentorian tone says: "L'chayim!"

"That's it?" says Marla, laughing.

A staggered chorus of L'chayims. We clink and drink.

"Delicious!" says the fake mom, draining her glass and licking her lips. "Who wants a refill?"

"Everyone does!" Joel hoists the bottle and pours.

"This is terrific champagne," says Marla.

"Almost as good as Freixenet," I say.

"Yeah right, almost as good as that Baby Duck," says Joel, laughing and setting the bottle back in the ice. He settles back into his seat and watches us drink, hands folded over his belly, a satisfied smile strung across his face like a popcorn wreath on a Christmas tree. "This isn't so bad, eh?"

"No," says the fake mom, "this is lovely."

"That lobster was pretty fine."

"Fantastic," says the phony father. "Best I ever had."

"You guys liked it, eh?"

"What's not to like?" says Marla.

"It was delicious," I say.

"Yup," says Joel, "it's been a good day. You guys had fun today, right?"

Yes yes yes, we all had fun.

"Me too," says Joel. "This whole weekend has been great, don't you think?"

Yes yes yes, the weekend has been great.

"And that stuff we bought today is really gonna make a difference in here. Ma, you'll finally have a piano worth playing, eh?"

"Oh well, that'll be nice," says the fake mom, glancing nervously at the faux father.

"Yup," says Joel, patting the pockets of his suit, "I could get used to this. Couldn't you guys get used to this?"

"It's been a good break," says Marla.

I set my glass down. I don't say anything.

"You know," says Joel, "I've been thinking things over and I can't say that I'm overly anxious to get back to California."

"Really?" says the fake mom with a pinched and pained smile.

"But you must have work to do," blurts the phony father. "People you want to see!"

"Nope. No work to do. And all the people I want to see are right here in this room."

"Well," I say, "you don't have to go back right away. You could take a trip somewhere."

"A trip? Why would I take a trip? Where the hell would I go?"

"Wherever you want. Fiji, Peru, Iceland, Bora-Bora."

"Bora-Bora's a bore and Iceland leaves me cold."

"Well, whatever. Norway. Botswana."

"No way on Norway and Botswana is a yawna."

"Uch."

"Well, travelling alone is no fun!"

"That's not true," says Marla. "I've travelled alone and it was great. I met a lot of interesting people."

"Well, bully for you, but I've met all the people I ever want to meet. The last thing I want to do is meet more peepholes."

"Oh come on, honey, there must be somewhere you want to go?" chirps the fake mom, sounding more and more like Nurse Ratched.

"Where would *you* like to go, Ma? Where would you go if you could go anywhere at all?"

Her face says *Home!*, but her mouth says, "Oh, I don't know... I always thought Greece would be nice."

"Greece, eh? Hmm, I've got an idea. Why don't we all go to Greece together? We could go tomorrow!"

"Joel, I can't. I have to get back to Winnipeg."

"*Winnipeg?* Michelle, I'm talking Greece here! The Mediterranean, the Parthenon, Mykonos, moussaka. I'm talking ouzo, Plato, tzatziki and potato."

"Yeah, I know-o, but I'm still not going to Greece, OK?"

"OK, fine. Fuck Greece! I wasn't even thinking of Greece, anyway. I mean, who needs to travel, we have everything we need right here, don't we?"

"I have to get back too," says Marla. "A colleague has been looking after my listing. I don't want to push it."

"You have one listing? That's it?"

"I just started. Give me a break."

"You know, the real estate market in Toronto is just as hot, if not hotter than in Vancouver."

"So?"

"So if you're really hung up on this real estate thing, it's not like you couldn't do it here quite easily."

"Yeah, so? What are you saying, Joel?"

Joel stands up, refills our glasses and sits back down. "Actually, I have a proposition to make."

Nobody responds. I feel my neck and shoulders tightening. I watch the bubbles in the champagne race to the surface and pop. Little puffs of carbon.

"I've been thinking," says Joel, wiping sweat from his forehead. "Thinking about my life, and all of our lives, actually. I guess you could say I've been rather depressed lately — well, not just lately — so I suppose that's what started it all. Anyway, I started to think about when the last time was that I was happy — truly happy, not just success happy or fame happy or money happy, you know? And I discovered that it was here. Right here. Here in this house with all of you." Joel sad-smiles, watery eyes in a bloated boy face. "I remember a time when we were all happy here. It's very clear to me, actually. Very real, you know?" Joel gulps some champagne and continues. "At first I thought, well, so what? It's impossible to go back. You know what they say: 'You can't go home again,' and all that. But then I started to mull it over and I realized that it wasn't impossible, that we could go home if we really wanted to. I mean, here we are, right? Here we are, *n'est-ce pas*?"

"Well, sort of," I say, gesturing with a glance towards the fake mom and faux father. Joel ignores me.

"I *have* unlimited resources — well, practically unlimited. If you think about it there is no good reason why we couldn't stay here if we wanted to. If you wanted to practise real estate we could arrange it. If you wanted to open a bookstore, no problemo. Or we could all take early retirement. Do whatever the fuck we want. Travel around the world or not travel around the world. Work or not work. Whatever your little hearts desire. You see what I'm saying?"

"You're saying you want us to move back in here? Stay here indefinitely?" asks Marla.

"Correct-a-mundo."

"You can't be serious."

"I can and I am. I've never been more serious."

"But you're not talking about your father and I?" says the fake mom, attempting to take it all in.

"Naturally. We're a family, aren't we? I'm talking about all of us, together. That includes you, Michelle."

"Oh come on, Joel..." The idea is ludicrous. Totally insane. I study my brother to see if he really means it. He looks serious, but he can't be. This must be a joke — the big joke of the weekend, like the capper at Maple Leaf Gardens — "a shtick, a caper, a painfully obvious burlesque." He doesn't expect us to take him seriously. He'd probably be surprised if we even considered his ridiculous proposition. Clearly, Joel is screwing with our heads, testing us. My brother is not certifiably insane. "You know, we're not children any more. We have our own lives now."

"What lives? You call sitting around a bookstore in Winnipeg a life?"

"Yeah, as a matter of fact I do."

"It's not like you have a relationship happening or a ton of friends. It's not like you couldn't open a bookstore here and do the exact same thing."

"But I like it where I am. I'm happy there."

"Bullshit. You're not happy."

"What? How can you say that?"

"I can just tell."

"Oh, that's rich."

"You said yourself that you were glad you stayed. You said yourself that you had a great time this weekend. I mean, didn't we have a wonderful day, you guys? So why not have a wonderful day every day from now on?!" Joel's eyes are glassy and bright. He's sweating like crazy in the fiercely air-conditioned kitchen.

"I'm afraid it's simply not possible, honey," snips the fake mom.

"Anything is possible," answers Joel, vaguely exasperated, glowering.

"Well, it may be possible for the rest of you," says the phony father, "but I'm going home tomorrow and that's for sure."

"But Daddy," says Joel darkly, "you're already home."

The faux father locks eyes with Joel. Their contract is wordlessly reviewed — a clause about staying in character at all times, no matter what. I can practically see it in front of me, printed on the page.

"Well, yes, of course, forgive me. What I meant to say was that I'm sure, I'm very very sure that Marla and Michelle are going to have to get back to their homes soon."

"Yes," says the fake mom, "I'm sure of that too."

"Well, we'll see about that, won't we?"

"There's nothing to see," says Marla. "I mean, it was very nice to have this weekend and I really really appreciate it, Joel, and I'm sure everyone else does too, but we can't stay here forever. I mean, the idea is totally absurd."

"Why is it absurd? Think about it, Mar. What's in Vancouver that you can't get here? Wheat germ? Reiki masters? Kotex pads stuffed with sphagnum moss?"

"Funny. How about Stanley Park? How about the ocean?"

"So, we have Earle Bales Park. So, we have a lake. Big deal. You want a sailboat? We'll get a sailboat. Don't you get it? You can have whatever you want here. You can do whatever you want! What is wrong with you guys? Do you know how many people would jump at this opportunity? I am offering a chance for us to be happy again. You guys can pretend all you want, but I know you're not happy. What's in Vancouver that's so important? What the hell is in Winnipeg? Think about it. This is it. Our big chance. I can't believe you're not jumping at it!"

"What, I'm supposed to move back to the burbs and live here forever like a little kid? Has it not occurred to you that I may actually meet somebody someday, that I might want to get married and have my own family?"

"I thought the surgeons took care of that."

"So I'll adopt, for Christ's sake. That's not the point!"

"It's not that I haven't thought about that, but let's face it, you guys, if we were gonna have the big relationships and marriages and families and all that crap, we would have had them by now. It's obviously not in the cards for us. Besides, if one of you happens to meet somebody and fall madly and badly in love, we'll deal with it, build an addition or something. We'll take it as it comes, OK? One day at a time."

"Oh come on, Joel. Get real. This is not gonna happen. If you're actually serious about this — which I doubt — but if you are, if you really want to stay here, then fine, you can. You should! I mean, why the hell not? We'd come and visit, right, Michelle? You'd come and visit, right?"

"Yeah, sure," I say, playing along, watching the game unfold.

"It would actually be nice to keep the place," says Marla. "But you can't possibly expect us to abandon our lives and move into this house. I'm pretty sure 'Mom and Dad' have places to go and people to see. I mean, come on, Joel, you know the whole thing's crazy."

"So I'm crazy now, is that what you're saying?!"

"I didn't say *you* were crazy, I said *the idea* was crazy."

"What do you think, Michelle? You think it's crazy, you think I'm banana-fruity-flavours, or what?"

"To be honest, Joel, I think the whole thing is a big joke. Some kind of weird experiment, which in itself is a little twisted, if not exactly crazy. I think you want to know how we're going to respond to your proposition, but I don't think you really mean for us to all move back here and carry on with this improv. I don't believe for a second that you're serious about that."

"Oh really? Well, you're wrong, Michelle. Dead wrong. I'm serious all right," says Joel, laughing bitterly and patting his suit-jacket pockets. "You'd better believe I'm serious."

"OK, fine, you're serious, whatever you say. It's a moot point really, because you already have your answer. It's fairly obvious that none of us is prepared to move in here, even with all the perks and goodies. So there you go, there's the answer to your big question."

Nobody says anything for a few seconds. I watch my brother's face. Wait for him to explode into laughter, admit the whole thing was a farce and pour another round of the bubbly, cut the fake parents a fat cheque and summon up the camera crew that's been hiding in the basement. But he doesn't. His face darkens and his eyes brim with tears. He starts nodding his head, sharp rapid nods signalling some kind of internal conversation, a conversation punctuated by resentful little breath-laughs that come up from the chest and escape staccato through the lips. Marla kicks my leg under the table and looks stern into my eyes. As I watch my brother I realize that I might have been wrong. Joel appears to be completely serious, utterly genuine. Either he's lost his balance and slipped off the tightrope of sanity or he's the greatest actor on the planet.

"OK, OK, OK, you guys, forget what I said before..." Joel drains his drink and dabs his hot face with a napkin. "I see where I made a mistake. I mean, I probably scared you off by the term 'indefinitely,' right? Obviously a weekend, no matter how great, wasn't enough of a taste for you people to commit indefinitely. OK, fine, that's cool, I can understand that. My mistake. A slight miscalculation. So how about this: we set a time period, say, a year — fuck it, six months even! OK? Say, six months. We agree to stay for six months and at the end of that period, if you're not totally satisfied, we will refund your money, no questions asked. In other words, if you want to leave after six months you can. No problemo. Personally, I don't think you'll want to — that's how much fun we're going to have here! — but if you do I won't try to stop you, I swear. Moreover, as an act of good faith, I'll even take care of the rent on your places, so they'll still be there if you want to go back to them at the end of the six months — which you won't, I guarantee it."

The phony parents wait tense and frozen for us to rescue them. I don't say anything. I've never seen my brother so rattled.

"Listen, Joel," says Marla softly, "I can't speak for anyone else, but if this is that important to you, *which obviously it is*" — a sharp glance in my direction — "I suppose I could stay."

"Wonderful! You made the right decision. You're going to be happy here, I swear!"

"Oh boy," says the phony father, cradling his head in his hands. The fake mom fills her glass and sips fast through pursed lips.

"Michelle?"

I need time to assess, time to dissolve the tense doom that has stretched over the table like a net. "Look," I say, "I'll think about it. Why don't we sleep on it and see how we feel in the morning?"

"Yes!" blurts the fake mom, coughing up champagne.

"No! No 'thinking about it.' I need to know now. Tonight."

"Why?"

"Because! It's now or never. I've already decided that. I want to know now. I need to know tonight."

"Well, in that case, I'm sorry, Joel. I'm sorry, but I just can't—"

"Six months, Michelle? What the fuck is six months in the scheme of things?"

"I'm sorry, I can't."

"You can't or you won't?!"

"Marla said she'd stay. I'll come for a visit."

"OK, fine. Three months. Three fucking months, OK?"

"No. I have to go home. I can't live here again."

"Well, this is just classic. I knew this was gonna happen. Are you that selfish, Michelle?! Are you that fucking selfish?!"

"Please don't yell at me."

"I'm not yelling!" thunders Joel. "I'd just like to know why you have to fuck everything up! Why, Michelle? For what? For a lousy three months you have to run away and fuck everything up again?!"

"Look, I'm sorry, OK?"

"All right, two months, then," says Joel, running his fingers fast through his hair. "Two freaking months, Michelle. I'm giving you the chance to make the right decision for once in your life."

The chance to right all the perceived transgressions of my past.

"Come on, Michelle," says Marla, her face full of fear and urgency.

I think about all the years in this house and two months more. All the screaming and yelling and eight long weeks. All the bashing and thrashing and fifty-six days. Sugar-daddy Joel and phony parent replicas. Marla's diamond wrist and sad scraped womb. Lobsters and sailboats and truffles and champagne. No silence. No solitude. No time to recover. And then what? Then what? Another night like tonight? Another round of plea bargaining and thumbscrew persuasion? Held hostage by Joel's impending emotional tailspin? On and on and on, a forever and ever trap. I can't do it. I can't. I'll go crazy. I want out.

"I'm sorry, Joel. You guys can stay, but I can't. I'm really, really sorry…"

"So that's it, then. You're sorry!" Joel starts to laugh — mad and distraught. "That's it. Fade out. End of story. She's fucking sorry! Yeah, maybe you will be sorry," says Joel, exploding into tears. "Maybe you will be sorry for once in your life…" Sobbing, Joel reaches into his jacket pocket and pulls out a gadget — shiny and high-tech. "Well, I'm sorry too. I'm very sorry it didn't work out…"

In the nanosecond that it takes for the image of the remote control to register, I realize with an icy jolt of clarity what is locked in the basement. Joel's surprise ending. I am absolutely shocked.

"What the hell is that?!" I hear my sister demand.

And for the first time in decades I hear my own mouth scream.

"I love you," says Joel, smiling.

He flips back the safety and pushes the black button.

—

I survive. Blown out of the house by the force of the explosion.

Nobody else survives. Marla gone. Joel gone. The fake parents gone. The real parents gone.

I'm lucky, they say. I don't feel lucky.

Fractured ribs and a punctured lung. Cuts and contusions. Severe concussion. A dislocated wrist and two perforated eardrums.

I don't remember how I got here. I didn't understand what the hell was going on. I saw things moving — doctors, nurses, trolleys, equipment, hands moving, mouths moving — but I was totally disconnected, my head full of pain and a powerful ringing, a screaming echo that wouldn't diminish. Some kind of alarm? Some kind of emergency alarm? I tried my voice, but it was gone. Vanished. I yelled as loud as I could, but my voice was gone. Then it was three or four hands pushing me back onto the bed, holding me down, keeping me still. Then a note of explanation scrawled on a clipboard, scrawled in red ink and held in front of my face: *Ruptured tympanic membrane: Acoustic Trauma.*

Two weeks of scans and stitches, incisions and chest tubes, X-rays and bandages, painkillers and bedpans. Poking, draining, peeling and patching. Audiograms and tympanoplasty, antibiotics and food through the veins. Nobody knows if my hearing will return. It may or may not. I am advised to prepare for a "Permanent Threshold Shift." I just nod and nod. At least the ringing has stopped.

Now I float here in silence. Disjointed. Alone. I have been installed in a private room with a guard outside the door. I have no idea who arranged this. Joel's assistant? The OPP? *Hard Copy*? The media is slobbering to get at me. I'm big news. The hot ticket. CBC, Global, CFTO, CITY, the *Globe and Mail*, the *Toronto Star*, the *Los Angeles Times*, the *New York Times*, *American Journal*, *Inside Edition*, *Extra!*, *Oprah*, *Sally*, *Geraldo*. Giant gift baskets and floral bouquets arrive with offers for "my story." Exclusive interviews. Movies of the week. Hardcover tell-alls. I watch the fruit rot under the Cellophane. Shrink from the fat-faced flowers and their suffocating hothouse breath. I've already given my statement to the police. Take it all away. I don't understand.

Now somebody in Willowdale has started a fund in my name. Total strangers send me Get Well messages and smiling Mylar balloons. Personal managers deliver pen sets and quotes from satisfied clients. A woman dressed as a nurse snaps my photograph and runs out of the room. Someone videotapes me sleeping and sells the footage to *Entertainment Tonight*.

Sometimes I skim the paper or watch closed-caption on the box — pretty journalists attempting serious expressions: *what was once a two-storey home is now just a hole in the ground*... Interviews with ex-lovers, television shrinks and television lawyers, fragments of explanation, fragments of information — *Schafer was addicted to Halcion... Believed to have suffered from borderline personality disorder... Emotionally traumatized by his father's suicide... Families of the victims suing for wrongful death*... Mostly I just lie here trying not to think. Trying to block the images that keep appearing in my head. Every five minutes I have to try not to think. Marla and Joel, torn up, ripped apart. Guts, blood, brains, teeth, my sister's hair, my brother's fingers — all torn and ripped apart. All because of me. Why should I remain intact? Why should the killer live? Why not Marla, who offered to stay? Why not the actors, who had no idea? I'm the drunk driver who annihilates a carload and stumbles away with barely a scratch.

Maybe if.

Why didn't.

If only.

I should have.

Perhaps Joel was right. Maybe I am destruction. Maybe that's what I do, my so-called "MO."

No, no, says the hospital therapist, with her pink-and-white pen, her appliquéd teddy-bear sweater and her false, reassuring smile.

—

I don't cry. Not while I'm conscious. But I keep having the same dream. Every night the same dream, in which I discover, to my great relief, that Marla and Joel aren't really dead. They've just gone away somewhere. California or Texas. I run into them on the street, but they don't want to have anything to do with me. They're bitterly angry. They won't even talk to me. They're so angry that they won't even look at me.

I wake in the dark hospital night with a twisting in my gut, salt water in my mouth and no sound of the moaning.

—

Three weeks after the explosion I am allowed to go home. Something of a celebrity now, the *Free Press* refers to me as "Winnipeg's own." I hide out in the bookstore. Keep it locked up tight. Go down at night to pick up the flowers and the letters left at the front door. I still can't hear a thing, but the doctors inform me that it could take several months to heal. I wait and I wait. I have nothing but time.

I still dream the dream, though not as regularly. I think about going to see a shrink, but ultimately decide against it. There's really no point. What could they tell me that I can't figure out for myself? That I feel intensely guilty? That I miss my family? That Joel was desperately sad and dangerously deluded? That it's not my fault? That I'm not to blame? I think it all over. Again and again. Trace it back and back, down to the roots. Was everything sunny perfect before I moved out with McCollum? No. No, it wasn't. We lived in a haunted house. Holocaust haunted. Dark and damaged. Do I blame my father? No, I don't blame my father. Did my mother get cancer because I left the house? No, my mother got cancer because she wanted to leave. Do I blame her for leaving? No, I don't blame my mother. And I don't blame Marla and I don't blame Joel. And I suppose, when all is said and undone, I can't really blame myself.

If I had agreed to stay the result would likely have been the same, just postponed. Joel had a Plan A and a Plan B, and that was that. Plan A was a fantasy, a false memory that couldn't possibly have been sustained, even with all the cash in the world. It would have been Plan B eventually. It was only a matter of time. I think I've figured out the reasoning behind Plan B. I don't think the explosion was punishment. I think death was another way for us all to be together. Subject X was grievously misguided, but he did believe in blue. He must have believed in blue.

I just hope that he experienced that "monumental recognition." The overwhelming relief. The freedom, peace and joy.

—

Being unable to hear has accentuated my isolation. I feel detached, invisible. Like I'm moving through some foreign land. No reason to speak or interact. Stripped of sound, the ordinary activities of people and their machines seem more absurd than ever before. It's like seeing everything for the first time. Chewing is absurd, high-heeled shoes are absurd, dogs, buses, bicycles are absurd. I witness a gang fight in the alley outside my open window. Arms pounding, teeth flashing, fist in face, bat to the back. It looks like nothing. Harmless. The violence is in the sound.

I used to crave this kind of peace. But as the long days slog by, all I want is to hear again. I miss music. I need music. What an idiot I was to banish music for all those years! The greatest of all the arts. The most direct and elemental. The cheesiest pop song more stirring and evocative than the finest book, painting or play. Take *Romeo and Juliet*, give me "1,2,3, Red Light" by the 1910 Fruit Gum Company. Take Picasso's entire blue period, give me Earl and Jean's "I'm Into Something Good." Give me "Nessun dorma," "Cow Cow Boogie," "The Chicken Cordon Blues" and "Tango Till They're Sore." Give me "God Only Knows" and "You Go To My Head," "Betchya By Golly Wow" and "Big Yellow Taxi."

I play the songs in my head so I won't forget. I start walking to the record store and loading up on music, all the music that I shunned before when I was dead.

—

Joel's assistant has couriered me some of his personal effects. Photographs, correspondence, the first eight pages of an aborted attempt at memoirs, and a hard copy of his last screenplay, sealed tight with packing tape in a large manila envelope. I keep looking at the envelope and not opening it. All day long I've been wandering over to the kitchen counter, picking up the envelope and not opening it. I want to know and I don't want to know.

I decide to read it in the tub, before bed. Pour some Bushmills and run a hot one with lots of bubble bath. Sink into the warmth and inhale the good mango scent. Hold the heavy envelope in my damp hands and stare at the thing for a good four minutes before deciding not to read it in the tub. It might be the only copy. It might get soaked.

I toss it far across the bathroom floor so I won't drip on it when I get out. I lean out of the tub and pull the garbage bag full of unread cards and letters closer to me. I brought them with me from the hospital. I've been reading them on the john in the morning. Some of them are from children. Crayon stick figures with smiling faces and bandaged arms on lined notebook paper. *Get Well Soon!* Most of them are from women. Women with nothing better to do than pray for my speedy recovery. A few are from men, men who would like to meet me, maybe go for coffee when I'm feeling better, when I'm up and about. I fish deep into the bag and pull out a large handful. As I'm flipping through, feeling for letters — the letters are usually more interesting than the cards — one of them slips from the pile and falls into the tub. I pluck it out of the water and squeegee the bubbles away. My name and the hospital address have been laser printed. The stationery is from the University of Montana.

I leap from the tub and lunge for terry cloth, sandwich the envelope between the folds of the towel and pat it dry. Careful with the soggy paper as I peel the thing open and gingerly remove the enclosed missive. Not in ink, thank Christ; laser printed as well. But what the hell is it?

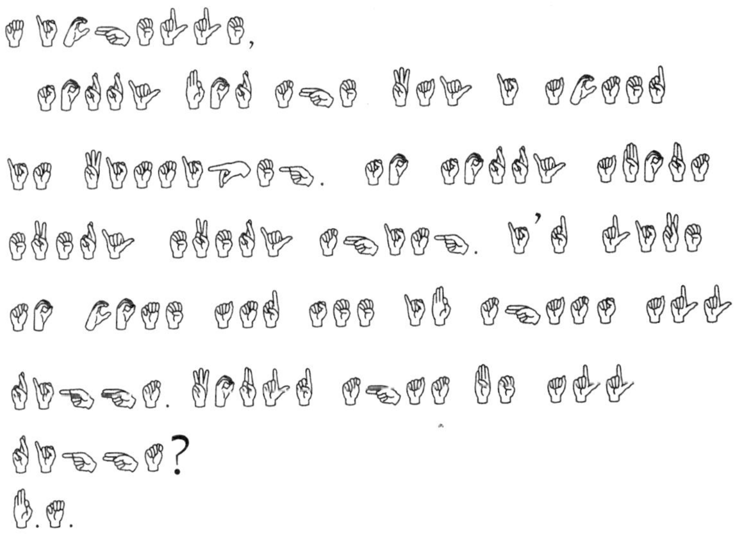

I recognize the symbols. It's American Sign Language. Finger spelling. I have a book downstairs! I wrap myself in a towel and zip down to get it. *A Basic Course in American Sign Language*, sitting untouched on the shelf for over four years. I kiss the dusty cover and hope to God this is the last time I ever have to use it. Settle into bed and decode the letter as quickly as I can:

> Michelle,
>
> Sorry for the way I acted in Winnipeg. So sorry about every every thing. I'd like to come and see you if that's all right. Would that be all right?
>
> F.M.

I read the letter ten, twelve, fifteen times. Bury my face in the original, press the page to my forehead, press the tiny hands to my lips. I tear off the *F.M.* hands and put them in my mouth. Chew them up and swallow them, laughing at my lunacy. What if I never saw this? What if I left it at the hospital? Oh God, oh God, what if McCollum thinks I don't want to see him?

I lunge for the telephone before I realize that I can't use the damn thing. I can barely make out motorcycle roar, let alone voices on the phone! I take my notebook and pen and get back into the bath. Run some more hot and try to compose a reply. Stare at the blank page, chawing on my nails. Christ! All those snappy letters I used to write to McCollum and now I can't think of anything to say. Everything I think of sounds Harlequin Romance! *Of course I want to see you... I adore you, come at once...* Jesus! I set the notebook aside and try to calm down. I want to dunk my head, but I'm not allowed to get my ears wet. I pour another shot of Bush and drink it down. Pick up the decoded letter and read it once more. *I'd like to come and see you if that's all right. Would that be all right?*

Suddenly I flash on something from the past. One time in the bath, in the basement with McCollum. We're talking about the most powerful word in the English language, wondering which word of all the words is the most powerful. And now, all of a sudden, I know for certain what it is. I pick up the notebook and pen my reply. One word is all I need:

Yes.

—

McCollum and I don't have to speak. We use the mouths for kissing, tasting and smiling. Twenty seconds of awkward when he first arrived, then one warm embrace and all the years went away. Instantly reconnected. Two drops of mercury melding.

We went directly to bed and stayed there for four days, slowly constructing a moat around the mattress-island. A moat full of whiskey glasses and coffee cups, pizza boxes and used condoms, notebooks and Bic pens, ashtrays and dirty plates, moisturizer and bottled water, chicken bones and orange peels, juice cartons and candy wrappers and greasy paper takeout bags — a beautifully fetid, bed-picnic mess. Disgusting and wonderful. We hooked up the Selectric to an extension cord and dragged that into bed too. We typed notes to each other. Notes of explanation. Notes of forgiveness. There was no mention of Edie and I didn't bother to inquire. I guess she couldn't have been that perfect. Or possibly she was too perfect.

Today McCollum was in cleanup mode. He showered, plowed out the moat and did a load of laundry, made a ridiculously long shopping list and went off to The Forks. He claims to have become an excellent cook. We'll see, we'll see.

I spend the morning in bed, reading Joel's last screenplay. The story of a boy growing up in Budapest during World War II. A heartbreaking story. My father's story. Terrible and true and no happy ending. Joel was right, this film would never be made. Too sad. Too subtle. Too complex and well written for Hollywood. Not enough schmaltz. Not enough obviousness. I marvel at my brother's good words and clandestine talent, think about all those soulless blockbusters, and what an appalling and galling waste.

I read through the script again, then set it down next to the Selectric. The good old garage-sale Selectric, still clickety-clacking after all these years. I turn it on and off a few times, remembering the sound it used to make, the warm contented hum, the satisfying crack of letter punching paper. I think about the missives I used to write for McCollum, and the file of newspaper stories that I've been saving for some promising local writer. I turn the thing on again and feel the vibration, feel the concave keys familiar under my fingers. It feels good, actually. A pleasant tingling sensation in the tips of my fingers.

I make a mental note to pick up a box of new ribbons.

—

McCollum is back from the market, back with eleven bags of groceries and a twenty-piece fondue set. We're having fondue for dessert. Ridiculously sublime.

Now he's busy in the kitchen, furiously concocting some elaborate meal, something involving jumbo shrimp and fresh mango, real ginger and chopped peanuts. I'm not allowed to help. He's got it under control. Good. I'd rather watch the mad professor go at it.

My mission, should I choose to accept it, is to set the bed/table and assemble the fondue set, but I just sit here drumming my fingers on the box and watching McCollum cook. It's a beautiful sight and I don't want to miss a frame. He leaves tomorrow and then who knows how long before I see him again.

Now he has some kind of music going. He's bopping lanky to the music. Cranking the salad spinner and singing out loud. I watch the mouth form the words, but I can't guess the tune. I check the empty CD box in front of the stereo. Rhino Records, Special Editions. *70's Smash Hits*, Volume 2. It's track nine. Charles Wright & The Watts 103rd Street Rhythm Band.

Love Land.

I go full on the volume and crank up the bass.

I can't really hear it. But, God, I can feel it.

—

Acknowledgements

A giant thank you to David Johnston, Sarah Davies and Anne Collins. Much gratitude to the reading squad: Daphne Floros, Esmé Keith and Ron Barry, and to everyone who assisted in the title search (you know who you are). A case of Jim Beam is on its way to my music guru, Ben Hamper. Huge and special thanks to Paul Quarrington who encouraged me to write the novel in the first place, and whose generosity and kindness made it possible and easy. And finally, heartfelt thanks to Jeff for believing that I could do it.